VANQUISHED

S. E. GREEN

CHAPTER 1

HOT. That's the first thing that enters my mind as I come to gradually, my lashes fluttering open. *Thirsty.* That's the second.

"Hi," comes a whisper to my right, and I roll my head toward it. A blond-haired woman about my age holds a tin cup to my lips. "Water. Drink."

I do. Gladly.

"Where am I?" I croak, searching the crevices of my brain, trying to remember something. Anything. But my thoughts are foggy.

"I don't know. They haven't told us anything."

Us? It's then that I hear them. Whispering over to the left and quiet crying behind me. I'm lying on a shallow bed of straw on a coarse stone floor with rough wood beams stretching above me. *Where am I?*

"My name's Camille," the woman tells me. "I was assigned to care for you. They renamed you Valoria. They said you fought them and they had to knock you out. They think you had a reaction to the sedative."

"I'm allergic to most all medicines," I say more to myself than her. Wait a minute. They *renamed* me?

Suddenly it all comes rushing back—Miami.

My sister flips on some sugary pop music and we both slide into our own thoughts as I navigate us through Coconut Grove toward Vasquez's estate. I've never been outside of South Florida. I don't want to get too excited, but this job as a live-in maid could be the start to a real future for us. I might even be able to enroll in some night classes.

How long ago was that? Hours? Days? There was a prick in my neck.

"My sister." I struggle to sit up, frantically looking around the cramped, shadowed room, searching for her.

Blood surges through me. I don't see her! "Lena!" I cry out, and the sound resonates off the walls.

Camille slams her hand over my mouth. "Shut up," she hisses.

I claw at her hand, kicking up the straw, and fight to get to my feet.

"*Shut. Up.*" She presses her palm harder against my mouth. "They will come in here. The last time they did, they took one of us out and she hasn't returned."

I bite down on her hand and she slaps me hard across the side of the head. "Calm. Down. Your panic is *not* going to risk the rest of us."

I don't know if it's the slap in the head, the horror in her eyes, or the fear in her voice, but I clench my teeth and nod my head.

Camille shoots me a warning glare before sliding her hand away.

My panting breaths fill the air around us and I look around again. There're only women in here—twenty or so—and we're all wearing matching brown tunics and leather sandals. They look about my age—late teens, twenties. Most of them sit huddled in clumps, clinging to each other, quiet, some looking at me and others staring off in a shocked trance. Silent terror fills the atmosphere.

We're in some sort of holding cell, like a dungeon, with stone walls and floors that have been weathered by the elements. A row of tiny windows along the top let in the only sunlight and fresh air.

Piss. The place smells like piss. I wrinkle my nose as my gaze drifts to the corner where a woman squats over a bucket. The smell hits me even harder, and my stomach pitches.

What the *hell* is going on? "How long have we been here?"

But before Camille can answer, the door to the dungeon creaks open, and a huge man dressed in leather and metal armor steps into our cell. He bizarrely looks like an ancient Roman soldier, but it's no costume.

"Let's go," he barks, pointing his very real sword, and my muscles immediately tighten.

Several of the women shrink back. Others start to cry. Camille grabs my arm and pulls me to my feet. "Just do what they say," she whispers, and I can feel her fingers shaking as she tugs me toward the door.

Instinct has me pulling back, and she only tightens her grip.

The soldier snatches up a few of the sniveling ones and shoves them outside.

The bright sun pierces straight into my skull. I hold up my hand and squint at the same time I gulp in fresh ocean air. However, the reprieve is short lived as another soldier grabs me and shoves me to the side where I stumble into line with the other women. Camille again grips my hand and together we straighten our spines.

We're standing in a sandy courtyard in what looks like an old world marketplace. To the left and in front of us sit multi-level stone buildings. To the right is the holding cell we came from.

On the balconies of the buildings stand people. Men and women dressed in long colorful gowns and sashes, like they're in Roman cosplay.

They are laughing, drinking, eating, talking—oblivious to us terrified down here in the courtyard. Though I know she's not up there, I search every face for my sister.

Two soldiers pull a wooden platform over and situate it between us and the people on the balcony.

I glance over my shoulder to see the ocean spreading in an endless black. There is no other land in sight.

One of the soldiers yanks the woman at the end of our line and shoves her toward the wooden platform. Shaking, she stumbles up, looking back at us, eyes dry but so full of fear it twists my gut.

She's tall, easily six feet, and big boned with short dark hair.

"Take your gown off," a man barks and I snap my gaze to him.

He's fat and dressed in a white wrap with a black braided belt. He's got his hair combed forward in a slicked style and holds a whip.

The tall woman doesn't immediately move as she looks around, seemingly waiting for someone to intercede.

"Take your gown off," he barks again and unravels the whip.

My heart leaps into my throat. *Just do what he says!* I want to yell.

Quickly, she lifts the hip-length dress over her head and clutches it in front of her as she stares down at the fat man.

He sneers. "Turn around."

She does, slowly, her face pale and terrified. She makes eye contact with a few of us before returning to the front. She's wearing a white band across her chest and white underwear. But her breasts are big and the bra barely supports them.

The fat man looks up to the balcony where most of the people aren't even paying attention.

"Ten!" A short skinny man up and to the left yells.

Ten what?

"Fifteen." Another man...

"Twenty."

My God, we're being auctioned!

The fat man scans the rest of the balcony, but when no one else yells anything, he motions the tall woman down and over to the left where—I'm just now noticing—a muscular bald man stands.

Fierce describes his strong jaw and stature. A trained fighter. Someone who could defend all of us women standing here in line. Wearing leather armor over a bare chest and baggy black pants cut off at the knee, he's dressed different than everyone else.

The tall woman puts her dress back on and the bald man snaps shackles on her ankles and motions her to sit.

I glance down the line to the next woman. She's got long dark hair and olive skin like me, and is small, too. Probably not more than five-foot-two and one-hundred-and-ten pounds.

She starts screaming and shaking her head and backing away. A soldier yanks her across the sand and shoves her up on the wooden platform. Her uncontrollable sobs fill the air and the fat man cracks his whip across her body.

I gasp.

"Shut up!" he snaps and motions for a soldier to wrangle her out of her tunic.

Sun glints off something and I track my eyes up to the balcony where an immaculate red-haired woman stands. Her bright hair is piled on top of her head in some fancy complicated knot pinned with jewels, and where everyone else wears colorful gowns, she has on the only silver one.

She lifts a golden rod in the air and doesn't shout out a number like the skinny man had.

The fat man doesn't wait for a counter offer and instead nods to a soldier. He pulls the small woman off the platform and tosses her over to the right where she's shackled and shoved down to sit in the dirt.

I want to run. But instead I stare at that small woman and the red welt across her face. I'll be of no use to my sister if I don't stay strong.

One by one it continues. Each of us going up to the wooden platform, the people on the balconies bidding, and we being separated into clumps.

I notice, though, the skinny man is buying most of the bigger girls and the red-haired woman is purchasing the majority of the petite ones. Is that where my sister went? With the red-haired woman?

A soldier approaches the next woman in line, the one standing beside Camille. Before he can yank her away she whispers to me, "*He* took your sister," and rolls her eyes up to the balcony and the skinny man.

I jerk my gaze up to where he stands. He's laughing and drinking. *He* has my sister. A bead of sweat slides down my back and I continue watching him. I *will* be bought by him. I'll figure it out.

Camille releases the hard grip she has on my hand and I snap out of my trance. I flex my fingers and feel them flash hot, then cold as the circulation comes back to them.

Without anybody telling her, Camille walks right up on the auctioning block, strips her tunic, and stands proudly in her white undergarments.

She's not big or small. She's average and muscular. A few people bid and she ends up owned by the skinny man. Exactly where I want to be.

I'm the tiniest of us all and I know deep down in my gut that the red-haired woman is going to make a bid on me.

I do exactly what Camille did. I straighten my shoulders, walk up on my own, strip, and though every muscle fiber in me quivers, I toss my dress aside and stand defiantly for all to look.

The red-haired woman up in the balcony raises her golden rod, and I blurt "No!" before I know fully what I'm going to do.

And pray it doesn't get me killed.

CHAPTER 2

THE FAT MAN with the whip narrows his eyes. "Excuse me?"

The laughter and chatter gradually dies down from the balcony. The captive women still crying grow quiet. And all eyes slowly turn toward me.

My nervous throat fights the urge to swallow, and I raise my left arm and point to where I want to go. Where my sister is. "I want to go with them."

The fat man's eyes narrow even more to two seedy slits, and then he laughs, deep and evil, as he unravels his whip and snaps it above his head.

I dig my nails into my palms and concentrate on not flinching when the whip's *crack* reverberates in the air around me and vibrates through my skull.

The fat man turns and looks up to those on the balcony, like he's waiting to be told what to do. No one does or says anything for a good solid few seconds. And then the red-haired lady starts to raise that golden rod again.

Determination replaces any lingering fear. "No!" I repeat and jab my finger over to the left. "I said I want to go with them." I lock my jaw muscles and keep my eyes fastened on the lady while all around her people start to whisper.

She smiles, but nothing pleasant comes across in the curve of her lips. And though nearly twenty five feet separate us, her wickedness curls around me.

I scowl. No, I definitely don't want to go with her.

She nods, ever so slightly, and the fat man slings his whip through the air. I register its lash a second's fraction before I back flip off the platform and drop and roll across the dirt.

I come up on all fours, staring, concentrating on keeping my loud breaths steady, like my father taught me. The crowd on the balcony laughs like they think it's the funniest thing in the world to see a little woman about to get beat.

Blood rushes through the fat man's face, spreading red all the way to his hairline. He nods to two soldiers who each grab one of my arms.

They're enormous and I'm nothing next to them, but I still fight their hold. I yank at it. Jab the heel of my foot into one of their legs. And sink my teeth into the other one's bicep.

The fat man stalks toward me, his eyes clinging to me as he slowly winds his whip and makes a show of fastening it back onto his hip. Blood pounds in my ears, echoing in my head, muting the lingering laughter and whispers from the balcony.

He steps right up to my face. "You're a little bitch. And I *will* break you," he promises.

I hike my chin. "Give it your best."

He rears his meaty hand high in the air. I catch a glimpse of a gaudy silver ring right before he backhands me across the face.

Blood flies through the air. From my mouth, my nose, I can't tell, but I snap my head up and spit right in his face.

I won't go down easily.

The fat man brings his fist back and punches me straight in the gut, lifting me off the sand. A grunt escapes my lips and I wish more than anything I could draw it back in. I don't want him to know he's causing me pain.

I kick out with my sandaled foot and my heel connects with his shin. I concentrate on the most defiant look I have. Little does this fat man know the training I used to do with my dad. My pain tolerance is high.

"That all you got?" I sneer in full on provoking mode, which earns me another backhanded slap.

This time his ring catches on my cheek and I feel a sliver of skin peel away.

"Fifty thousand!" someone yells from the balcony and I look up to the short skinny man.

I smile. *Yes.*

Everyone just stares at him, like fifty thousand is a ridiculous amount to spend in this twisted marketplace.

"Fifty thousand," he says again, staring right at me.

The fat man gazes up to the red-haired lady, who gives me a long menacing look but doesn't raise her rod. Relief washes through me as the soldiers sling me over to the clump of women going to where my sister is. *My sister.*

The bald fierce man roughly slides my tunic back on me, and after he shackles my ankles he stands and looks down at me. His gray-eyed gaze traces the cut on my cheek and the blood seeping from my nose. But his stoic expression gives no clue as to what he is thinking.

In our shackles, we're led from the marketplace into a back alley and loaded into a wooden cart attached to horses.

"Are you insane?" Camille whispers as she slides in

beside me.

"Wherever we're going, my sister's there." I don't want to think about what they may have already done to her.

The bald fierce man closes the hatch, climbs up beside the driver, and we're off.

No one talks as our cart rolls down a dirt alley and out into the countryside, and it's like I've literally stepped back in time. Stone villas dot the hillside, encircled by lush lawns, gardens, and fountains. Small cottages are scattered here and there and attached to farms. Horses and cows graze within corrals.

People dressed in cream and white gowns tend the animals and gardens. Others like the ones on the balcony in the marketplace lounge on terraces. Yet others dressed like me, like a slave, scurry about carrying stuff. I wonder if they were bought and sold in the same marketplace.

An elaborate carriage passes us going in the opposite direction. Inside of it I catch sight of two beautiful women, laughing and eating grapes. Neither of them even glances our way.

We peak the hillside and I take in more of the same. Villas. Cottages. Gardens. Farms. A round structure that seems to be some sort of small arena, and thick woods off to the left surrounded by a tall wall. I wonder what that wall's about.

We're definitely on an island. A very large island. I can barely make out where it starts and stops. Dark ocean surrounds us, spanning all the way in every direction to the horizon. I catch a glimpse of a galleon with all sails hoisted going away from land. Is that how I got here? On that galleon?

But more importantly, where in the hell am I? And what is going on?

CHAPTER 3

"Where you from?" Camille asks, bringing me from my perusal of the island.

"Miami, Florida," I say.

"I'm from Denmark," she tells me, and it only just now occurs to me that she has an accent.

"How did you end up here?" I ask.

"I don't know. I was in Berlin hopping hostels and partying. Met these guys. Got drunk. Woke up here." She nods. "You?"

I take a second to piece together the details. "I went for a job interview. My sister was with me. It was at this big mansion owned by Mr. Vasquez. I was interviewing for a live in maid position." It was going to be great. A nice place for me and Lena to live. A good new school for her... wait, is Vasquez behind all this?

"What about your family?" she asks. "Your parents? Surely they know you're missing by now."

I shake my head. "It's only me and Lena." Mom left way back when Lena was just a tiny girl. Dad died two years ago, putting me at nineteen in charge of raising a pre-teen. "What about you?" I ask.

She gives a harsh laugh. "I got nobody. Been a system kid pretty much my whole life."

I look around at the other young women in the cart. Are they the same? No family? Does no one know they're missing either?

The cart turns right and clumps down a stone-laid driveway. A multi-level villa comes into view with outbuildings attached. A soldier sees us coming and opens the gate. We enter a circular outdoor area that I'd say is about fifty feet in diameter.

Other women and men dressed like us in short brown tunics are busy training with wooden swords and kicking and punching posts. I count fourteen in all. Four women and ten men. All with either shaved heads or very short hair. They collectively stop when they see the cart come to a stop.

The fierce bald man climbs down, circles around, and unlatches the door. "Out," he says in an accent I can't quite place. It's the first time I've heard him speak.

He unlocks our shackles as we climb down and indicates we should line up for whatever's next. Of the twenty or so girls in our original holding cell, only six were brought here.

The cart pulls away, the gate to the outbuilding bolts shut, and we stand confronted with the other men and women captives. They begin walking up and down our line.

One of them pokes a woman standing two down from me. "Look at this one all scared."

"This one's fat," another taunts.

"And this one smells," yet another sneers.

What are they doing? They're one of us. We're one of them. Aren't we?

An enormous black woman stops right in front of me. "What was Master thinking getting *this* one?"

I narrow my eyes.

She throws her head back and laughs.

I stare up at the roof of her mouth, her white teeth, her dry lips, and something just snaps. I shove her in the chest, she stumbles back, but doesn't waste a second coming right at me.

I crouch down, ready. My father always warned me my temper would be my downfall. She goes to shove me, and I back flip away and come up with a smirk that makes her full on charge.

"Enough!" The fierce bald man barks, and the big black woman immediately halts.

She scowls at me. "This isn't over."

"Whenever," I challenge, and she snarls.

"Greetings!" someone shouts, and I glance up to see the short skinny man who bought us at the marketplace standing on a terrace overlooking the training area. Beside him is a gorgeous dark-haired lady and behind them two young girls.

Like me, both girls wear a tunic, but where mine is brown, theirs are blue. Neither of them is my sister.

"Welcome to Saligia," the short skinny man says. "You may call me Master and this is my wife who you will refer to as Mistress. Each of you are lucky enough to have been bought by this camp. You have been blessed. This is sacred ground. We do not fear death, we embrace it! We are warriors."

The big black woman and all the other fighters in the

training area give a guttural war cry. Camille and I shoot each other a confused look.

"We are the proud owners of Sera, the serpent of Saligia." He points to the big black woman and she sticks out her unusually long tongue. "And Ignatius, the fire of the arena." He indicates an enormous man who has to be at least six foot five and has horrible, jagged scars all over his face and body.

Master waves his arm through the air in a grand gesture. "We are a self-sustaining society here in Saligia. A decadent one where desires can be explored, fantasies lived, and perversions satiated."

"I'm now a slave?" I ask. "Because nobody has told me anything."

Master smiles down at me. *Smiles.* "Welcome, Valoria."

My jaw clenches. "That's not my name."

"Valoria, my little defiant one. My little warrior."

That's what my dad used to call me. His little warrior. I don't like that this man, Master, is using the same term.

"You will find, *Valoria,* that this can be a good new life. You will be well cared for *if* you do as you're told. Let me ask you, what did you have going for you back wherever you're from? Bills paid? Roof over your head? Food in your belly?"

"Not always," I answer back. "But I was free. You don't own me. You *can't* own me. I don't know what kind of sick fantasy world you have going on here, but it's not right. I want to go home."

"And freedom you can have again," he answers, totally ignoring everything else I just said. "As soon as you pay back your expenses for bringing you here. But you'll find you'll want to stay. Ask anyone in the training area. Ignatius was freed and now chooses to stay on his own will. There's nowhere else you can have such worth than right here with me and on Saligia."

I look down the line at all the warriors, staring with rapt attention. These people are brainwashed. And Ignatius, the scarred man, why would he stay if he is free?

"Alexior is in charge of your training." Master looks over to the fierce bald man. "He will turn each of you into the type of warrior that gives us our outstanding reputation. But make no error in judgment. You are slaves. You belong to me. You *will* be executed if you try to escape. Do *not* cross me in any way."

I swallow, and the sound gurgles in my head. I don't doubt that for one second.

Master nods to Alexior. "Bring me Valoria."

"What?" I take a step back. "Why?"

Alexior ignores me and begins calling out other names, pairing each of the trained fighters with one of us new women. Camille gets paired with Sera, the serpent of Saligia.

When he's done he points to me. "Let's go."

I don't move.

"Let's. Go," he warns.

Forcing my feet forward, I follow him into the shade of an outdoor room with wooden tables and benches piled with bowls and cups and spoons.

We step through an archway and walk down a long tunnel. Iron bars barricade the left side and through the bars I see what must be our living quarters. Canvas cots line the walls, and above those span long skinny openings that let in sunlight and fresh air.

Next sits a big open room with a large in-ground stone bath tub containing clean clear water. Along the wall hang white towels and blades attached to leather straps. My gaze zeros in on those blades. I could use those for a possible weapon.

In each corner of the large room sits a brick stand with a hole in the center. A sponge attached to a wooden handle hangs beside each one.

"This is where the women sleep," Alexior speaks and his Australian accent really comes through now. I couldn't quite place it before with his one and two word commands. "Men are on the other side. Men and women do not interact unless you are training or eating. Or unless Master allows it. You are required to bathe and shave once a day."

"And if I don't?"

Alexior stops and turns to me. Sunlight illuminates the left side of his face and body, accentuating his bunched muscles. I take in his strong jaw and the hollows caused by the tunnel's shadows. He's younger than I originally thought. Maybe mid-twenties, just a few years older than me.

"You need to control your temper and your mouth," he quietly speaks. "This place is no joke. And that's the last time I'm going to say that to you. Got it?"

Who does he think he is speaking to me that way? But I set my jaw and remind myself I'm here for my sister. "Yes, I got it."

I follow him the rest of the way down the tunnel and we come to a stop at a locked iron gate. A soldier on the other side unlocks it and we step through. We climb a long flight of stone steps to yet another locked gate where a different soldier unlocks and opens it.

I continue following Alexior through the villa as I take in the spaciousness and opulence. Slaves quietly mill around. Some polish floors while others carry trays of food or pitchers of drink. No one looks at me. I search each of them, but don't see my sister.

Where my tunic hangs loose, they all wear a gold rope tied around theirs. I suppose that signifies they work in the villa.

We cross through yet another spacious room with a shallow pool running the length. Rose petals drift along the surface.

An open skylight illuminates several naked women reclining in the water, one of whom is Mistress, the wife. A few slave girls stand nearby, ready with food and drink.

My gaze darts around. Where is Lena? Where is my sister?

CHAPTER 4

As if sensing my thoughts, Mistress glances up from the pool and looks right at me. I stop for a second, but then she moves her gaze from me to Alexior and gives him a long desire-filled once-over.

He doesn't return her stare and instead seems to pick up pace.

"How many did you bring in today?" one of the naked women asks.

"Six," Mistress responds, taking her eyes off Alexior.

"Any men?"

Mistress sighs. "No. I don't know why he's dead set on fighting the women."

"All the men seem enthralled with it. My husband made nearly half a mil after the last round of fights."

Half a mil?

Mistress rolls her eyes. "Enough of this. I'm bored. You." She points to one of the slave girls. "Take off your clothes and get in the water."

My heart skips a beat and I turn. *What?* That slave girl

can't be more than fifteen. They can't make her get in the water with them.

Alexior death grips my arm, and I jerk back as he roughly drags me from the room.

"But—" I fight against his hold.

He pushes me up against a wall, and my head hits the stone behind me. I cringe. "But—"

"Stop it," he warns, planting his muscular arm across my chest. "There is nothing you can do. They will kill you if you try. What about that don't you understand?"

Anger and frustration and fear boil through my body and tears come to my eyes. I fist my hands to stop them from shaking. "What are they going to do to her?"

Alexior doesn't immediately respond as his gray eyes search mine. I don't know what he sees in them, but whatever it is causes him to lessen his hold on me. Just a little.

"They are going to do whatever it is they want," he tells me. "Whatever it is that pleases them. That is the reality of this place. The sooner you comprehend that, the easier this will be for you."

The tears wetting my eyes begin to fall. *My sister.* Oh, God, my sister. I start to slide down the wall, but Alexior grips my arm and hauls me right back up.

"Master is waiting," he says.

I barely register him pushing me through one final archway until I'm standing in an office. Master sits behind a dark wood desk with a calico cat perched on the corner. I look around for a phone, a computer, *anything* modern, but it's just as historically accurate up here in the villa as it is down below in the slave's quarters. They're really taking this role play thing seriously.

Off to the right spans the terrace where Master

addressed us all only moments ago. Training noises echo up from down below.

Master glances up from his paperwork. He puts a pen aside and studies me. Gone are the smiles he had on the terrace. In his sunken face I see his true self. Up close like this I realize he's older than I thought. I'd say he's in his sixties.

He doesn't stand as he begins addressing me, "Tell me, Valoria, why did you want to come with me so badly?" He looks pointedly at the dried blood still on my face. "Enough so that you took a mild beating."

"Mild beating? I'd say the fat man did more than that."

Master doesn't respond to my snippy remark.

I tug my arm from Alexior's grasp, and he backs off a step. I take in a deep breath and straighten my shoulders. "Because you have my sister."

Master lifts his gray brows. "Do I now? And who is your sister?"

"Her name is Lena. And she looks just like me." My throat unexpectedly swells, and I try to clear it. "She's only thirteen. She's innocent." I swallow and fight the tears I feel forming in my eyes. "Please don't hurt her. I'll do anything you want."

He just continues looking at me, unfazed by my switch in emotion. Then his eyes roll up, like he's thinking, and it fills me with dread.

"No," he says, bringing his eyes back down to mine. "You are mistaken."

"What... but I was told you had her. That *you* bought her."

He lifts his brows. "Told by whom?"

Slowly, something expands inside of me, widening, pressing out. "The wo—the woman in line."

He shakes his head in a deliberate back-and-forth motion. "Again, you are mistaken."

The reality of what I've done slams into me. *Lena's not here.* I open my mouth, but words get lodged in my throat. Whatever is expanding in me bursts, and I cry out as it buckles me forward and I sink to my knees. *No! Then where is she?*

Master scoots his chair out and slowly makes his way around the desk to my side. Gently, he touches my shoulder and it strikes me as an odd thing for him to do. "Shh. It's going to be okay."

I squeeze my eyes shut and try to stop myself from crying, but I can't. I bury my face in my hands. *My sister. She's not here.*

Master runs a soothing palm down my back. "Valoria, look at me."

I ignore him, rocking back and forth, my catching breaths echoing in the room around us. *My little sister. How am I going to find her now?*

"Valoria," Master repeats, "I don't have your sister. But I'll do you a deal. I'll find her if you fight for me. Win. And I'll bring her here."

His words slowly sink into my grief, and I swallow hard. My fingers scrape down my face as I lift my head and look up at him. Escape. I could escape. But where would I go? I can't just jump off the shores of Saligia—wherever that is— and swim.

He smiles. "You like the way that sounds?"

I sniff and wipe my nose. No, I don't like the way that sounds. But what other option do I have? Right now he is the only link to finding my sister.

I make myself nod. "Yes."

"Good." He helps me to my feet and remains standing

in front of me. "I paid a lot of money for you. Don't disappoint me."

"I won't."

He motions for me to step out on to the terrace with him. Down below everyone practices with wooden swords and shields just like they were when our cart first pulled in.

"Sera!" Master calls out, and she glances up. He doesn't say anything, just nods, and before I have time to blink, Sera grabs Camille and puts her in a head lock.

I suck in a breath and stare down into Camille's wide frightened eyes.

Master turns to me and holds his thumb out sideways. "If I turn this up, Sera will snap that girl's neck. Is that what you want?"

"No," I immediately answer. "Please let her go."

"Then you need to control yourself. Do not *ever* speak unless you're spoken to. You can be defiant in the arena when you're making me money, but not here. Here you train, you learn, and you do *whatever* I ask."

He tilts his thumb down to Sera, she releases Camille, and I simultaneously breathe out.

"I won't be kind the next time," he tells me.

Frantically, I nod.

Master looks over my head to Alexior. "Get her cleaned up. She stinks. You know how much I hate filth. And get rid of all that hair."

"How many fights do I need to win to get my sister back?" I ask, already disregarding the rule of when to speak.

But Master ignores the transgression. "It comes down to money. The more you win, the more money you make me."

"And for us both to go free?"

He smiles, but there's nothing kind in it. "Between your expenses in bringing you here. The fifty thousand I paid for you. Your general upkeep and training. Locating your sister. The money I will then have to pay to purchase her. We're talking over a mil."

I think of my sister. Camille. That girl in the pool with Mistress and her perverted friends. *A million dollars...* "I'll do whatever you want." If that means keeping everyone safe.

Master smiles. "Exactly what I wanted to hear."

CHAPTER 5

I PULL *into my sister's middle school and there she is slumped against the chain linked fence. Alone. Always alone.*

She hears my clanking car before she sees it, and pushing off the fence, she slings her backpack over her shoulder.

All the other kids are saying goodbye to each other for the day and no one spares her a glance or a word as she shuffles across the parking lot toward me.

Lena's the mini version of me. Short. Dark features. In my hand-me-down clothes, it's like looking in a mirror.

She creaks open the door, tosses her pack in, and slides into the torn seat. "Hey," she says.

"Hey, Lil' Bit." I put the car in gear and putter off. "Good day?"

She shrugs a skinny shoulder. "Made an A on that algebra test."

"An A!" I grin over at her. "That's awesome."

She shrugs that indifferent shoulder again and tries to hide a proud smile. God, she reminds me so much of myself.

"You want it bald?" an old lady asks, and I blink from my memory.

I'm now sitting just outside the women's bathing area. There's an old lady here and she's cutting our hair. She just did the other women who were bought today, and now she's doing mine.

"Bald?" she impatiently prompts.

I shrug as I glance down at all my dark hair on the floor. I didn't think I had a choice.

She pats my head that now has inch long choppy hair. "This is the longest Master allows. We'll leave it. If you decide you want bald, just let me know."

The old lady gives me a shove, and I get up off the wood bench and walk into the bathing area.

Sera is here along with the other women warriors. Camille, too, and those who came in on our cart. Ten of us females in all. I assume the men are in their own bathing area.

Some of the women are in the large stone bath cleaning themselves. Others sit on wood benches, meticulously shaving their legs, underarms, and pubes.

Master wasn't kidding when he said he doesn't like hair.

I watch those who are shaving as they scrape the arched blades over their skin. I'm going to kill myself with that medieval looking thing. Or use it to escape...

One of the warriors looks up at me, catches me staring, and barks, "You like to watch? I'll give you something to watch."

Gritting my teeth so I don't bark back, I turn to the bath. Camille's already in there, shooting me a warning look. Her blond hair is cut just like mine instead of bald.

I return her warning look with one of my own that I

hope conveys I'll be good. Hers softens then to a sad relieved smile and she ducks her head to give me privacy.

I strip and walk right in the hot water. I've never minded being naked. I'm not self-conscious. I close my eyes, breathe deeply, and just soak the heat into my exhausted body.

Without a word, I grab a bar of soap, lather a rag, and viciously scrub my skin. I want the filth of this place off of me.

Naked, Sera proudly strolls across the bathing room straight toward the woman who had to go first on the auctioning block. The one whose breasts were too large for the white band they gave us all to wear.

"What's your name?" Sera demands.

"F-F-Felicia. That's what they named me." She grips the towel in front of her naked body, much like she had her tunic when she was up on the block.

"F-F-Felicia," Sera parrots and the warrior women all laugh.

I clench my jaw.

"*Don't* get involved," Camille cautions me.

Sera yanks away Felicia's towel and throws it across the room.

"Leave me alone," Felicia whimpers.

Sera rakes her intimidating gaze down the length of Felicia's shaking, naked body. "You're fat."

There was a big girl back home in our neighborhood who used to bully and terrorize some of the kids. I caught her picking on my sister once and punched her in the eye. "Leave her alone," I grit out.

With one hand, Sera shoves Felicia and she stumbles back.

I shoot up out of the water, fueled by everything. Sera's

harassment. My meeting with Master. My sister. This whole place. "I said leave her alone."

Slowly, Sera pivots and pins me with her dark gaze. "You are nothing." She stretches out one long muscular leg. "*This* is bigger than your whole body. You think just because Master paid some stupid money for you that you're special?"

She points to a large S shaped scar on the back of her shoulder. "*This* is the mark of a true champion. Only those who win in the fights get to bare it."

"I could care less about some stupid branded S on your shoulder."

Sera comes right at me, and I step completely out of the bath to meet her. I don't care that she's enormous. I've had enough.

She towers above me, her eyes too wide, her lips curled back like a snarling dog. Logic tells me I can't beat her, but I sure will give it my best if that's what this comes to.

She opens her mouth, like she's going to take a bite out of me, and instead unrolls her unnaturally long tongue. She waggles it at me and makes some weird satanic sound.

"Is that why you're called 'Sera the serpent?'"

Alexior steps into the bath room. "Stop." He looks straight in Sera's face, then into mine, not even glancing down at our naked bodies. "You'll settle this on the training ground, not in here. Now be done. Dinner's out and ready."

Sera and I glare at each other. This is one score far from settled.

CHAPTER 6

FEELING CLEAN AND NEAR-HUMAN AGAIN, I take my place in the dinner line at the back and wait for all the men and women warriors to load their bowls with chunks of meat and rice and stalks of broccoli. Despite this entire horrible day, my stomach audibly growls at the spicy scent.

Sera goes right before we newcomers, and when we finally step up, there's only a couple scoops of rice and some broccoli left. They did it on purpose.

Camille's eyes water. "I can't do this," she whispers.

"Yes, you can," I assure her.

Behind the long table stands a small old man I assume cooked everything. He grabs a spoon and slings a wad of rice into Camille's bowl, but nearly half of it falls to the ground.

The cook scoffs. "Recruits eat whatever is deemed left." He nods to the rice on the dirt beneath our feet. "And off of wherever."

I glance over to Alexior who has been silently standing along the wall. He doesn't do anything. Just stares straight ahead. Isn't he in charge? Shouldn't he do something?

Camille kneels down, like a dog, and scoops the rice into her bowl.

I unclench my fist so I don't punch the cook who merely raises an eyebrow in challenge.

The veteran warriors have left no room for us at the wooden tables, so we recruits, as I now know we're called, find a spot over in the corner on the floor. None of us speak as we inhale the meager dinner and shamelessly lick the bowls.

With a sigh, Felicia puts her empty bowl down on the ground. "I miss my boyfriend."

Her comment makes me think of the conversation I had with Camille in the cart. "Do you have any family?"

"No." She shakes her head. "Just my boyfriend. We've only been dating a month."

"How'd you end up here?" Camille asks.

"My boyfriend and I were camping in Canada, and when I woke up, I was here. Wherever here is." She straightens, like an idea just hit her. "Do you think they took him, too?"

None of us respond. Who knows? Maybe. Or maybe he's the reason why she is here. Like Mr. Vasquez is for me.

I look at the other three women sitting in our circle. "Any of you? Family?" I ask, and they all shake their heads. Just what I thought. No one knows we're missing. No one knows to come looking for us.

"I have a daughter," the woman sitting directly across from me quietly says. She looks older than the rest of us. Maybe late twenties. She has features like she's an Asian-Caucasian mix. "My name's Gem by the way."

Up to this point she's been the most silent of us all. I think about her in the original holding cell in the market-place and then up on that auctioning block. She hadn't seemed terrified like the rest of us. More like she was going through the motions. None of that had occurred to me until just now.

She runs her eyes over all of us sitting around her. "I... I was in prison. Ten years for something I promise you I did not do. I signed a one year contract to come here."

Her words curl through my brain, confusing me. "What do you mean you signed a contract?"

"Some man came to visit me. Told me I could come here for a year, my ten would be wiped, and then I could return to my daughter. I took it. She's only eight. She'll be nine when I get home versus eighteen if I would've stayed in prison."

"Who has your daughter?" I ask.

"She was placed in foster care."

"So then, do *you* know where we're at?" Camille asks.

"No." Gem shakes her head. "I knew I would be sedated and transported to an island where I would become a house slave in a role play environment."

"But you're not a house slave," I point out the obvious.

"I know," she sighs and the meaning really hits home. They get us here and then they can do whatever they want with us.

"No other family?" Camille asks, and as expected, Gem shakes her head.

United States, Denmark, Australia, Canada... Saligia seems to have their fingers everywhere.

Alexior crosses the outdoor eating area to tower over us. "Enough talking. Get up. You will rest when you prove yourself."

CHAPTER 7

IT's DARK OUT NOW. I don't know exactly how much time has passed. Hours for sure. The warriors have long gone to bed. Me and the other recruits are in the training area, pacing in a circle with each of us gripping ropes attached to small boulders.

Though it's cooler out now that the sun has dropped, sweat drips off my bowed head.

Each boulder can't weigh more than ten pounds, but with the hours that have passed, the continuous pacing, and the rough rope wrapped around our hands and wrists, it feels more like a hundred pounds.

In front of me Felicia crumbles to her knees. I clench my jaw so I won't yell at her. That's the fourth time she's done it. If I can do this, so can she.

"Get up," Alexior demands. "Every time you fall, the others suffer. That's one more hour everyone will pace."

I close my eyes. I knew that was coming.

Alexior hauls Felicia up by her arm. "I can do nothing with you as long as you're showing such weakness. In the fights you will be a team. You have to have each other's back. Right now no one can depend on you. You're making that clear."

The first couple of chastisements, I wanted to defend her. Now I want to kick her myself. Another hour. *Jesus.*

Grunting and moaning, Felicia stumbles forward and rejoins our pacing circle. I shoot her a death glare that I hope she *really* gets. She must because the next hour goes by, and she manages to stay upright.

"Halt," Alexior speaks into the night. "Sit." We all fall over instead. He walks around and unstraps the ropes from our wrists. "You may sleep right here in the dirt."

I don't think twice about arguing. I curl up in a ball and close my eyes. A million to get my sister back and earn our freedom. *Would they really let us go?* It's the last thought that goes through my brain before I am gone.

———

A splash of water wakes me, and I jerk upright. Sera stands over me, laughing, the sun beaming down behind her. I hate her.

"Valoria," Alexior calls. "Someone's here to see you. Come with me."

I drag my weary body up and am immediately aware of my blistered hands. I try to flex them and wince. I don't bother looking at them. I don't need the visual reminder of the pain. I can only imagine the bruising and burns from the ropes.

As I drudge across the training area and under the overhang where the warriors sit eating, I gaze longingly at the fruit and bread and cheese on their plates. Hungry acid burns through my stomach like its eating my lining from the inside out.

I step through the archway where Alexior waits and he opens an iron gate. I glance into the tiny holding cell and to the shackles attached to the wall and immediately back away.

"Don't worry," he tells me. "I'll release you as soon as she's done speaking to you."

I hesitate. "She?"

He doesn't answer and instead nods me inside. He shackles my ankles and wrists to the wall. Instinctually, I give my chains a tug and discover I can only come out about a foot.

He stands on the other side of the cell, and we both fall silent. I glance around at the murky stone interior, at another door on the other side, and at a dark stain in one corner. As the moments pass, I get more and more anxious. What are we waiting for?

Alexior rotates his neck ever so slightly, like it's tense, and I wonder if he wishes he could reach up and rub it. Somehow I don't see him doing such a natural act.

The door on the other side of the cell opens. My muscles tense in expectation.

The red-haired woman from the marketplace steps in. Today she has her bright hair down in long curls and wears a gold gown instead of the silver one. Her makeup is immaculate and she smells like a peculiar mixture of pot and jasmine.

It only serves to remind me I was up sweating through the night and my mouth is dry and dirty.

She stands a careful distance in front of me, like she knows the exact reach of my restraints.

Casually, she takes in my choppy black hair, my filthy

tunic from sleeping in the dirt, and my equally filthy skin. Her lip curls, like I stink so powerfully she can barely stand being in here with me.

Her disgust washes over me and makes me angry. How dare she be offended by me! I hike my chin and proudly return her stare.

"My name is Bareket, and I am the richest person in Saligia."

I want to give into my tendency toward sarcasm and snide, *How good for you*, but I refrain.

"You are the very first person who has ever defied me in the marketplace." Her red brows climb up her forehead. "That displeases me."

Well, what does she want to do about it? Beat me? Is that why I'm shackled?

"I understand from your Master that you wanted to come here because of your sister."

A lump slowly begins to thicken in my throat.

She tilts her head. "Is this true?"

"Yes," I whisper.

"Then you'll be disappointed to know that you didn't come with me. Because I bought your sister the day before I was going to buy you."

The lump in my throat tightens to near pain, but I manage to ask, "Is she okay?"

Bareket's red brows drift back down and then she half smiles. "I wouldn't know. You see, there were a couple of men who took a liking to her. They had quite the time with her."

My chest constricts. *No...*

"Indeed they enjoyed her so much," her voice lowers to coldness, "they offered a fair price to take her with them."

I yank at my shackles. "NO!"

Bareket laughs. "If only you would've come with me instead of defy me."

"NO!" I jerk against my chains as hot tears burn trails down my cheeks. "Where did they take her?" I scream.

Bareket backs away. "I wouldn't know." She opens her hand and tosses my sister's bracelet toward me, and it lands at my feet. "That's all she left behind. You can have it." With that she walks out.

I scream and wildly pull at my restraints. Scorching terror surges through me, blistering my veins. "Unlock me," I sob to Alexior. "Unlock me."

Anguish buckles every muscle inward, gutting me of any last hope. I sag against the chains, crying, the clanking metal the only thing holding me up. I peer at Alexior through blurry eyes.

He doesn't react to my grief and instead crosses the cell to where I sag. He leans in close and unlocks my now bloody wrists.

"I hate you," I tell him. "I hate all of you."

He releases my ankles next. "Use the pain to take you to the next level. That's what will turn you into a warrior. Hate will keep you alive. It will make you a champion."

"I don't care if I'm alive anymore," I speak so quietly I barely hear my own self.

"Yes you do. Bareket didn't say your sister's dead. You stay alive for her."

Crawling forward, I grab Lena's bracelet. I gave it to her for her tenth birthday. I run my finger over the alternating leather and silver and turn it inside out to read the inscription. *Sisters forever and ever.*

Through my tears, I stare down at the fuzzy words. Alexior is right. Bareket didn't say Lena is dead. "Master will still find her, right?"

Alexior nods. "If he said he would, he will."

I fasten her bracelet around my wrist and cradle it to my chest. *For you, Lena. I will stay alive for you.*

CHAPTER 8

ALEXIOR LEAVES me alone in the cell, and hours later I finally drag myself up and out. He's right. I need to stay alive for Lena. She is not dead. She is *not*.

Everyone is out training in the courtyard with wooden swords and shields. Over to the left sits a large wooden box filled with more practice swords and shields. In front of the box lay a pile of spears.

Dad throws his arm around my neck and knuckle rubs my head. "Thata girl. Way to take first place. The other team never expects you for a javelin thrower."

Laughing, I poke my dad in the ribs and repeat his own words, "I'm short and scrappy, but deadly."

My dad was a cop. From the time I could throw a punch, he worked with me on techniques and skills. He wanted me strong and able to defend myself. Lena never got into it, but I loved training with him. He was also very skilled in gymnastics and taught me a lot of those moves, too. He was the one who encouraged me to join the heptathlon team in high school. And though I was the shortest javelin thrower, I held my own. Actually took first in a lot of competitions.

My father's laughter floats through my mind. It's been two years since he died of pancreatic cancer. I miss him more and more every day. It doesn't seem to get any better. If he were alive right now, I wouldn't be here and Lena would be safe.

Though everyone's using swords and shields to train, I lean down and pick up a spear. It's a little smaller than a javelin, but the most familiar thing here. I turn and look at Alexior, and he nods his approval.

I take a second to familiarize myself with the difference in weight and shape and center of gravity. I'm used to throwing a six foot javelin and this spear is about a foot shorter. It's also lighter. The grip's what I'm familiar with, though, and wrapped with leather.

Wiping my sweaty palms on my tunic, I put it in position overhand and turn toward the training area. I need running space to gain momentum. I step on the other side of the large wooden box where no one is training and back all the way up.

I take off in a jog, feeling the bounce and weight. Yes, it's definitely smaller. I point my left finger where I want it to go, leap off the ground, and bring my arm back as I use my shoulder and triceps to throw it through the air.

It sails a respectable distance and skids across the dirt. I frown. That's not where I was aiming.

Laughter fills the air and I turn to see Sera. I glare at her. *This one's different than I'm used to throwing!* I want to snap at her, but instead ignore her and go retrieve my practice weapon.

As I stalk back to my original spot, I glance up to the

terrace to see Master and his wife and several more of the rich and elite.

They're drinking and talking and idly watching us train. Behind all of them stand a row of slave girls. I see the one who was forced to get in the pool. She is staring straight ahead in a brainwashed haze. I wonder what her name is.

Two women over to the left are giggling and eyeing several of the men warriors. It hadn't occurred to me until this second that the men captives are used and discarded just as us women.

I push their disgusting rich selves from my brain and resume my spot. I try again, jogging, throwing, and do better this time. I actually spear the dirt.

My dad always coached me to fine-tune my "distance" weapon skills for self-defense. Things I could throw. Things that would injure my opponent without hand-to-hand combat. Though he taught me plenty of that as well.

Again and again I reacquaint myself with the spear until I'm consistently spearing not only the ground, but specific spots on the ground. Next I want to try an actual target. I turn and glance up to the elite on the terrace. Those are some good targets.

"Halt!" Alexior commands.

I put my spear down, use my tunic to wipe the sweat off my face, and go stand in line with the other warriors and recruits.

Master addresses us from the terrace. "My esteemed guests," he indicates those who are standing with him, "would like to see an exhibition." He turns to the heavyset man on his right. "Who is your first pick?"

CHAPTER 9

THE HEAVYSET MAN looks right at Sera. "You know the Serpent of Saligia is my favorite."

Sera waggles her snakelike tongue and steps forward out of line.

"Who shall she go up against?" Master asks the others.

A tall skinny woman standing beside the heavyset man points right at me. "Isn't that the one you paid fifty thousand for? I want to see that little one go up against her."

My heart skips a beat and then starts racing.

Alexior steps forward. "Master, Valoria has only just begun training. She is not ready for an exhibition."

Master looks from Alexior over to me and then at the tall skinny woman who delivers an ugly pout. "Please. We'll pay double," she says, slipping her arm through the heavyset man's. "Won't we, darling?"

He chuckles indulgingly. "Yes, yes we will."

Master nods to Alexior. "As they wish."

Camille shoots me a worried glance that I purposefully turn away from. The last thing I need floating in my brain is doubt. Will I beat Sera? Probably not. But I will give this, whatever this exhibition is, my best.

If this is part of getting Lena back, doing whatever Master says, then I'll do it. Of course I'll do it.

The warriors and the recruits go to stand along the perimeter of the training ground, leaving me and Sera alone in the courtyard. Alexior hands a wooden practice sword to Sera first and then brings one to me.

"She's a stronger opponent," he quietly tells me. "Do not allow advantage to your back. You are small. Use that to your benefit. Draw her to you then use her strength against her." With that, he backs off, leaving me to wonder how exactly I'm supposed to execute what he just said.

"I would like them to use *real* weapons," someone calls out, and I snap my eyes up to the terrace.

Bareket is there now, standing off by herself, staring her beady eyes right at me.

Every single one of my tendons and muscles tense in fiery anger.

Master lets out a nervous laugh. "Bareket—"

"It's what I want." She flings her jeweled hand through the air. "If it's their lives you're worried about, I'll reimburse you double should one perish."

My mouth goes completely dry. I can't help myself from looking over at Sera who seems as stunned as I am.

Master nods. "As you wish." He looks down at Alexior. "Let them choose their weapon."

My feet stay rooted to the dirt as frenzied blood throbs through me. *I'm going to die.* My world tilts, then everything mutes. I'm going to pass out.

Alexior appears again in front of me. He peels my fingers off of the wooden sword and hands me a smaller spear than the one I just practiced with. This one has a blade attached to the end.

"Look at me," he commands.

I bring my dazed eyes up to his.

"Focus. Think of your sister. Neither you nor Sera have to die. When it comes time to surrender, do so with the show of an index finger." He wraps my hand around the spear and goes to stand with the others around the perimeter of the training ground.

"Begin!" Master commands from the terrace.

"Valoria!" Sera shouts. "You will die here in this dirt."

Indeed they enjoyed her so much, they offered a fair price to take her with them.

Bareket's voice echoes around me and tears spring to my eyes.

"You're crying?" Sera laughs. "What were you all thinking giving me this one?"

I clench my jaw and focus in on her standing some twenty feet away. Behind her I see the other warriors and recruits and their images slowly blur until Sera, in all her hugeness, is the only thing in my line of sight.

I feel my sister's bracelet around my wrist, and it's like warm water slowly washes over me, cleansing me, taking with it any last remnant of panic and replacing it with rage and strength and power.

I welcome the renewed control.

"Valoria!" Sera taunts again.

With a yell, I take off in a full sprint toward her.

She throws her sword through the air at me. End over end it hurtles, and I dive to the right as it whistles past. I come to my knees and sling the spear. She ducks, and it sails past straight toward Gem.

"Gem!" I yell.

She doesn't react quickly enough and the blade nicks her leg. Guilt twitches inside of me, and I push it away. Focus.

Sera uses the second of distraction to retrieve her sword.

I whirl on her. "You're pathetic," I spit. "I'm unarmed and half your size and you feel like you need a sword? I thought you were Sera, Serpent of Saligia."

Up on the terrace people laugh, and Sera's jaw tightens. I know she won't use that sword now. It would make her look like a fool.

As expected she tosses it aside, and we charge each other. I hurl myself through the air and our bodies slam together. She picks me up and flings me to the dirt and my head bounces off the ground.

Her fist comes back and straight into my face. Blood slings through the air. Something crunches. My nose. She broke my goddamn nose!

I press all ten fingers into her face and scream as I dig in hard. She grabs my wrists and slings my arms away and I come right back at her with a punch to the esophagus.

She gags and I use the momentary reprieve to curl my legs in and roll away. I sprint over to my spear, snatch it up, turn and whip it through the air. It flies toward her and before she has time to dodge, it slices open her upper arm.

She doesn't even give the split skin a glance as she jumps to her feet and runs at me. I try to sidestep her, but for a big woman, she's quick. She catches air in a round-house kick, her sandaled foot connects with my jaw, and the momentum flings my body up against the stone wall.

Then she's on me, punching me. I feel her fists every-where. My face. My chest. My stomach. Blood spurts. Somewhere deep down I find the will to bring my knee up hard straight into her groin. The contact stops her.

With one hand she holds me up against the stone wall, towering above me, panting, glaring at me. I don't fight back. If it weren't for her hand holding me up, I would be a boneless, lifeless pile in the dirt.

When it comes time to surrender, do so with the show of an index finger.

Stubbornness struggles within me. I can barely see her through all the blood and swollen skin. I've never been the type of person to give in. But if I do not, those people up on the terrace will gladly let her beat me to death, and she won't have a problem doing it.

With everything in me, I raise my quivering arm to try one last time. Sera must think I'm going to surrender because she glances over her shoulder and up to the terrace at Master. He starts to give a thumbs down—

I jab my thumb straight into Sera's eye socket and keep right on jabbing until I hear *pop*. She lurches away, simultaneously holding her eye and thrusting a finger straight up in the air.

My body slides down the wall. *She surrendered...*

"No," Bareket cries. "I want to see Valoria die."

I close my eyes and think of my sister. The last thing we ate together was an orange. She giggled when it squirted me in the eye.

"I want to live," I whisper, my lips so puffy it barely seeps out.

Bareket's smirk is the last thing I see before I pass out.

CHAPTER 10

THE SAME OLD lady who cut my hair tends to me when I wake up. I'm lying on my back in a room I haven't been in yet. I try to move and end up groaning instead. My entire body feels like I've been trampled by bulls.

"Bruised rib, broken nose, bashed eye, stitches." The old lady tisks.

I turn my head on a grimace.

"Stay still," she snaps.

Groggily I stare from the corner of my eye as she purses her lips and stitches up my cheek. I don't even feel it. She tugs the thread, ties it off, and snips it.

Beyond her I see a couple of empty cots, shelving with bottles of herbs, and various utensils I assume are her medical tools.

I try to swallow but my throat is dry and swollen.

She sees the movement and limps across the cell to her desk. I hadn't noticed her limp before. Or the fact her shoulders sag and hunch.

She hobbles back over and holds a battered goblet to my

lips and I try to drink, but most of it dribbles out of my numb mouth.

"What's your name?" I croak.

She frowns down at me in confusion, like no one's ever asked her name.

"Talme," she tells me.

"That's a pretty name."

She just looks at me, and I wonder what could've brought her here to Saligia. Was she kidnapped like me? Did she sign a contract like Gem? Or does she work for them like Alexior does?

"Master has given you three days to heal and rest." Talme lifts the thin material draped over my naked body, checks my bandages, and walks out.

I close my eyes. *I wish I felt like crying.* That's the thought I have before I drift off.

When I open them next, Alexior stands over me. I try to smile. I don't know why. He and I are certainly not friends.

His gray gaze takes in my battered face. He holds the goblet to my lips and I eagerly drink the entire thing.

I breathe and roll my tongue around in my mouth. It doesn't feel as swollen as the last time I woke up. "How long have I been out?"

"A day."

Master said I only get three. I can't imagine I'll be ready to go back out there and train in two days. I shift a little on the cot, and my shoulder sparks with fire. I lift it off the table, cringing, trying to see.

Alexior puts a stern hand on my chest. "Lie still."

"My shoulder," I gasp.

"It's the branding. You have the mark of Saligia now. It's a true honor." He turns to show me the S branded on his shoulder as well. Just like the one I saw on Sera in the bath house.

"*What?*" I don't understand. "I thought only those who win in the fights get that."

"Or those who beat a warrior."

My brows come down, and my stomach lurches at the thought of what I did to Sera's eye.

"Yes, she lost it," Alexior tells me, seemingly reading my mind.

I wince. "I can't believe I popped someone's eye out."

He turns to leave. "I'll leave you to your rest."

I close my eyes and even though Sera and I are enemies, even though she would've killed me out there, guilt still twinges through me.

The next time I wake, Talme is gently dabbing something on my cheek. It's an ointment and smells—I crinkle my nose—like shit.

"I know," she says. "But it's good."

She grabs a bowl and a spoon and begins feeding me soup. The broth slides over my tongue and down to soothe my raw, starving stomach. I haven't eaten in days, I realize, and impatiently open my mouth for more.

"Easy," she coaches and makes me eat the rest painfully slow.

When I'm done I close my eyes and once again am gone.

Daylight shines in the narrow window and flashes across my face. The warmth and brightness is what has me opening my eyes and simultaneously squinting against the beam. I give myself a few minutes to orient and carefully push up to a sitting position.

The sheet slides down me and I note I'm still naked underneath. I look around the cell and find that I'm alone. I flex my body, my neck, arms, and legs. The sharp pangs have dulled now to a sporadic throb. I wonder if it's day three.

I slide off the cot and on unsteady legs, stand.

The door opens and Talme walks in. Her eyes widen when she sees me.

"What day is it?" I ask.

"You're on day five. Master came in to see you on day three and granted you two additional healing days. Be glad. He's never done that before."

She checks all my stitches and bandages and cuts and bruises, then grabs my white undergarments and brown tunic and helps me get dressed.

The last thing she hands me is Lena's bracelet.

There is no mirror so I have no clue what I look like. I imagine it's not good. But for a person who has been in bed for five days, I don't feel unclean. Talme must have bathed me.

"Why are you here?" I ask her. "In Saligia." She doesn't seem like the others.

"I've got no other place to go," she answers simply before handing me a goblet and walking out.

I take some healthy gulps of water, pondering her response. I should've asked how she came to be here in Saligia. Next time I'm alone with her I will.

The warriors are eating breakfast when I emerge, and the recruits sit in their usual spot on the ground in the corner. My fingers trail up and over my shoulder and across the scabby branded S. I'm one of them now.

I don't consider it an honor at all. But I will fake that I do. I will try to be proud of it. And I will keep my mouth shut and stay out of trouble.

The warriors catch sight of me and all stand. I hesitate

at the incredibly awkward and unexpected greeting. I glance over to the patch covering Sera's eye and make myself hard against the sight. There is no place for weakness here in Saligia.

I look to the ground where Camille and Gem and all the recruits stare at me with tense expressions.

I gaze to Alexior next who as usual remains stoic. Then I turn back to Sera and Ignatius and the other warriors. They clear a spot at one of the tables for me where a plate of fruit and cheese and bread already awaits.

Just the sight of it makes my stomach growl.

I walk straight toward it and pick it up. "Thank you," I tell them all.

My resolve to keep my mouth shut and stay out of trouble immediately dissipates. It's just not me. I turn to the recruits sitting like dogs on the ground with empty bowls in front of them that I know barely had a crumb to start.

I cross the eating area and set my plate down in the center of their pathetic circle. "Eat," I tell them, then walk right back over to the serving line and fill a new plate with more food. I turn to the warriors. "Where's your compassion? Dogs eat better than them."

Sera narrows her eye. I glance over to the recruits who out of fear have not touched what I put in front of them.

"Eat," I tell them again, proud my voice comes across clear and firm.

With one last hesitant look toward the warriors, the recruits dig in.

I stand, eating my own, fully aware everyone is staring at me and not caring.

Starting today, things will change around this place. Something inside of me loosens with the realization and then tightens right back up with determination. We may be in some twisted cosplay of the rich and elite, but that doesn't mean we have to lose our humanity. We are not animals.

CHAPTER 11

OVER THE NEXT WEEK ME, Camille, Gem, and the other recruits settle into the pace of training from sunup to sundown.

We practice with the wooden swords and shields. Throw nets at each other. Toss leather balls heavy with sand. Climb knotted ropes. Traverse an obstacle course with swinging mallets. And practice fighting formations.

We eat, bathe, sleep, and get up and do it all again the next day. I throw myself into the training, singularly distracted by one goal: to win money to purchase mine and Lena's freedom.

In the background Alexior repeats the same thing over and over, "Forget everything you were before. You study. You train. That is how you become a champion. And you accept the humility of surrender when required."

Camille shoots me a look as if to say, *he's talking about you.*

"I'll never surrender," I answer her unspoken thought.

"The only voice I should hear," Alexior snaps, "is

mine." He gives me a pointed look. "Grunting is what I should hear from *you*."

I grit my teeth. I know I shouldn't, *I know*, but I can't help myself from returning his pointed look and following it up with a loud grunt.

Alexior stalks across the training courtyard until he's right in front of me. "Perhaps a lesson in obedience is in order."

My stubborn temper flares even more. "Perhaps," I agree.

He switches his eyes to Camille. "For both of you."

All the warriors laugh, and Camille just glares at me. *I'm sorry*, I mouth, feeling horrible. I didn't mean to get her in trouble too. I glance over to Gem, and she quickly looks away like she knows better than to get involved.

Alexior nods to Ignatius and Sera who grab Camille and me and drag us across the training area over to a latched metal shed. I've seen this here every day. I assumed it was storage or something.

Alexior opens the door and we get tossed inside the empty area. The door bangs closed, locks, and hot blackness engulfs us.

"Remind me why I'm your friend?" Camille tensely whispers through the darkness.

I wipe the sweat that's already beading. "I'm sor—"

"I don't want to hear it," she cuts me off. "Just don't talk to me."

"Okay." At least Gem didn't get thrown in here, too.

I rotate my sister's bracelet around my wrist, running the pads of my fingers over the alternating softness of the leather and hardness of the silver. Everything I do, I do for her.

"What is your deal?" Camille snaps, even though she just said she didn't want to talk.

"I have to win. It's the only way I'll get my sister back. We've been training hard. I'm ready. Getting into the fights is the only way to earn the money to buy her back."

"But how can you even trust that?"

"What other choice do I have?" I *need* it to be true.

"You're not ready."

"How do you know?" I snap.

Her sigh echoes around us. "Look at what Sera did to you."

"And look at what I did to her."

"She beat you to a pulp."

"But I won!" I angrily point out.

"I didn't say you didn't," Camille snipes. "But she is bigger and more powerful and if you went up against her or someone like her again, they would do the same thing to you."

Irritation swells through me, and I don't respond to her point. Sera is enormous. Yes, I popped her eye, but she did beat me senseless.

That thought circles my brain for the next several quiet, hot, tense moments until I finally ask Camille, "You really think I'm not ready?"

"Yes," she quietly responds.

The truth of her answer niggles around inside of me, and I don't want to admit she's right. But I know she is.

"You're obsessing," she says. "I can tell."

Despite the blackness, the intense heat, and the sweat now dropping off of me, I laugh a little. "Why don't we talk about something else?" I suggest.

"Okay. How long do you think they'll keep us in here?"

"Not that," I jokingly whine. "Something that'll keep our minds occupied."

"Ignatius," Camille mumbles. "I heard he was set on fire in the fights. That's how he got all those disgusting scars."

"Jesus," I breathe. "How horrible."

"Suppose that's why he's called the 'Fire of the Arena'."

I think about Ignatius outside training. I think about his enormous height with every muscle and feature mangled with scars. "Do you think that's why he stays even though he's free? Because he's so disfigured?"

"Maybe. But then what would someone like him do away from this place?" People would be scared of him.

The thought of that saddens me. All things aside, he's been okay with us newcomers. He's far from a gentle giant, but he certainly hasn't been cruel like Sera and some of the others.

"How big do you think Saligia is?" Camille whispers.

I think of when I arrived and all that I saw while traveling in the cart from the marketplace. "I have no clue." It seems to go on for miles in all directions.

Heavy silence falls between us, each lost to our own thoughts. I don't know how much time passes, but I close my eyes and simply focus on Camille's quiet raspy breaths.

I must fall asleep, or maybe I pass out, because the next time I open my eyes I'm sprawled outside of the shed with my cheek pressed into the dirt. It's dark out now and the air is warm and moist.

Groggily, I push to a sitting position. Everything spins and I close my eyes. I give myself a second and when I feel steadier, I get to my feet.

Up on the terrace I spy Mistress drinking from a jeweled goblet and staring down at me. She raises an eyebrow when our eyes catch. She's not wearing her usual colorful gown and instead has on a long, see-through, yellow one.

Behind her stands a completely naked slave girl with gold body dust sparkling in the moonlight. It's a different girl than the one I saw at the pool.

Master steps out onto the terrace too. His chest is naked, and though the railing prohibits me from seeing below his waist, I assume he has nothing on.

His wife turns to smile at him and then nods to the slave girl who sinks to her knees in front of him. With one last look at me, Mistress turns and watches the slave girl give her husband a blow job.

Staring up at the terrace, I swallow hard. I want to scream. I want to yank that girl away, but all I seem able to do is stand rooted in the dirt, staring up in disgust and horror.

My sister... I close my eyes, but I see her on her knees and not that slave girl. Violently, I shake my head. I can barely think straight.

When the slave girl is done, Mistress turns and looks down at me, then swerves her attention over to Alexior, who, I just now realize, stands in the shadows. Has he been there the whole time?

"Bring us Ignatius," Mistress tells Alexior.

He nods and disappears into the men's quarters. I frown at his back. Ignatius? What are they going to do with him?

Several minutes later, Ignatius steps from the men's quarters. Instead of his usual tunic, he wears a cloth that wraps around his lower body. It's the first time I've seen his chest and it's just as mangled as the rest of him is.

He doesn't even glance at me as he strolls past and straight into the tunnel that will lead him up to the villa. I want to chase after him. I want to tell him he's free. That he doesn't have to go.

"Valoria," Alexior quietly says and I jump. "You need food, a bath, and bed." He nods to the terrace where Master and his wife and the slave girl have now gone back inside. "That's none of your concern."

"What are they going to make Ignatius do?" I ask, even though I already know the answer. *Whatever they want. Whatever pleases them.* "Why is he here if he's free?"

"He doesn't know anything else," Alexior answers with a voice that seems deeper than usual. "He's been on Saligia since he was ten. This is his life—pleasing others."

Everything going through my mind I've already said. I've already thought. *This place is sick. It's wrong.* But I don't put words to any of it, and in fact find myself more numb than anything.

What does that say about me? I've only been here a couple of weeks and I'm already becoming desensitized to the depravity. What will I be like in a couple months? I don't want to know.

"Is Camille okay?" I ask.

Alexior nods. "She's already in bed."

For some reason, the question she whispered in the shed comes back to me, and I ask, "How big is Saligia?"

He doesn't answer and instead just stares down at me. "Do you need another lesson in obedience?"

I clench my teeth. "No. I do not. Why is my question considered disobedient?"

Alexior widens his legs and folds his arms across his chest, which only makes every muscle in his upper body bunch. Is he standing that way to be intimidating? "Why do you want to know? Is the reason a disobedient reason?"

I mull that question around. If I were to somehow escape, I wouldn't even know where to find my sister.

Why do I want to know? Because I'm thinking of escaping, and, yes, that is a disobedient reason.

Without answering his question I turn away. An unexpected shudder drives my feet and I move forward across the training area to the women's quarters.

When I get to the archway I glance back to see Alexior standing and staring up at the stars. He closes his eyes and mouths a few words as if in prayer.

CHAPTER 12

AT BREAKFAST THE NEXT MORNING, Alexior makes an announcement. "Master has put together a demonstration to officially introduce our recruits to the rest of Saligia's society. This will be your opportunity to win the mark of Saligia and also money."

He holds up one finger. "Please remember surrender."

"Who's the visiting camp?" one of the warriors asks.

"There isn't one. You will be fighting each other." He pulls out a piece of paper. "I have the pairings here. There will be six rounds, each round increasing in earnings. Camille and Valoria will fight in the first round—"

I look over at Camille and we exchange an uneasy glance.

Alexior continues listing the rounds, "Gem with Felicia. Then Sera and Ignatius will fight in the last round with a ten percent prize."

"Tonight in the villa there will be a gathering of Saligia's elite where they will place their wager on each warrior and recruit. You are expected to be in attendance." He tacks the paper on the wall and walks off.

"I'm with Felicia," Gem mutters. "I hope I don't hurt her too badly."

Camille leans into me. "For some reason I never thought we'd actually be fighting each other."

"Me neither..." I can't imagine beating up Camille. "Why don't we flip a coin to see which one surrenders? Then we could put on a little fighting show, surrender, and neither of us gets harmed."

She nods. "But it's too bad we're not fighting in the last round. Ten percent?" Camille's brows lift. "If Master bets a million, ten percent of that will give you a good chunk toward your sister."

The last round. I cut a glance over to Ignatius and then Sera. Camille's right. If I can somehow figure out how to fight in the last round...

"If you fight one of them, you will die," Gem whispers in panic. "I hear Sera's never lost in the arena."

"Yes, but she surrendered to me."

Camille shakes her head. "I'm not having that conversation with you again."

Master comes through the archway leading to the villa with a soldier on each side. He takes a moment to speak with Alexior and then heads toward the locked gate that we all came through weeks ago on the cart.

"Be back in a second," I tell Camille and approach him. "Master, may I have a moment?"

He nods to the soldiers and waves me toward him.

"Is there any word of my sister?" I ask.

Master huffs a laugh. "And why would I have word of your sister? I told you to fight and win and *then* I'd find your sister. At this point whatever little money you've made me has gone to your upkeep."

He takes a step closer. "Do not *ever* approach me again. When I want to speak to you I will summon you."

Icy anger jolts through me, but I set my jaw and lock every one of my muscles so I don't shake with the fury of it. I train my eyes on the ground and take a submissive step back. "Yes, Master."

After he leaves, I lift my head. *I will fight in that last round, and I will win.*

CHAPTER 13

THAT NIGHT we are instructed to bathe and oil our bodies. The men fighters are dressed just like Ignatius was when he visited the villa in white cloth that wraps their waists. We women are dressed in similar cloths but with an additional one across our breasts.

Our wrists are shackled, and we are lined up women first according to size and then men after us. Being significantly shorter than every other fighter, I am, of course, right in front.

No one speaks as we wait in the tunnel for our cue to enter. The gathering upstairs has been full on for a good hour now, and the laughter and voices and music echo through the tunnel around us.

A soldier unlocks the gate, and everyone behind me moves, pressing me forward. Nerves twitch through me as I lead the way up the stairs. The other gate opens, and I step into the villa.

The place doesn't fall silent, but it does quiet. Alexior is already here waiting. He's in his usual soft leather body armor and black baggy pants. A brilliant purple scarf wraps his neck and marks the only change in how I usually see him.

"You are to stay in line at all times," he instructs. "Do not leave formation unless one of the elite requests it."

He steps in front of me and begins leading us on a march through all the rooms in the villa. I take in the polished brass goblets and platters, the gleaming marble floors, the white walls with gold inlaid leaves, the colorful curtains blowing in the breeze... After weeks of living in bare-boned quarters, the luxury up here is even more evident now than when I first arrived.

The place is packed with the richest, all dressed in their finest vibrant gowns. Most of the women wear their hair up in order to better display gaudy necklaces decorating their necks. Everyone's drinking and eating and staring at us as we march through the rooms. Do these people live on Saligia full-time or do they come and go? I can't imagine they could just disappear from society altogether.

There are twenty of us trained fighters and by my rough estimate about a hundred of them. None of them look armed. I think we could probably take them if we really wanted to, even with our wrists shackled. Especially if the house slaves joined in. Am I the only one who thinks this way? Have others tried and failed?

I'm sure the punishment is enough to scare everyone into obedience.

My gaze trails over the soldiers next, armed and at attention, one for every five or so elite. The soldiers would definitely be the problem.

We come to a stop in the room with the shallow pool where we're told to line the perimeter. Women on one side and men on the other.

The house slaves linger in every corner, dressed differently as well. Gone are their blue tunics to be replaced by gauzy white gowns. I glance over my shoulder at the young slave boy occupying the corner behind me.

He can't be more than fifteen.

Through the near-transparent fabric his private area is on display for anyone who wants to look. I think of Ignatius. He's been here in Saligia since he was ten. That was probably him once upon a time. The whole thing makes me sick.

"Greetings!" Master sweeps into the room flanked by seemingly the most elite. "Welcome to my home. My wife and I are excited for the upcoming demonstration. Please," he indicates us, "walk around. Feel. Touch. Place bets. Eat. And definitely get drunk!"

If anyone *feels* me, *touches* me, they're going down.

The elite laugh and slowly begin spreading about the room. Master claps his hands and two slave girls emerge from the shadows. In their gowns, they slide into the shallow pool and begin seductively rolling and crawling through the water covered in rose petals.

I know I should be observing my surroundings, but I find myself fixated on the two girls. The more this immorality settles in, the harder of a person I become, and the better chance I have at adapting and surviving and finding my sister.

"This is the little one he paid fifty thousand for," a man speaks from beside me.

I turn away from the girls in the water and look up into deep set eyes framed by bushy black and gray brows. The woman standing beside him looks young enough to be his granddaughter.

They both reach forward and touch my bare stomach and my muscles contract, which makes them laugh. It's all I can do not to shove their creepy hands off of me.

They continue on down the line and more elite follow, discussing us like we're inanimate objects. Bareket glides right in front of me, sliding me a haughty look that I glower at.

She stops in front of Gem. "You. Come with me."

Gem doesn't immediately move and then with a deep breath she steps out of line and follows Bareket. I watch as she picks out a man warrior, and then with a small group of elite they disappear into a back room.

My whole body tenses and I keep my eyes focused on the archway they all went through. I don't bother asking myself what they want with Gem in that private room. I suspect I know. And I also know if they *ever* pull me from line, I will not go easily.

Gem gave herself to this place for a lesser sentence. I think I'd rather spend ten years in jail than one here.

"Not surprising, the elite aren't happy with the list," I overhear Master tell Alexior. "They want to see Sera and Valoria. Their fight from a couple of weeks ago is all anyone can talk about."

"Valoria isn't ready," Alexior answers. "If you put them together again, Sera *will* maim her, surrender or not, and then you'll be out fifty thousand plus some."

Master nods. "I know." He laughs. "But you should see the bets people are willing to place on Valoria. I'll triple my money in one exhibition."

Triple the money. At ten percent that means I'll have a lot going toward my sister. I glance down to where Sera stands, and a thought forms...

Ten percent.

I lift my sandaled foot, and even though Alexior told us not to, I step out of line and stride down to the end.

"Valoria!" Alexior reprimands, and I blatantly ignore him as I come to stand right in front of Sera.

She lowers her one good eye to mine. *What am I doing?* sneaks into my mind, and I push it out and replace it with *Lena*. I lift my shackled wrists and punch Sera in the neck.

Several of the rich scream and back away, and Sera charges.

She slams her shoulder straight into me. Our bodies fly through the air in a weightless moment, and we land in the shallow pool. The jarring impact knocks the wind right out of me, and we roll through the rose petals as the slave girls scream and scramble from the water.

Immediately hands fall on both of us, yanking us apart.

"You little bitch," Sera spits. "I will kill you."

I jerk at the two soldiers holding me, purposefully putting on a show. "Let's do it."

In the background I see some of the elite backing further away.

"Enough!" Master shouts. "You two will settle this tomorrow in the final round." He jabs a finger toward the tunnel gate. "Now get them out of here."

Soldiers drag me from the villa. I'm thrown in the same cell that I was in when Bareket visited me. Sera is thrown in a separate one.

I close my eyes and try to focus on everything my dad taught me, on everything I've learned here, but all I can think of is Sera and how badly she beat me up. I shake my head. I can do this. I have to do this.

In the morning Alexior lets me out. "I'm fully aware you've done all this on purpose. You need more training. You're not ready."

I tilt my head and look up at him, ignoring the truth of his words. "I'm as ready as I can be."

"No you're not." He steps to the side. "Go eat."

Though nerves have taken over my hunger, I grab a bowl of oats and fruit and sit down across from Camille and Gem.

"We don't know if we should offer you cheers or sympathies," Camille says.

I make my lips curve into a reassuring smile. "We'll go with cheers."

Gem holds up an index finger as a show of surrender. "Please remember this."

I nod even though I know I have to win this thing.

We eat in companionable silence for a few minutes and my thoughts trail to last night. "How are you?" I ask Gem.

A faint, sad smile curls her lips. It's been so long since I've seen a simple thing like an easy smile.

"I'm all right." Gem glances over to the warrior who went in that back room with her. He's shorter than the others, but just as layered in muscles, and his accent is odd. Like he's from a mixture of countries, not just one. "Razo was kind to me."

"What did they make you do?" Camille uneasily asks.

Gem presses her lips together and moves the oats and fruit around in her bowl. I shake my head at Camille indicating we should just drop the subject.

Gem glances back over to Razo. "They made us have sex," she quietly admits, "and they watched."

Camille gasps.

My throat tightens and I reach out and take Gem's hand. I squeeze a little too tightly. "I'm so sorry, Gem."

She brings her eyes to mine. "Like I said, he was kind."

My gaze tracks over to Razo. He's just as much a victim as Gem.

CHAPTER 14

I STAND at the iron gate that leads from the holding cell out into the sandy fighting area of the small arena. Actually it's more like a large, circular, outdoor theater. It's definitely the structure I saw the day I arrived and was transported across the island.

The sound of stamping feet vibrate above me. The cheering crowd echoes off the stone walls down here in the holding cell. I try to block it out and focus on preparatory thoughts, but I end up watching Gem fight one of the other recruits instead of Felicia.

Because of me the original pairings got jumbled around now that I'm fighting Sera.

There're several hundred people here. In the stands sit an array of men and women all dressed in ancient Roman outfits. Above the stands are private balconies filled with the most elite. I twist my head to see up to where Master sits along with his wife, a few others, and Bareket.

I look back down to the stands, wondering how all this works. I imagine people come here to "vacation", and like any resort—how much money you cough up determines you're experience while you're here. Obviously, the people up in the private balconies have the most to spend.

"I can't believe I broke her arm," Camille solemnly mumbles from beside me.

My eyes shift over to the corner where Felicia sits huddled, sniveling, cradling her awkward, disjointed arm. She was half hysterical with wails when they dragged her off the sands.

Weeks ago I would've felt pity. Now, I don't. She's weak. She spends every day complaining and half assing. I have no more patience for her.

"She won't last in this place," I tell Camille as I take in her bloody face. "You fought well."

She shrugs. "Suppose I get branded now."

"True."

We both go back to watching Gem as she submits her opponent. One finger goes up. The fight is over.

"You're next," Camille tells me.

Jitters spark through my nerve endings and I use the sensation to fuel me. Focus. I beat Sera once. I can beat her again.

I watch as Gem exits via a wooden door on the other side of the fighting area and then Master begins speaking. "Good people of Saligia, the fight you have been waiting for. Some of you have heard of Valoria, the defiant one. She is the tiniest fighter I have ever owned. She is the only fighter to have bested Sera."

He points to my gate and a soldier opens it.

I inhale a deep breath, blow it hard through my lips, and enter the arena. The crowd goes wild. They jump to their feet, stomping, screaming, leaping up and down. I absorb their energy and lift my fists into the air, and they scream even louder.

I do a back flip. "Yeah!" I yell, and the crowd echoes me.

Master waves them quiet. "And we have Sera, the Serpent of Saligia. She's never lost in this arena. Let's see how she does with one eye, courtesy of Valoria." He motions across the fighting area to a different gate that slides open.

Sera steps through, and the crowd goes from wild to uncontrollable insanity. She stomps around in a circle, snakes her tongue out, and waggles it at the people. Several of the women flash Sera their boobs and wiggle their own tongues. *Sick.*

"Sera. Sera. Sera," the crowd chants.

Obviously they favor Sera. I tell myself not to let it get to me. *Focus.*

A slave comes out pulling a wagon that holds our weapons. My footsteps falter as I go to approach him. I search the wagon for my spear, but don't see it. He hands me a heavy metal helmet, a just as heavy chest plate, a hefty sword, and an enormous shield.

My shoulders drop. "Where's my stuff?"

He shakes his head. "This is what they gave me."

"But..." I glance up to the balcony where Master sits to see Bareket smugly smiling down at me.

I clench my jaw and she merely grins wider in return.

"Fine," I grit and lift out the weighty supplies. Why is Bareket doing this to me? Just because I defied her in the marketplace? She's had her fun with my sister, what more does she want from me?

The slave moves the wagon on to Sera and while she quickly dons her helmet and armor, I struggle into mine, stumbling back with the weight of it. The crowd chuckles.

With a soft grunt, I pick my shield up and let it fall right back down. It's too heavy. The crowd laughs even louder.

Through the tiny holes in the helmet, I look over to Sera who stands tall and proud in her armor. She easily lifts her shield and sword high into the air and the crowd leaps to their feet. They love her. She looks over at me and sneers.

I narrow my eyes and switch my gaze back up to Bareket, who is full on giggling now. I hate her. I hate all of them.

Master lifts his hands for quiet. "Good people—"

I snatch the sword off the ground and charge. The armor is heavy and dulls my usual quick speed to near slow motion. It only aggravates me.

With a yell, I lift my sword and swat it at Sera. Right. Left. Right. Left until my arms shake and my heart seems as if it's going to burst right out of me. She blocks each blow with her shield and on my next one, shoves me, and I stagger back.

She looks right at me through her helmet and lets out a deep chuckle that's meant to be a scare tactic. It doesn't work.

The crowd echoes her amusement, and she stalks a wide circle around me, lifting her sword and shield and enthralling the onlookers.

I use the break to surge to my feet and attack. With a yell, I ram my sword straight up under her armor. She spins at the exact second of my lunge, and my sword slices her side instead of puncturing an organ.

Blood immediately gushes, and the crowd goes wild. This time for me, not her. The sound of them and the sight of Sera's blood provoke me. I don't wait a single second before I go in for another stab.

She blocks it with her shield, and her eyes bore deeply into mine. "You have no idea who you're up against." That's the last thing she says before she full on attacks.

Her sword swings and stirs the air around us. Right. Left. Right. Each powerful motion driven by her enormous muscles.

I duck and swing and duck some more, struggling to breathe, but she's fast and I can't keep it up. My heart pounds so quickly it hurts, and our muffled grunts fill the air. Her sword clangs off my armor again and again and again, and my ears ring.

The blade connects with my lower leg and my skin splits open. The searing pain trips me to the sand. I inch back, and her foot slams down on my hand that's holding the sword.

She grinds it into my fingers and I clamp my jaw so I won't scream. I release the sword and she kicks it to the side. I struggle and kick and she comes down on top of me, planting her knee right into the armor covering my chest.

Though I know the sword is out of reach, I still fumble my fingers for it.

She puts the tip of her sword at the edge of my helmet and pries it off. Cool air immediately soothes my bared head.

"Stupid, stupid cunt," Sera sneers. "They're not going to let you live."

The tip of her sword presses into my throat, and I concentrate on staying very still. One millimeter more and she'll puncture my voice box.

I'm allowed to surrender. I need to. She will kill me if I do not.

I've heard life flashes before your eyes upon near death. But that doesn't happen to me. I feel only the bracelet burning into my wrist. I see my sister giggling as we swam in the ocean. I would rather be dead than live without my sister.

My sister. I have to live.

I lift my arm straight into the air and hold out an index finger. It's the first time in my entire life I've surrendered at anything.

The crowd boos. They don't want to see me live. They want to see Sera cut my head off. They're beasts. All of them.

I don't dare move my head. I stare up into the side of Sera's face as she looks up to where Master sits. The crowd's boos get even louder.

Then she's off of me, strutting away, and I lay in the dirt gazing up at the sun in the sky. I'm alive. For now.

CHAPTER 15

THAT NIGHT I sit on my cot, staring at the stitches in my calf. Pain prickles through the puffy skin. Other than that, a few bruises, a stinging elbow, and tired shaking muscles, I am unharmed. The armor saved me.

"Valoria—"

"That's not my name," I mumble.

Alexior sighs. "You needed more training."

I glance up to see him standing in the tunnel looking at me through the iron bars. I nod. "I know."

"What did you learn?"

"That Sera's good. Armor's heavy." I think of my spear and how Bareket purposefully didn't let me have it. "That the rich and elite call the shots. Always."

I think of my index finger. "The humility of surrender. And that my pride gets me into trouble." Though I already knew the last one.

Alexior nods. "Good. The best warriors, the ones who survive, are vicious, cunning, and know how to use their disadvantage for success."

"What's Sera's disadvantage?"

"That's for her to know. Not you."

"And mine?"

"What do you think they are?" he prompts.

"My temper," I immediately answer. "My size."

"I concur." He casts me a long determined study. "You needed to lose. Losing makes you stronger. More focused. You come out tomorrow ready to train. You listen and do everything I say, and I will make you into a winner. I will make you into a champion. Agreed?"

I breathe deeply. "Agreed."

CHAPTER 16

ALL THE NEXT day Sera struts around like she has a golden vagina, and Master lets her. She's allowed privilege into the villa to watch our training from the terrace. She's handfed by a house slave and drinks so much wine I hope she pickles her liver.

The rest of us are back to training. Felicia is over by herself, practicing against a wooden post with her one good arm. She stops to bite a cuticle and then starts back up. For such a strong looking woman, she's the weakest among us.

I try my best to block her and Sera out and concentrate on training with a sword and shield and in full armor, as that's clearly where I'm lacking strength.

Alexior walks among us. "Study your opponent. Use your wits. It is the intelligent warrior that conquers. Always maintain eye contact. That is an act of challenge. Of power. There is power in control."

He stops right beside me and studies me in a very concrete way as I lunge toward Camille with my wooden sword. She blocks with her shield, sweeping down, and catches me off guard by bringing the blade straight to a stop at the side of my neck.

I nod. "Good job." She won that round.

"Power should be given to those who do not abuse it," Alexior tells us. "Mutual respect and trust is the most powerful of all."

He walks off, and Camille and I hold each other's studied stare. *Power should be given to those who do not abuse it.* I think of Master and the others abusing their power every day.

Then I think of me and Camille and Gem down here. If we were given that kind of power, what would we do with it? We'd set everyone free and bring this place down.

Respect and trust. Though I feel that for Camille, I know she hasn't been able to maintain that of me. Because of me she spent a day in the sweat box. She hasn't been able to trust me to keep my temper in check. I'm ashamed to admit it.

Respect and trust. Alexior's quiet, assured way has earned my respect. I do not trust him, though. While he might have some begrudging respect of me, he doesn't trust me either. I've done nothing to earn it. If I'm going to figure a way out of this place, Alexior is someone I could use on my side.

Camille cuts her sword to the ground, bringing me from my thoughts, and I leap over it, spin, and soft kick her shin.

She goes down to one knee, rolls, comes right back up and our swords collide. Both of our arms shake as we hold our stance, muscle pressing muscle, staring at each other through our soft practice helmets.

She crosses her eyes and sticks out her tongue and a laugh bursts from my lips. She laughs, too, and we both drop our swords. *God,* it feels good to laugh. I can't remember the last time I did.

I take off my helmet and laugh some more, enjoying the heat rushing to my cheeks, and it occurs to me, I'm probably about to get into trouble. About to get both of us into trouble.

"We better stop," I tell her, glancing across the training area to Alexior. His lips twitch, and he turns away, and I find myself smiling at the simple fact we amused stoic Alexior, if only for a second.

"Alexior!" Master shouts from the terrace. "Put Valoria in the cell."

My laughter immediately dies. I glance to Camille and her expression flattens to caution. The last time I was in there, Bareket visited me.

I strip out of my practice gear and follow Alexior into the cell. He doesn't shackle me to the wall like last time, but he does secure my wrists behind my back. Do they think I'm going to hurt Master? Probably.

I won't, though. But it would do no good to say that.

Like last time, Alexior stands over in the corner and I stay in the center of the cell staring at the door Bareket came through.

Minutes tick by and finally the door opens. Master nods to Alexior and then looks right at me.

Submissively, I nod my head. "Master."

He huffs an unamused laugh and shakes his head. This can't be good. Slowly, he begins pacing the cell, circling me, studying me. My eyes follow his movement, but I force my body to stay extremely still.

"*You* have cost me so much money." He levels chilly eyes on mine. "The fifty thousand I lay down on the block for you. The training and general upkeep. The failed arena fight cost me over a million. I was counting on you *not* submitting so Sera would slice your neck off. That's right. I didn't bet *for* you, but many of the elite did. And they are pissed. They hate you. The crowd hates you." Master gets right in my face. "*I* hate you."

Though I try very hard not to, I can't help from nervously swallowing. Master tracks the movement with his wicked gaze and his lips curl into an equally wicked smile. Why confront me now? Why not last night after the fight?

He chuckles. "Oh, I bet you thought you were doing just fine. Nothing like getting comfortable only to find out your master is pissed at you."

"Master—"

"I thought you and I had an agreement," he keeps going. "You fight. You win. I find your sister."

Panic surges through me. "We did. We do!"

He takes one step away, puts his hands behind his back, and gives me another long study. "I'm just not seeing it. I'm more inclined to send you back to the auction block and end my arrangement with you. At least then I'll make back some of my money."

I look over to Alexior who stares back at me with a grave expression. My eyes flick back to Master. "I'll do anything," I plead.

"Hm." He purses his lips. "Anything?"

Hope rushes through me even though my gut clenches with his calculating tone. "Anything."

"All right." He unclasps his hands. "I'm sending you to fight in The Hole."

Alexior steps forward. "Master—"

He cuts him a dark look that effectively shuts him up and then glances back to me. "You survive three days there and I'll let you back to training here."

He turns to Alexior. "I want *everyone* out there to know that a day does not go by where they should feel comfort. And if they *ever* defy or manipulate me The Hole is where I will send them as well."

Master rakes me with a haughty, disgusted look. "Have her ready for tonight." Then he turns and exits the cell.

Immediately, I look at Alexior. "What's The Hole?"

Solemnly, he crosses the cell and unlocks my wrists. I'm used to him being quiet, stern, stoic, but something is very different about him right now. Whatever The Hole is, it is not good.

I listen to the clank of metal as he unlatches my wrists. When they go free, I turn and stare up into his gray eyes. The somberness in them makes my heartbeat begin throbbing in my ears. "What's The Hole?" I repeat.

He straightens and pulls his shoulders back, like he's reminding himself to be hard. "It's filthy. It's vicious. It's gory. It turns humans into beasts. There is no surrender. One lives. One dies."

I catch my breath, and the bones in my body give way, and with that I slowly begin to fall to my knees.

Alexior digs his fingers into the front of my tunic and hauls me right back up. He brings me close to his face. "Do you want to survive?"

It's vicious. It's gory. It turns humans into beasts... His words fog my brain and my head lulls back.

Alexior gives me a hard jerk, and my head snaps back up. "Do you want to survive?"

I nod.

"Then forget honor. There is no index finger. You are hard. You are cold. You are an animal. You *have* to kill to stay alive."

Heat presses through my eyes and though I don't want them too, they blur with tears.

Alexior grabs both of my arms and shakes me almost violently. "Stop it." He pierces me with a steely look. "Don't cry." Another hard shake. "Stop it right now."

I try to focus on his words. I try to get my emotions in check, but I can't seem to. *One lives. One dies.* I'm done. I can't do this anymore.

He lets go of me, grabs my sister's bracelet, and yanks it right off my wrist. My entire body and all my thoughts snap to attention and I hurl myself at him. "Give that back!"

He spins and pushes me up against the stone wall, pinning his arm across my chest just like he did the first day I was here. My breaths come in pants as I struggle against him and he plants the side of his lower body against mine to hold me in place.

"There," he says, holding the bracelet up in front of my face. "Now you're back."

His words filter in and with them my breaths begin to even out. I stop struggling and he steps back.

"Who goes to The Hole?" I manage to get out.

"A variety. Some are sold on the auction block and go straight there. Some of the elite use it as discipline. Others are banished there to never return. You are fortunate Master has sentenced you to three days."

Fortunate? That's laughable.

"Ignatius will be your escort." Alexior puts my bracelet into a black leather pouch tied around his waist. "I'll keep this for you. You don't want this in The Hole. The fact I'm keeping this for you should be proof enough that I have no doubts you will return."

I fix my eyes on the pouch, aching at the thought of my sister. "Promise me if I don't return that you will one day give that back to my sister and tell her how much I loved her."

I know he can't really make me that promise, but I *need* to at least hear it.

He nods. "I promise."

CHAPTER 17

As ALEXIOR SAID, Ignatius goes with me to The Hole. I'm blindfolded for transport, but by the length of the trip I guess the location to be back toward the marketplace.

Blindly, I'm led down the length of a long tunnel. By the shuffle of my feet and weight distribution in my thighs and shins I can tell we're descending.

The smell hits me first. Puke and piss and feces and decay. Before I know it's happening, my cheeks puff and I throw up in my mouth and have to spit it out underneath my hood.

The sounds hit me next. People yelling and cussing and screaming and laughing. It's a demented combination.

Ignatius slips my hood off and it's only then that I realize he's dressed differently. Gone is his brown tunic and in its place is a cream one. I wonder if the difference in color has anything to do with being out of the camp and walking around freely. He gives me a nudge, and I stumble straight into a cell. As I turn, he flips the bolt. He stands with his back to me, arms folded, legs wide, and surveys the room.

There're fifty or so men and women tightly pressed

together in a circle cheering on the fight in the middle. There are too many bodies, and I can't see who is fighting. Up high sits a tiny balcony with only two of the most elite. I don't recognize either one of them.

I tear my gaze away and land on a wall to the left where —my eyes widen—human skins hang from nails. Faces. Breasts. Butts. Strips that must have come from the stomach or the thigh. From some of them blood still trails down the stone wall making it evident they are fresh.

Acid rolls right up my esophagus and I heave what's left in my stomach.

Ignatius glances over his shoulder. "Don't look around. Close your eyes and focus."

Every muscle in my body begins violently, uncontrollably shaking. I spit and wipe my mouth.

The crowd parts just a little and I glance up to see one of the fighters swing a sledgehammer up and straight down into his opponent's skull. Blood squirts, an eyeball flies, and seemingly every bone in the man's head collapses.

The crowd goes from wild to crazy insanity, and I grip the iron bars and dry heave. The sound increases and I flatten my palms over my ears. It physically hurts to hear them.

Someone in the crowd hands the winner a knife and he slowly fillets the skin right off of what's left of the dead man's face. Then he struts the skin over to the wall and ceremoniously nails it.

The crowd jumps up and down, pumping the air with their fists, screaming, chanting the winner's name. He yells back, raising his fists. He's naked, except for a cloth winding his mid-section. Through the dirt and blood smeared on his body I see tattoos. Dozens of them. He walks away from the wall and comes right past me and is locked into the cell beside mine.

He's a prisoner, too.

What did he do to be sent to this hell? Has he been here in Saligia forever like Ignatius or is he a new slave like me?

There's no wall that separates his cell from mine, only bars. I watch as he sits down on a bench and brings his blood shot eyes up to mine. Gone is the cockiness of a few seconds ago. His eyes are lifeless now. Flat. Like he's been fighting in The Hole night after night. Killing. Tearing people's faces off. He doesn't even acknowledge me and instead closes his eyes and drops his head.

I wonder if he has to fight again tonight.

I wonder if I have to fight him.

Ignatius opens my cell. "Let's go."

I take a deep breath and force it out steady and strong. *One lives. One dies.* I am cold. I am hard. These things stick in my mind. I will do whatever it takes to stay alive.

Every tendon, every muscle, every artery in my body is so tight I'm amazed I can walk. I use the tenseness to hold myself straight and powerful. I don't look anywhere but straight ahead as I'm led through the crowd.

They recognize me from the arena and immediately begin booing, spitting on me, pushing me. I ignore them.

Ignatius comes to stand in front of me, and I crane my neck to look up at him.

My pulse pounds so loudly I can barely hear myself hoarsely ask, "Have you ever fought here before?"

"Yes." He rolls his eyes down to a chain I just now realize is hidden in the sand and then just as quickly brings his eyes back to mine. "They won't give you a weapon for this first fight. Use whatever you need to."

I nod, but I don't glance back down at the chain. I don't want anybody to know what Ignatius just showed me.

He disappears back into the crowd and I'm shoved into the middle of the ring. I want to dissolve into the shadows and pretend I'm not here. But I'm very present and accounted for.

My eyes trail over to the pool of blood that marks the spot where the other man just died. His body is gone now.

I turn a slow circle, taking in everyone's faces. Laughing. Sneering. Still spitting. I channel it all inward and it boils vehemence through my veins.

The chain Ignatius pointed out runs the circumference of the circle and marks the fighting area. He was right, no one gives me any weapons.

A woman steps into the circle. She looks like the dirty version of Camille. Average height. Muscular. Short greasy blond hair. She's topless and her breasts are even smaller than mine.

She wears only a leather thong. Filth streaks her arms and legs. From the way the crowd chants her name —*Odonna, Odonna, Odonna*—she's obviously a favorite.

She sizes me up. "Only one of us leaves this circle alive. This is my sixteenth fight. That's all I have to say." From behind her back she holds up a squirming mouse by its tail. She tilts her head back, and I watch in horror as she bites off the rodent's head. Even through the roar of the demonic crowd, I can hear it squeal.

She flings the hairy limp body over her shoulder and spits the head in my direction. Rodent blood drips down her face. She catches it with her dirty forearm and then licks it right off.

Inwardly, I grimace and wonder what she was like on

her first fight. How long did it take her to become this possessed person standing in front of me?

Odonna charges me then, hissing, teeth bared, her hands up and dirty nails ready to scratch my eyes out. I give those nails another look. They are metal and attached to her fingers. Her weapons.

I crouch, eye the hidden chain in my periphery, and calculate three—two—one. I drop and roll, grab the metal links, and am back on my feet before she's barely stumbled past.

Do not allow advantage to your back. That's exactly what she's done and I don't give her a second of reprieve.

I'm quick and I'm little. I use both as I leap through the air and snake myself around her from the back.

She screams and claws at me and tries to shake me off. I cringe as her nasty metal nails rake down my bare arms and I fight to wind the chain around her neck. The weight of it in my fingers, the roughness of it, feels deadly.

She pulls at it and tries to buck me off and I just fight harder. I get the chain wrapped once around her neck, then twice, grit my teeth, and pull as hard as I can.

She won't choke out.

I struggle for one more wrap and adrenaline spikes through me erupting a yell from my very core. I squeeze both ends of the chain in opposing directions so hard my hands bleed. She falls to her knees, then flat onto her face, and then stops moving altogether.

The violent roar of the crowd buzzes energy through my body and I don't stop pulling the chain. She's dead. I know she's dead. But I can't take any chances.

I scream a sob, and it grates my throat. I keep yanking until my arms throb, until the chain bites deep into her skin and her blood mixes with my own to coat the metal links.

I fall off of her and scramble away. My heart bangs my ribs and I gasp for breath as I stare at her lifeless body. All around me people yell their senseless cheers. Chanting *my* name now. "Va-lor-i-a. Va-lor-i-a. Va-lor-i-a."

Shut up! I want to scream.

I close my eyes and shake my head. No! I just killed another human being. *Nooo...*

I open my eyes and through tears see my sister sitting just a few feet away, tears streaking her own dirty face. Her dark and sad yet frightened eyes look down at the dead woman and then back at me.

She reaches a gentle hand toward me. "It's okay," she whispers.

I reach out, too, but I touch only air. And then she's gone.

Filthy. Vicious. Gory. Turns humans into beasts.

Alexior is right, and the realization stabs me with hot pain. I am now a beast.

CHAPTER 18

For three whole days I live and breathe the same cell in The Hole. Around me the other prisoners scream to be let out. Shout for the fights. Yell threatening and intimidating things at each other. There is no sunlight or fresh air. Only the flickering of torches illuminate the underworld we are all in.

We don't bathe, and we're given a bucket for a toilet. We're allowed one meal a day and though I have no clue what it is, though it looks and tastes horrible, I still eat it. I need nourishment if I'm going to survive. Not having walls between our cells only elevates the fear and insanity. We do nothing but stare at each other during the day, waiting for night to settle in, waiting for the next round of fights to begin.

In my head I practice everything I've learned from Alexior. I think of all the fighting techniques my father taught me. And then I repeat it all. It's the only thing that helps me block out my surroundings.

The crowd loves me. They roar my name at the vile things I do. I try not to be brainwashed by the sick adoration, but I am a beast now and I raise my fists in victory and ignore the bile that whirls in my mouth. I *am* going insane.

On night one after the metal finger girl, I'm "treated" to a weapon. I pretend my next opponent is Master and I kill him with a large spike. He knocks out one of my teeth. When he takes his last breath there's this terrified look in his eyes that I know will always haunt me.

On night two, I imagine Bareket as I beat a woman to death with rusted brass knuckles. She gives me a swollen eye. Her quiet frown and muffled groan will linger for eternity in my mind.

Tonight is night three and my last night here. If I survive tonight, I'm done. If I had to go beyond tonight, I'd probably willingly give my life to end this torturous hell.

The vision of my sister hasn't returned since that first night. I try and conjure her image or a memory—especially the one where I use to poke her and she'd giggle—but nothing will come.

Her face is just a blur. Her voice mute.

I wonder if it is because she's so horrified by me now she doesn't want to visit even in my mind. I wonder if it is because she's dead and I truly have nothing to live for.

If she's dead I wish someone would tell me so I could die too.

Into the fighting circle steps the man from day one. The man who filleted his opponent's face and hung it on the wall. If he wins, will he do the same to me? My stomach squeezes. Probably.

He's been in the cell beside me for the last three days, and he's never said a word. He fights. He wins. And he goes back to his cell. We've been beside each other for three days and I don't even know his name.

We survey each other across the circle and in his eyes I

now see my own vacant, stony ones. We are both desperate. Callous. Numb. But something way deep in his is different than mine. Whatever he was fighting for is no longer there. This man is done.

The realization pangs my chest and I welcome it. It's the first bit of humanity I've experienced in three days. He is how I would look if I found out my sister was dead.

He's given the same sledgehammer I saw him use that first night. I'm given a double bladed spear.

He lifts the sledgehammer straight up and comes toward me. I crouch and lift the spear. His sledgehammer swings through the air and I duck and lunge and he walks straight into my double blade.

I suck in a breath and stare into his bloodshot eyes as the sledgehammer thuds to the sand. "I'm sorry," I whisper.

"Okay now," he gasps, grips my hands, and forces me to twist and push the spear further in.

Familiar pressure warms my eye sockets and I blink the tears free. A short laugh puffs from my lips and it sounds insane to my ears. I'm weirdly giddy with fatigue and the knowledge this is officially over. I'm alive.

More tears slip out and I look up into his face to see him crying, too, smiling, and I wonder if he's seeing heaven right now.

His whole body freezes and then he slouches toward me. I try to catch as much of his weight as possible so he doesn't crash into the sand.

When I look up, my sister stands across the pit, smiling through tears of her own. She's alive. She's still alive. I know it in every inch of my soul.

"Va-lor-i-a. Va-lor-i-a. Va-lor-i-a."

The crowd parts and relief rushes through me when I see Ignatius. He's come for me. Without a word, he leads me through the tunnel and away from the hell of The Hole.

He doesn't blindfold me on the way back to the villa, and I discover I was right. We were under the marketplace the whole time. I imagine being sold on the auction block and immediately transported to The Hole. I likely wouldn't have lasted one fight.

Master and Alexior are waiting for me when I return. It's late and everyone is already asleep. They're standing in the middle of the training ground in the exact spot I saw Alexior staring up at the stars. Ignatius walks right past us and goes into the men's quarters.

The air seems very thick and warm tonight. Or maybe it's just Master' presence.

I'm exhausted. I'm sore. I'm starving. But I make myself stand in front of the two of them. Master wrinkles his nose. I know I stink. I know I'm filthy. I don't care.

"Ignatius tells me you fought well." He raises both brows. "In fact, you've made me quite a bit of money."

I don't like where this is going.

He shrugs a shoulder. "Maybe I'll send you back just to make more."

What? My world tilts. My head spins. I fall to my knees. "*No.*"

Master laughs like he thinks The Hole is the funniest joke ever. "Get cleaned up. You have no days of rest. I expect to see you out here training tomorrow. And... I have news of your sister."

Shakily, I reach for his foot and he steps back as if just the thought of my touch is repugnant. I fist my hand into my chest. I don't want to do anything to offend him.

I look up at him, pleading. "What news?"

"I know she was moved off of Saligia and is currently

somewhere in Taiwan. That is all I know. It's not much, but it's something."

Graciously, I nod my head. "Thank you." Tawain. Is that close to us? Is it far? I don't know, and I don't want to ask. I don't want to do anything to upset Master.

He strolls indifferently past and I stay right where I am, kneeling in the dirt of the training area.

"You can get up now," Alexior quietly tells me.

I don't think I can. Maybe I can just curl up and sleep right here with thoughts of my sister swirling through my head.

Alexior kneels down beside me. He takes my dirty hand and opens my stiff fingers and places my sister's bracelet in the palm.

He doesn't immediately release my hand and we both stare down at her bracelet, my smaller hand, his larger one, the callouses on his, and the cuts and blisters on mine.

It's been so long since I've had simple human contact. I wish I could drop my head into his lap and have him run his fingers along my scalp.

He releases my hand and I breathe out as I unsteadily get to my feet.

"Go get a bath," he tells me. "I'll find some food for you."

CHAPTER 19

BEING filthy for three days makes a person truly appreciate cleanliness. This is my one and only thought as I recline in the hot water and give into the heaviness of sleep. I don't worry about drowning. Surely inhalation of the water will wake me up.

A tap on my chin has my eyelids slowly opening. How long have I been out? Seems like a whole night, but from the darkness outside, it must've been only minutes.

Alexior hands me a hunk of bread with a slab of cheese and puts a goblet of water down. As I greedily tear into it, I wince at the rawness in my mouth. I'd forgotten about my missing tooth.

He paces away. "The Hole is not something you'll ever forget. But you can train your mind to not think about it. Find new thoughts. Use the distant memory to form new habits, new rules, a new you."

He looks back at me. "I've been to The Hole. I know what you had to do to survive."

I swallow a chunk of unchewed bread and follow it with a gulp of water. "You fought in The Hole?"

"No, I was a spectator."

My lips curl in disgust and my body stiffens.

"It's not what you think," he reads my mind. "And I'm not explaining it to you. Just know I've been. I've seen. I know."

"Is that what Ignatius did? Trained his mind not to think about it?"

"Yes. Ignatius has had to train his mind not to think about a lot of stuff. It's how he survives."

Sadness creeps through me, followed by confusion from old thoughts. "I don't get it. He's free now..."

Alexior glances toward the bars that separate our bathing area from the tunnel, like he thinks someone might be lingering, listening. "No one is ever really free," he speaks so quietly I barely even hear him.

Before I have time to ask what he means, he is gone.

CHAPTER 20

ME AND LENA *pull up to a security gate outside of Mr. Vasquez's estate. The officer takes my name, checks a list, and then motions us on through.*

Simultaneously, we both lean forward. The cobblestone driveway gently curves along a path of swaying palms and colorful gardens, and beyond the gardens I catch sight of a glistening pond.

A final turn reveals what can only be described as a mansion, or a small hotel for that matter. It sprawls in front of us, all white stucco and gleaming clean, with private balconies off of every room on the second floor.

I looked it up online and know it's thirteen thousand square feet with seven bedrooms, eight baths, a movie theater, a wine cellar, six-car garage, and an Olympic-size lap pool.

"*That's a lot of rooms to clean," my sister whispers and we both laugh.*

"What are you smiling at?" Camille asks.

I shake my head, "Memories," and dig a fig out of my breakfast bowl.

Gem glances over to where Razo sits before pulling her

attention back to me and Camille. She's been doing a lot of that lately, ever since that night in the villa. Razo must sense her gaze because he too glances up, and then averts his eyes.

Other than while training or eating, we are not allowed to interact with the opposite sex. Alexior is the only one permitted in the women's quarters. If something's developing between Razo and Gem, I'm not sure how that's supposed to work.

Normally these types of things don't matter to me (guy and girl stuff). I've always had more important issues to worry about. Like taking care of Lena. But in this sick place, if Gem and Razo can somehow make each other happy, then they should.

There's no telling how long either one of them will be alive. We could *all* be dead this time next week.

I see Sera's shadow a fraction of a second before she shoves me so hard I fall off the bench I'm sitting on. My bowl of figs and oats tumble to the dirt.

"Only warriors get to eat here," she sneers coldly. "Not dogs from The Hole."

Camille shoots to her feet, her face red with indignation. "Leave her alone," she snaps. "Master released her. She's one of us again."

Sera picks up a fig and throws it at me. "She'll never be one of us."

Ignatius steps between me and Sera and hands me what's left in his bowl. Then he turns to Sera in a silent challenge and she narrows her one eye at me before turning and striding off.

"Thanks," Camille says to Ignatius.

He doesn't respond, but he does look down at me.

Quick images of The Hole flash through my brain, and I cringe.

Following Alexior's advice, I consciously shove the images away. Ignatius nods, just once, like he's watching my thought process and approves, before turning and walking off.

"That was strange," Camille whispers.

I poke through the bowl he gave me. Maybe Ignatius and I could talk sometime. To my knowledge he's the only other one of us who has been forced to fight in The Hole. Somehow I can't see him peeling skin off someone. What did he do to get sent to that hell?

Then again, I don't want to talk about it. I want to cram it far away, just like he apparently has.

"You know," Gem quietly says, "if you ever want to talk—"

"I don't," I immediately cut her off, looking at both her and Camille sternly. "Never. Don't ever ask me again."

Camille swallows hard. "Okay. We won't."

I grab both of their hands and squeeze too hard. "Don't ever do anything to get sent there. Do you understand me?"

They both nod and try for small forced smiles.

The corners of my mouth tug down and I release their hands. I don't want them to see me as anything less than strong. I get to my feet and head straight to the training area.

Respect and trust. I will gain that from everyone. That is my new goal. Whether I want it or not, I have a new identity. Saligia has given it to me. The Hole has, too.

There is power in control. I will control my thoughts. I will control my body. People may think they have power over me, but they most certainly do not.

CHAPTER 21

"SWITCH!" Alexior shouts.

I race down to the end of the line and crash my sword into Gem's. She blocks, swat kicks my legs, and I leap into the air.

"Switch!" he shouts again.

Gem steps out of line and sprints to the end and Sera takes her place.

Right. Left. Right. She assaults me with her wooden sword, putting all her weight behind it, making it obvious this isn't a practice round for her. I block with my shield, sideswipe her shin, and she palms my ear.

My neck cracks, my vision blurs, my ear rings, and then everything goes mute. *Dammit.* I clench my jaw and lunge.

"Pick!" Alexior barks.

Sera snickers and spins away, grabs a ball and chain, and twirls it toward a wooden post. Everyone else takes their chosen weapon and executes.

I dash toward my spear, snatch, and fling it toward the round leather target. It whistles through the air, hits in the exact center, and I smirk. Damn, I'm getting good.

"Back!" he yells.

We tear into line, pick up our swords, and begin again. On and on we practice—*switch, pick, back*—until sweat drips, heart pounds, and breaths come in pants.

"Halt!" Alexior hollers.

Simultaneously, we all breathe out.

Sera shoves Felicia. "Make this one into a house slave. She's *nothing*."

"I'm trying," Felicia says through gritted teeth and holds up her wrapped arm. "What do you expect?"

"I expect you to man up. We all have injuries." She motions around the training area. "Broken ribs, bruises, gashes, stitches, swollen muscles." Sera takes an intimidating step toward her. "You don't see any of us whining."

Felicia cowers, and Camille and I exchange a fed up glance. If Sera wants to beat her up, go ahead. I'm not getting into this. There is absolutely nothing I agree with Sera on, but she does have a point about Felicia. She would rather surrender than even try. I have no respect for her. She's weak. I know it. Camille and Gem know it. All the warriors know it. It's only a matter of time.

"Warriors!" Master greets us from the terrace, and we take that as our cue to line in formation. Weeks ago I didn't understand how they could stand in rapt attention, staring up at him, but now I naturally do it, like I'm becoming brainwashed, too.

Several of the rich elite stand with him and I study their faces. I recognize a few of them from the auctioning block. I do not see Mistress or Bareket, though.

"We've put together a new exposition," Master addresses us. "There will be several pre-show fights and then the main event. I have one word for you..."

Grinning, he glances to the elite standing on his right

and then the ones on his left, like he can barely stand whatever demented news he's about to deliver. "Zebulon."

Beside me Ignatius stiffens. It's slight and if I were not inches from him, I would not notice, but whoever Zebulon is, that name does not sit well with Ignatius.

"Zebulon is the *only* undefeated warrior in Saligia. He has killed more fighters than anyone else. He is the one warrior to be in the arena with ten others and to kill them all. He is a god among us. He is revered." Master looks down at Ignatius. "One of you knows him very well."

Though I do not, I want to glance over at Ignatius.

"This event is Zebulon's idea," Master says with a chuckle. "I believe his exact words were, 'I'm bored. I need a good fight'."

This Zebulon, I can see it now—being brought here, times goes by, years even... fighting, winning, becoming seduced by the accolades and violence and gore.

"There will be no surrender," Master continues. "Either he dies or the opponents die. That is the only option."

Wait a minute, *what?* Buried memories from The Hole creep forward.

"Zebulon has requested two fighters from this camp to stand against him. The first—" Master looks to the end of the line—"Sera, the Serpent of Saligia."

Sera grunts and steps forward to waggle her infamous tongue. For Ignatius' sake, I hope he's not the second choice.

"The second." Master runs his gaze down the line and lands on... *me?* "Valoria, the defiant one."

My stomach drops.

"You have one week to prepare." Master claps his hands, indicating he's done talking, and Sera and I turn to face each other.

"Fuck," she says.

With this, I agree.

The warriors head into the shade for lunch, and Ignatius turns to Alexior. Seeing the two of them stand eye to eye, chest to chest, is something. Ignatius is taller by a head but they are both just as broad. Just as intimidating.

"I should be the one who fights Zebulon," Ignatius tells Alexior in a voice that sometimes seems so deep it's nearly inaudible. "I request it."

Alexior holds his eyes level. "If it was my decision, I would allow it. But you know it is not."

Ignatius folds his arms and looks up to the terrace where Master was standing. Then he turns his hard eyes on me before switching them to Sera. "I want to be involved in their training."

Alexior nods. "Done."

"I'm the only who's fought Zebulon and survived. The only way to defeat him is to work as one. If you work separately, he'll kill you both. There's no surrender with him. Never." Ignatius turns his gaze back to me. "Do you see the scars on my body?"

I nod. "Yes."

"They were put here by Zebulon," he tells me. "He set me on fire and then he laughed while my skin melted."

I squelch everything in me that wants to comfort. Comfort is not something done in Saligia.

"He thought I was dead. That's the only reason I lived. Alexior dragged me from the arena." Ignatius glances back up to the terrace and I watch as every muscle in his scarred face clenches. "You two *will* kill him. It's not an option."

He walks off and I stay standing in the training area, visualizing the haunting scene. The fire. The melting skin. The laughter. Ignatius. Alexior dragging him from the arena.

I turn to Alexior. "I didn't realize you two have known each other that long."

"I've been here many years," he simply responds and follows after Ignatius.

I look at Sera. At her eye patch. At her perpetual disapproving sneer. "They're right. We have to work as a team. We have to kill Zebulon. For Ignatius."

Sera huffs. "I'm not working with you. I don't need you to kill Zebulon. I can do that all by myself.

I sigh. Of course she's going to be a bitch.

CHAPTER 22

ALEXIOR SWINGS both swords through the air, cracking them against mine and Sera's and spinning us both to the dirt.

"Work as one!" he shouts.

Sera jumps to her feet and yells as she charges. Alexior rotates his sword and uppercuts the heel of it hard into her chin. Her teeth crack together and she winces. He sidekicks her and sends her flailing backwards.

I roll, grab my spear, and fling. He snatches it right out of the air, twirls it in his fingers, and slings it back. I flatten my body to the dirt and it hisses the air above me as it glides past.

That was close. *Too* close.

"Idiots!" he spits. "Pathetic idiots. What don't you understand about 'work as one'?"

I do understand! I want to yell and point at Sera. *It's her!*

"We've been at this for hours and I've beaten *both* of you every single time." Alexior gives us a disgusted look. "Arrogant."

Ignatius steps up and waits for Sera and I to get back on

our feet. When we do, he slowly reaches over his head, grabs his tunic, and slides it off.

I've seen him without his tunic once before on the night Mistress requested him in the villa. But still, the sight of his scarring is unnerving.

Jagged, keloid patches mangle his olive tone skin in a horrendous maze. Though I try very hard not to, I can't help but grimace when I look upon him. The pain had to be excruciating.

And then there's the agony of what he must have gone through in The Hole. This man, who can't be more than twenty-five years old, has seen so much suffering.

Proudly, he stands before us in only his white undergarment, letting us look at him as the sun sets behind him. *Making* us look at him.

Several quiet, tense, uncertain seconds go by before he leans down and picks up one single sword and no shield. His voice is low when he speaks. "Prove yourself worthy."

Prove ourselves worthy to defend his name. To go up against the person who did this to him and obtain retribution. To take his place in this event. To kill Zebulon. Prove ourselves by working as one.

Sera and I exchange a resolute glance, and in that one determined look I see the care she has for Ignatius. Their friendship and respect runs deep. If she is truly going to work with me, he will be the reason why. She would risk death for him and vice versa. I would lay a good solid bet that *she* is the primary reason he stays here.

She nods, ever so slightly, and together we charge. She's on his right, I'm on his left, and we circle and duck and swerve and lunge.

The movement confuses him, as it was meant to, and he

blocks Sera on the right as I stab him on the left. We're using practice swords, but even wood is not comfortable.

He bends with the stab and Sera hooks her foot around his ankle and yanks. Ignatius falls to one knee and I quickly circle behind to place the tip of my sword at the base of his neck. Sera steps in front and mirrors my action at his Adam's Apple.

He holds up a finger. Surrender.

A satisfied smile curls my lips. I look over his shoulder at Sera to see her scowling at me. Fine. Scowl. But we *did* work as one and we actually won.

Ignatius nods. "Well done."

"I concur," Alexior quietly agrees.

Ignatius gets to his feet. "Zebulon's ruthless. He'll try to separate you. Don't allow it. Acknowledge his strength. Crave victory." He stabs his sword into the ground. "We'll practice again tomorrow."

A soft clapping has me looking up to the terrace where Bareket and Mistress stand, sipping from goblets, and staring down at us. Ice trails my spine and I don't stop myself from joining Sera's scowl.

It's nearly dark now and it's only me, Sera, Alexior, and Ignatius on the training ground. How long have they been standing there watching us?

"We would like to see Ignatius and Valoria after their baths," Mistress announces, and my whole body goes still.

Alexior turns to me. "To the baths then."

Ignatius and Sera start off and I stand rooted to my spot. "Why do they want to see me?"

"I don't know." Alexior goes about picking up all the practice weapons and putting them back in the large wooden box.

I think of Gem and Razo and what they made them do.

I absolutely will not have sex with Ignatius. They cannot make me. They can send me right back to The Hole if they want.

Alexior closes the box and turns to me. "You will bathe and you will go up there. There is no other option. Know that if you refuse, Master *will* send you to The Hole and this time you will not return. You will go, and you will die there. Or he will kill you himself for amusement and your sister will never be located. Think about all of those things before you refuse their wishes."

I physically feel myself hardening. My face. My body. My soul. I hate the person Saligia has made me into. I hate even more the person I know I'll be when this is over. "Don't you feel anything?" I ask with every angry molecule in my body.

Alexior doesn't immediately answer and instead looks away. "Just go."

CHAPTER 23

THOUGH IGNATIUS IS NOT, my wrists are shackled before I'm led into a private room in the villa where Mistress and Bareket wait. They both lounge on red fabric chaises in grand comfort, eating berries and gossiping. There are no walls to this room, only colorful bolts of fabric hanging from the ceiling and brushing the marble floor. They stir slightly with the cross breeze flowing through the villa.

I wonder if this is the room Gem and Razo had sex in.

There is only one house slave in here with us and I recognize her as the one who performed oral sex on Master on the terrace. She doesn't make eye contact and instead fixes her light eyes at a place above our heads. I was right. She can't be more than fifteen years old.

Neither Ignatius nor I say a word as we stand tall in front of Mistress and Bareket.

Like the slave, I focus my expression, showing them I am not scared. I am not intimidated. And no matter what they make me do, I will act like I don't care.

They will get no satisfaction out of their power.

"Take off your tunics," Bareket commands.

I stay stoic as I lift my shackled wrists and slip my tunic off. Ignatius does the same. We stand in our undergarments, side by side, continuing to stare straight ahead. I concentrate on steady breaths so they don't see my nerves.

Next to Ignatius, I am a dwarf. He is big. Enormous. And put together like a bunch of bulking, oddly shaped bricks.

"You," Bareket nods to Ignatius. "Naked."

I clench my jaw and in my periphery I see him step out of his undergarment and toss it on top of his tunic. I want to protect him from their leering eyes. But I do nothing except fist my hands, lock my muscles, and wait.

Bareket leaves her chaise and glides across the marble floor to where we stand. Her distinct pot and jasmine scent surrounds me and I want to gag.

She slips between us and her silky gown brushes my skin. It's all I can do not to step away from the creepy intimacy.

She circles around the back of Ignatius, caressing her fingertip over his scars, his muscles, and then comes back to the front to do the same to his chest and his arms. She looks straight down at his penis and smiles.

"Looks like *every* part of you is huge." Then she turns to me. "You're so *small* compared to him."

The muscles in my neck involuntarily constrict and she cruelly giggles at the anxious movement. God, I hate that I just satisfied her evil self.

The entry's curtains open and Master steps in. "What's going on?" he asks in honest confusion.

He didn't know we're here. That's interesting.

Mistress pushes herself up and sidles up to her

husband. "A little nighttime fun." She licks his ear lobe. "That's all."

Master grunts. "I want to speak with Valoria."

His wife pouts. "Oh, all right."

Relief washes through me and I very carefully, cautiously, reach down, grab my tunic, and put it back on.

As I walk from the room, I hear Bareket say to Ignatius, "Now touch yourself."

I close my eyes and struggle against every desire in me to go back. Instead I force my feet forward to Master and his office. I walk in, and my steps falter when I see Alexior standing in the corner.

Beside him cowers Felicia, sniveling, her face covered in blood. Her swollen nose has to be broken. She blinks, dazed, and looks at me. I narrow my eyes.

Master lifts his left fist and caresses his fingers over his knuckles, drawing my attention to the blood smeared across them. My gaze flicks back to Felicia.

"You may go," he lightly tells her, and she pinches her nose to stop the bleeding as she hurries out.

A warm breeze flows in from the terrace, but it doesn't calm my nerves. What is going on?

"Alexior has brought a couple of concerns to me. First: Felicia's lack of dedication, which," he cleans a nail, "I just took care of."

I quietly wait.

"Second: yours and Sera's inability to work as a team."

My eyes flip back over to Alexior. Why did he tell Master that? Sera and I *did* work as a team earlier. He was there. He saw it. If I'm in trouble, why isn't Sera here, too?

Master takes his time pouring wine into a goblet, sipping, studying me, and the silence in the room grows. I want to tell him we worked as a team, I want to somehow diffuse this tension, but I do not.

Does he want me to get indignant? Does he want me to call Alexior a liar? I don't understand, but something inside of me warns to keep quiet.

"You *will* fight as one. You *will* make it work. You *will* kill Zebulon. Do you understand me?" he asks.

I nod. "Yes, Master."

"You win this fight, and I'll have more than enough money to bring your sister here."

Hope surges through me.

He sips more wine, rolls it around in his mouth, and then swallows. "Who knows, you may just become a legend out of all this. You may be the next Zebulon."

I absolutely do not want to be a legend. I would never want to be another Zebulon. I would never live here in Saligia of my own choice.

Master nods. "You may go."

I follow Alexior from the villa, through the locked gate, and down the stairs. When we are in the tunnel, he turns and unlocks my wrists.

"Why did you lie?" I demand.

He lifts his eyes to mine. "If I would've told Master the truth, he would not have pulled you from that room to praise you. To reprimand you, though, he would. It was the only way I could think to save you from what they had planned with Ignatius."

His words wash through me. Warming me. Comforting. Nearly making me cry.

Alexior cares. Someone in this horrid hell cares.

Something way inside of me unravels just a little bit. But I don't say thank you. Instead all I can think about is Ignatius and what they must be making him do right now.

I wish Alexior could have saved him, too. But if it had to be one of us, I'm glad it was me. So glad. Yet I hate myself even more. I don't like that I'm the type of person who thinks that way.

CHAPTER 24

FROM MY BENCH AT BREAKFAST, I watch Razo step behind Gem and reach beyond her for an orange off the food table. It's barely discernable, but his body brushes hers and his fingers trail her lower back.

Just as quickly as it happens it is done, and he steps away. For a second she doesn't move and then she glances over her shoulder to catch his eye.

How very odd for Gem and Razo. Whatever they have, it is in reverse. They've already had sex and now they are doing the flirting thing.

My eyes trail to Alexior who is standing to the side in his perpetual strong stance as he stares off into the rising sun. I see him do that a lot, just stand and stare, and I wonder what he's thinking of.

Felicia sits silently eating. Yes, her nose is definitely broken. I detest that fact makes me glad. Maybe she'll really train today.

Ignatius and Sera sit down across from me, and I exchange a confused glance with Camille. This is a first. I want to ask Ignatius if he is okay after last night, but I don't. Perhaps later when we're alone I will.

It's odd, but I feel a connection to Ignatius I don't share with anyone else. I suppose our mutual experience with The Hole initially brought it on. But after last night and our ongoing training for the Zebulon fight, our connection is only stronger.

"I'll be working with you and Sera all day," Ignatius tells me. "Alexior will be conducting training as usual with the others."

I nod and glance to Sera who only glares back.

"What is your problem?" I ask. "Is it really that hard to fight with me?"

Beside me, Camille sighs.

"I fight to honor this camp," she proudly states. "You fight for ulterior motives. You're only driven by Master's promise of your sister."

"You're damn right." A laugh huffs out of me. "You're a slave just like me. All of you are. When did you become so conditioned that this is really your life? Do you have no independent thought? Who were you before? Don't you want that freedom back?"

Sera narrows her one good eye. "You're never leaving. None of us are. You seem to *still* be the only one who doesn't realize that."

"When did you start honoring this place? Is there nothing else *you* fight for? Don't you have family—" I stop myself.

Of course she doesn't have family. None of us seem to, except for Gem and her daughter. Nobody out there beyond the waters knows we're here. I look between Sera and Ignatius. They *are* each other's family.

My realization must show in my eyes because Ignatius nods. "It's why I stay."

"But if you were both free, you could have a life outside these walls. Away from Saligia." I look pointedly at Ignatius. "No one would ever make you do anything you didn't want to do. Your very existence wouldn't constantly be in peril."

That statement earns a tense few seconds of silence.

"If you think you're *ever* being set free, then you're naïve. This is your life now. Make the best of it." Sera's words send icy fingers creeping down my backbone, but I refuse to believe her. Me and Lena *will* go free. They could too, all of them could, if they would regain their focus.

Sera gets to her feet and brings her one dark eye down to me. "We will fight Zebulon and we will win and after that you and I go back to being enemies."

"Fine," I reply.

CHAPTER 25

OVER THE NEXT SEVERAL DAYS, Master watches from the terrace as Sera and I train. Sometimes a few of the elite show up to do the same. I'm sure they're already wagering bets. Down here on the training ground, Sera and I maintain a silent vow to work as one.

Literally every muscle in my body aches. But I am strong. I am ready.

The day arrives and we ride in the usual cart across the island toward the small arena. Outside the walls I take the opportunity to look around. The enormous galleon now sits docked on our shores. I catch sight of people dressed as elite disembarking. How often do they arrive and where does it sail from?

In Miami we have a couple of galleons that tourists go out on for a few hours of sailing aboard an ancient vessel. One of them even has faux pirates that sing and dance and serve booze. The rich people getting on this galleon obviously know it's coming here to Saligia. They wouldn't let just anybody enter, though. This is a secret society. Coming here must be by invitation only and require a ton of money.

Yes, there are those who come and go, but there are some who seemingly live here full-time like Master and Bareket. They are apparently the sociopathic masterminds behind this sadistic playground for the vetted evil elite. For what I'm sure is a *huge* amount of money, the rich get to come and live like ancient Lords and indulge in whatever sins.

Then there's the soldiers, the hired muscle behind this place. Here to keep us slaves in line. They're free, but I'm sure if they ever defy Saligia's secrets, they too will suffer.

Finally there are us slaves who get placed where the elite deem fit. In the house. In The Hole. As fighters. Out working the gardens and fields. And wherever else... From what I can tell there are more of us than them. But they've got this society fine-tuned. They know how to control. To keep us in the dark. To make us feel powerless and defenseless. If we put our minds to it, we *could* overpower this place. I know we could.

I focus back on the galleon and watch as slaves begin unloading large wooden boxes with holes. Either there are animals or produce or humans in those boxes. I would bet anything that's how I arrived here.

Our cart bumps over a rough patch and I blink from my thoughts. We pass a group of walkers on the road dressed as elite and they throw their hands up, cheering. They must be on their way to the event.

"Do you think," Camille whispers, "that we'd be friends outside of this place?"

Her softly spoken question takes me off guard and a second to digest, but when I do I grab her hand. "Absolutely." I've never had a friend like Camille. I don't trust easily. "When we *do* get out of Saligia, we will do it together."

She squeezes my hand back. "Good."

We pull into the small arena where I hear a crowd already cheering. We are led into the same holding cell as before where we can stand and watch the fights from the dirt level.

Soldiers are already out and sword playing for the crowd's amusement. I glance up to the boxes where the most elite sit and see Master and his wife. Bareket is there, too, and many familiar faces from our terrace, the villa's party, and the auctioning block.

A gate opens across the arena and four women slaves are led out. They are not shackled but neither do they hold weapons. Their eyes are wide with helplessness, with nerves, with weakness that I know is about to be exploited.

Though fifty yards or so separate us, I can see the sweat soaked tunic of one and the violent shaking of another.

I recognize one from that first day on the auctioning block. She was with Camille and me in that holding cell. I try to remember which of the elite bought her, but I can't.

I don't turn my back, but I purposefully distance myself. There is no stopping what's about to happen. I do the only thing I can do. I channel the anger until it is vibrating in me.

The soldiers circle them, taunting, one even cracks his knuckles. One of the slaves throws a punch and the soldier dodges it and kicks the slave hard in the side. She crumbles to the ground, sobbing, clutching her ribs.

Another slave lurches forward and a different soldier shoves her to a sprawl in the dirt. He grabs her hair and brutally begins punching her over and over and over again. She cries out as her blood darkens the sand beneath her.

The crowd roars, and my eardrums throb with their gross delight.

On it goes with all four slaves. The soldiers are greedy,

cruel, and show no mercy. The youngest slave sluggishly tries to crawl away, shrieking for help that won't come, and I'm disgusted at the repulsive, merciless show.

There is absolutely nothing I can do but watch and be happy my heart is banging with the fury of it all. Because if my heart ever stops banging I'll know I'm empty and just like these wicked people.

Beside me Camille catches her breath and I turn to see her lips pressed together and her face ashen and shiny with sweat. Another scream pierces the air, and she shudders. My eyes skirt her face as she stares blankly through the bars at the horror.

I wish I knew what to say to her, but I don't. It's good she's watching. I glance around. Everyone's silently watching. Sera, Gem, Alexior, Ignatius... Good. They all need reminding what a hideous place this is.

"It's over," Camille whispers and I turn to watch the corpses dragged through the bloody sand.

"What do you think they did to deserve that?" Gem whispers.

I shake my head. "Absolutely nothing."

Our gate opens, and Alexior says, "Gem, Camille, and Felicia, you're up."

I give Camille a nudge with my elbow. "You got this."

From the gate across the arena step three women fighters from another camp, reminding me that I need to figure out how many there are here. Our trio fights their trio in a good show. There's blood, which the crowd of course wants and loves.

One of their trio gets a broken ankle. Camille and Gem submit their opponents, and Felicia surrenders to hers after her already injured arm gets reinjured.

I stare at Felicia slumped in the dirt and try to imagine

fighting with an injured arm. I truly think I would do okay. I would hold my own. Any of us would.

Camille and Gem drag Felicia across the sand back to where we wait. They deposit her in the corner and I give her arm, swollen eye, and quivering lip a brief glance. I have no clue what Master will do with her now.

In the elite's box, Master stands to address the crowd and my body coils into a tight nervous knot. *Here we go.* I blow out a steady breath and go through everything Alexior and Ignatius said during our training.

Fight as one.

Don't let him separate you.

Crave victory.

I do crave victory. Which means I have to kill Zebulon. If that makes me a bad person, then so be it. Like The Hole, there is no surrender. Either he dies or we do. I never imagined I would be put in a position to reason out such evil.

Sera looks over at me. "Your sister is the reason you fight? The reason you live?"

I nod. "And to one day be free. Because despite what any of you say, I will."

The gate opens, and she doesn't respond. I step through first and the crowd boos. I block it out as I strut the circumference. I do a back flip and pump my fists in the air.

Sera steps out next and the crowd goes crazy wild. They love her. She circles in the opposite direction, waggling her tongue and just like before the crowd waggles back.

Out comes a slave wheeling the cart of weapons. We both strap on full armor and everything in me strengthens with the ferocity of the weight. To think weeks ago I stumbled under the bulk. I'm strong now. I'm ready.

I glance one last time over to the gate we just came through. Alexior gives me a firm nod, and I nod back.

"And now!" Master announces. "Zebulon, the god of Saligia. The unbeatable. The revered!"

The crowd's volume explodes. The gate across the arena opens and out steps the largest man I have ever seen in my life.

Ignatius is huge, but this man morphs him. Zebulon stands taller than seven feet and from the boulders he has for muscles, I'd put him at well over three-hundred pounds.

He is a black albino with a bald head and two white tuffs of hair fashioned into matching horns. He wears no armor and carries two single swords.

He stomps into the center and though I'm sure it's not actually, the ground seems to vibrate with his steps. I glance over to Sera and through her helmet I see beads of sweat already forming.

Zebulon turns a circle, egging the crowd on. Sera and I exchange a look and then we charge. Zebulon rotates toward us in snapped attention, and just like we did with Ignatius, we swerve and circle and duck.

He swings both swords and at the last second we spin direction, Sera cuts his left ribs, I slice his right, and he falls straight back. His enormous body bounces once and then goes completely still.

The crowd's cheering dies and Sera and I stand over him, cautiously eyeing his lifeless giant body. A few seconds go by and she takes her helmet off. I do the same. We look at each other. All that work, all that training, and *this* is it?

The crowd begins laughing, and we turn away from Zebulon's body and look up to Master to see him grinning as well. I think everyone's shocked.

We lift our fists in victory. The crowds' laughter becomes a roar of cheers. I turn to the gate and look straight at Ignatius. *We did it,* I mouth. But his expression doesn't seem relieved.

The caution behind it has me glancing over my shoulder to Zebulon's body at the exact second he slams into me from the side. Every ounce of air rushes from my lungs as my body sails through the air to smack into the ground.

Zebulon rears back his massive foot and kicks me hard in the side, sending me spiraling through the air again. I clench my teeth. Everything spins. This time when I land my vision spots.

I come to my knees and scramble to my feet. I can't think straight, I feel clumsy, but I sprint toward my spear. He's big, but I'm fast.

Sera yells and runs at us from across the other side of the small arena. Every muscle in her big legs bunch.

She snatches up her sword and leaps through the air. Zebulon dives too and they collide midair to fall and slide across the sand. He pins her down, head butts her, and then pummels her face with his meaty fists.

My hands slip into position on my spear and I sling it through the air. It pierces him in the side and he bows back. Sera uses the second to wiggle free. Dark blood covers her face as she arches her sword and swipes it crisscross over his chest.

His skin splits open in an X but he twirls his sword and slices her deep across the stomach right under her armor. She fumbles back, gripping her abdomen, and through her fingers her guts puff out in a glistening curl.

She shoots me a pained look before falling to the ground, and I know she's done.

"Zebulon!" I scream and he spins.

I dive and roll, snatch a sword, and race toward him. At

the last second I veer off and whirl, then slide between his legs and plunge the sword straight up into his groin. He hollers and falls to his knees.

"Zebulon!" Sera yells through her pain, and he snarls to where she's still sprawled.

I use the precious second to grab his sword and with two white knuckled grips, I stab it straight into the base of his neck and down his spinal cord. I don't wait to see if he's dead, I run over to Sera, grab her sword, race back, and I stab him over and over and over again.

I keep stabbing until his blood saturates the ground, him, and me. Until his eyes roll back in his head. Until my jaw hurts from my gritted teeth. Until it's hard to breathe. Until I'm soaked with sweat. Until Zebulon's body is just a pile of split skin, organs, and jagged bones.

It's the complete silence that finally leaks into my hazed brain. I drop my sword and take an unsteady step back. I swallow and look down at my shaky, bloody hands. I turn toward Sera. She's not moving and her guts are spilled out beneath her armor.

But she's breathing. She's not dead.

I turn toward the gate next to see Alexior and Ignatius and everyone else quietly, stoically, staring at me.

I inhale a shallow breath and it rasps in the air around me.

Slowly, gradually, the crowd begins making noise. It grows and grows and grows to a deafening level.

Finally, I glance up to Master' box to find him proudly smiling, Bareket sneering, and the other rich a mixture of celebration and shock, depending on who bet for or against me.

"Va-lor-i-a. Va-lor-i-a. Va-lor-i-a." The crowd chants my name.

The gate opens and Alexior and Ignatius step into the arena. Neither of them look at me as they rush to Sera, carefully each take an arm, and slowly slide her across the dirt and out of the arena.

If it weren't for her, I would not be standing here. There is no way I could've defeated Zebulon without her.

"Va-lor-i-a. Va-lor-i-a. Va-lor-i-a."

That's not my name, drifts like a fog across my brain. But I do the only thing I can. I do what's expected. I lift my fists in victory and let the crowd bathe me in their repulsive praises.

CHAPTER 26

WHEN WE GET BACK Sera is taken to Talme, and a soldier leads me through the villa to Master' office. Other than the very first visit, this is the only time I'm not required to wear shackles.

Perhaps defeating Zebulon grants me this privilege. If so, it's a good one to have. It means to some extent they "trust" me. That'll only make deception all the more easier.

The soldier knocks once, opens the door, and I step inside.

Master spins away from the slave boy he has bent over his desk. I recognize him. The night of the villa party. He stood in the corner behind me.

Master lowers his gown as the boy does the same to his tunic. He gives the boy a shove and growls, "Later," and the boy quietly slips from the room.

As I have learned I keep my repulsion and anger simmering. I keep my expression schooled. Only I know what's in my thoughts. Only I know that one day they will all violently pay.

Master throws his hands out in greeting. "Valoria! My

defiant one! I *knew* you'd pay off. I knew it!" He claps his hands and laughs in an ugly hoot that I despise. "Oh, do I have grand things in store for you."

I force my lips into a pleased smile. Now *I* apparently will be the one with the golden vagina.

He strolls over, grinning. "First, I will take you shopping for new armor. My champion deserves her own. We'll get it engraved, specialized, so anybody who sees it will know it belongs to Valoria, the defiant one. Then I'll parade you through the marketplace so everyone can congratulate and marvel at your excellence. You'll be going on a tour of the villas, too. The elite want to meet you up close and personal."

He clasps my shoulder. "I'll throw a party down on the grounds for the other warriors with wine and whores. Everyone will know you are the reason for the good cheer." Another bark of laughter comes out of him. "No other warrior has *ever* made me the money you did killing Zebulon. You have accomplished more than anyone in your short time here."

"My sister?" I simply ask.

Master' smile fades and then he immediately grins again and steps away, leaving a trace of sensation where his fingers dug into my shoulders.

"Of course!" he joyously agrees. "Of course you'd want to know. I've found her. I've bought her. And I've arranged transport. She'll be here within a few days."

I suck in a breath, my knees go weak, and I lock them into place so I don't fall. Relief and happiness and pure shock swirls through me causing tears to blur my vision. *Lena.* I step forward and reach out a shaky hand. "Th-thank you, Master."

He graciously nods. "You are very welcome. I said I'd

find her, and I did. Valoria, you will discover I am a man of my word. If I say I'm going to do something, I will."

I nod and something inside of me squeezes at the thought of my sister. "Our freedom? Did I make you enough to buy that as well?"

He gives me a sad look. "No, but at least your sister is coming. Now you can work toward paying off your expenses and upkeep and purchasing your freedom."

"Where will Lena stay?"

"Here in the villa. I will make her into a house slave."

"No!" I snap and immediately clamp my lips together.

Master narrows his eyes. "Excuse me?"

A bitter taste tangs my mouth, and I swallow and put all my energy into clenching my fists. I tell myself to calm down. "I mean, may I respectfully request she stay downstairs with me? She could clean our training weapons. Or assist Talme in the medic room. Or help serve food..."

Even I can hear the pleading in my tone. Anything but up here in the villa. Anything.

Master crosses his arms and studies me for an extremely long time and then finally, *finally*, responds, "Yes. Yes, I'll allow that."

I release an unsteady, relieved breath. "Thank you."

He holds up a finger. "Now I want you to remember this. I'm not hard to work with. I'm not unreasonable."

I nod. "Yes, Master."

He motions to the terrace. "Step out with me."

I follow him out into the windy night and my tunic presses to my body with the strong breeze. I look down to see all the warriors standing in formation. I've been up here before, but right now the height dizzies me. I imagine climbing over the rail and flying off into the night.

They look up at me and start chanting, "Va-lor-i-a. Va-lor-i-a. Va-lor-i-a."

I should feel victorious but I do not. There should be pleasure coursing through me, but there isn't.

Master reaches over, grabs my wrist, and lifts it into the air and I force my mouth into a triumphant smile.

CHAPTER 27

TRUE TO HIS word I am paraded through the marketplace like some goddess. People applaud. They stop to just touch me. It's revolting.

Master buys me trinkets that I don't want but I accept. He has specialized armor fashioned out of some sort of lightweight material and a giant V engraved in gold on the chest. He purchases two spears and engraves them with the V as well. He declares this is my new look.

The villas come next where I have a private audience with the various rich and elite. Some of them want to sit and play board games. Others want to mock fight. And yet others just want to look at me and hear my version of the infamous killing.

The whole thing is gross and strange. But I use the time to scope the grounds and layout. To look at the interior and exterior of the villas. To count their slaves. To calculate the best ways in and out.

I discover there are three more *ludi* in Saligia, but none have as many warriors as ours. Other than that, the other villas are just homes. Though a few of them seem designated for hosting feasts or spas or sexual fantasies.

Saligia *is* the seven deadly sins.

And like the villa I live in, there is no technology anywhere. Or if there is, it's hidden. I think about that, and it actually makes sense. Because where there is technology there can be pictures and film and possible leaks. It wouldn't surprise me if that's a requirement, leaving all that behind. When you come to Saligia you step back in time in all aspects. It's part of the lure.

"You're back," Camille says, and I blink from my ponderings. She gives me a small smile and sits down beside me on the training ground. "I hear your sister's coming."

"Yes," I say and tune into Lena's bracelet weighing warm against my wrist.

Camille gives me a one arm hug. "I'm so happy for you."

"Thanks."

"Did you hear about Felicia?" she asks.

"No."

"Master has made her into a house slave."

We exchange a glance. We both know what that means. Sure Felicia annoyed me, but I wouldn't wish that on anybody. Never.

I go back to staring at the dark clouds covering the setting sun. Between those and the strong winds, I expect a storm to hit either today or tomorrow. I think about the weather patterns, the summer month, and as usual come up empty with a solid hypothesis of where we are. The dark water is certainly not Bahamian or Mediterranean.

I think about Lena's arrival next, my tour of the villas, my limited knowledge of Saligia, and I whisper, "You and me. We've got each other's backs. Right?"

Camille glances around to make sure no one's listening. "Of course."

From beneath my fancy new armor that I have yet to change out of, I slip the handle of a small dagger. Camille sucks in a breath and I tuck it right back in.

"Where did you get that?" she quietly asks.

"From one of the villas I was at today." I turn to her. "Listen, we can do this. We can escape. There are more slaves in the villas than the elite and the soldiers who guard them. We can overpower these people. Let everyone free. Get on that galleon and get the hell out of here."

"And go where?" she whispers. "Plus, those house slaves don't know how to fight."

"We didn't either and look at us now." I grab her hand. "I guarantee you those slaves up in the villa would gladly stab Master or his wife if given the chance."

"You haven't thought this out. This isn't a viable plan. It's only me and you. We would need more people on our side."

"Then we'll get them," I command. "One by one. You know Gem would. And if she does Razo will. Of course my sister."

"But what about Ignatius and Alexior. You don't think they'd stop us? And Sera."

My thoughts instantly shift and my grip tightens. "Sera. How is she?"

"Not good. Talme doesn't think she's going to live."

An image of her intestines slipping out of her stomach flashes through my brain and I wince. That could've easily been me.

Camille sighs. "Why don't you just focus on purchasing your freedom? If you got your sister this quickly, it probably won't take you long to secure the other."

No one is ever really free. Alexior's words come back to me, and I absolutely believe them.

"Besides," she whispers, "we would need weapons."

My gaze tracks over to the large wooden boxes that hold all of the practice weapons. I study the bulky iron locks. Alexior has the keys.

"Please be patient," Camille implores. "I don't want you sent back to The Hole."

Master and his wife step out onto the terrace and draw my gaze away from my friend.

"Greetings!" Master calls. "To celebrate Valoria's grand victory I have arranged for music and drink and whores." He waves his arm over to the gate as it opens, and a crowd of people pour in. "Enjoy! Feel free to fuck wherever!"

Several of them march in playing flutes and guitars and pipes. Women dressed in skimpy gowns with thin gold sashes around their waists dance in behind them. Men wearing only leather thongs and carrying barrels of drink and platters of food follow.

What the hell?

Camille gets to her feet and I follow. "What's going on?" she asks.

Alexior approaches. "As Master said. A celebration of Valoria's victory. He's only done this twice before in the time I've been here. Enjoy. It likely won't happen again anytime soon."

"But who are these people?" I ask.

"Slaves," he answers. "But these are special slaves. They've been trained to party and entertain."

Music trickles through the area and I listen to it as I watch the visitors laugh and dance. None of them seem like they are here under duress. Then again if they did, they would just be punished or executed. They've learned to "entertain" as Alexior said.

Several of them pour liquid from the barrels and start handing out the goblets to us warriors. People are going to be hung over tomorrow...

A night like this would be the perfect night to escape. When everyone is distracted and getting drunk. But without my sister, of course there is no way.

Two very good-looking men gyrate over to me and Camille. She laughs and takes the hand of one and lets him pull her away. I shake my head to the other. He handsomely pouts and twirls away to find a more willing partner.

Over in the shadowed corner I catch sight of Gem and Razo in a passionate kiss. He takes her hand and leads her across the training ground and into the men's quarters.

I glance over to Alexior. Why I glance I'm not sure. I did that the last time I saw Gem and Razo exchanging an intimate act.

Alexior looks down at me and his normally hard face gentles into a very, *very* slight smile. An electricity fills the air. An awareness. The party around us slowly fades as I gaze up into his dark gray eyes.

"Would you like some wine?" he quietly asks.

"No thank you." I don't want anything impeding my senses.

"I'm very happy your sister is coming," Alexior tells me. "Master says she will be working down here cleaning weapons and whatever else I deem appropriate."

I nod. "Yes. It was his intention to make her a house slave, but I knew down here would be safer."

Alexior turns fully to face me. "Be prepared. Your sister will likely not be the girl you remember."

Sadness grips me and I shove the images from by brain

at what she's had to endure. I'll love her. I'll listen to her. I hold her if she cries. "Whatever she needs I'll freely give it and I will never let anything happen to her ever again."

"That's good," he whispers.

In the flickering light of the lit torches, we study each other's faces. I look at the shadows beneath his cheekbones, I take in the mystery behind his gray eyes, his clean shaven head, and I wonder as I have before how he ended up here.

"What about you, Alexior? Do you have any brothers or sisters? Anybody you fiercely love?"

He studies me for a long second, like he's wagering if he should answer, then quietly speaks, "I had a wife."

CHAPTER 28

ALEXIOR'S FACE softens with sadness. "We met when I was eighteen, she twenty. Fell immediately in love. Eloped. We were kidnapped on our honeymoon."

"Oh my God," I gasp.

He looks away. "That was seven years ago."

"Is she still here in Saligia?"

A muscle flexes in his jaw as he stares hard at the party waging on. Then without a word, he walks off.

Alexior! I want to yell, desperate for him to come back and tell me more. Is she dead? Is she alive? Which of the elite have her?

But if Alexior was brought here as a slave, why is he now working for them as a trainer? So many questions and way too little answers. I'd give anything to sit down with someone, ask a question, and have it properly answered.

Other than Master, I doubt anyone around here could answer every question. It seems like everyone is in some degree of darkness.

Music floats through the breezy air followed by bursts of

laughter and giddy voices. Over to the right Camille dances with one of the visiting men.

I want to be offended—how can people party in a place like this—but I can't seem to muster the fault. Who knows how long any of us will be alive?

I will refrain from the partying, though. I want to always be mentally prepared and alert. What good is this trained body if my mind isn't awake, too? There will be a time when I will use both to my advantage, and I will be ready.

Reaching over, I clasp my bracelet, and the slight movement shoots a pain through my side from my fight with Zebulon. I've gotten so used to the aches that I find them comforting. They remind me that I'm alive. They also remind me of Sera.

Making my way through the party, I head toward the tunnel that leads to Talme's medic room.

Up ahead I catch sight of two figures and squint to see. A naked man hoists a woman up, slams her against the stone wall, and plunges inside of her. A strangled gasp echoes through the tunnel followed by loud pleasurable grunts. I don't look to see who it is. I don't want to know.

Quickly, I skirt past them and silently open the wooden door that leads into the medic room. Candles flicker in each corner, casting shadows over the area. Sera lays half naked and unconscious on the same table where Talme tended to me.

Ignatius sits at her side, his voice low and gentle and soothing. I can't make out what he's saying but the care he has for Sera clearly runs deep.

In contrast to what's going on outside, the near silence in here is eerie. And calming.

I've seen her naked many times before but her taut and

defined muscles always cause me pause. Aside from her female parts she is built like a man.

Quietly I make my way into the room. Ignatius glances over his shoulder and then smoothly gets to his feet. I come to stand right beside Sera, and now that I'm so close I can barely, just barely, make out her raspy breaths fluttering in the air.

Even though her skin is ebony and gleaming with sweat, bruises overlap in Zebulon's patchwork of pain. On me they would be angry green and brown, but they are dark on her.

On her lower stomach, Talme has tucked her intestines back inside and sewn her up. But from the puckered, pussy skin, even I recognize infection.

"When she finally gets up," Ignatius says quietly, "it's going to hurt for her to even breathe, let alone bend or move."

I reach over and touch his shoulder. "Yes, but she *will* get up."

His brows furrow, but he doesn't respond. I give his shoulder a sympathetic squeeze and release it. If it were Camille or Gem standing here, they would probably offer a hug and more comfort. But I'm certainly not either of them.

He directs his usually emotionless eyes right into mine. "Thank you for killing Zebulon."

I nod. "You're welcome." Though I know if things could be reversed, he'd rather I be on this table instead of Sera. I know this, but I am in no way offended.

Something glints behind him and I glance over to where a thin, hammered piece of metal hangs on the wall. I don't remember seeing it here before. I shift my weight and something in the glint shifts, too. It's... my reflection.

I haven't seen myself since arriving to this place months ago. That thought has me numbly crossing the room to look.

A stranger stares back at me through wide, brown eyes with black circles beneath and choppy dark hair. I run my tongue along my dry bottom lip and turn my face to check out the bruise on my cheek. I didn't realize I had one. I touch the freckles on my nose. Those are new from all the hours in the harsh sun. In this moment I look just like my Cuban mother. Or at least what I remember of her. The last time I saw her was twelve years ago when Lena was one. Days later she just... left, and my dad did the best he could. No, he did a hell of a job. I really miss my dad.

The door opens and Talme lurches in. Her lips immediately pucker into a scold. "Get out," she snaps sharply and jerks her head to the tunnel. "Both of you. You know visitors aren't allowed in here."

Ignatius nods, and I heave a sigh. I really don't want to go back out to the party. I shoot Talme a mock scowl and she scowls right back but there's a hint of amusement beneath.

Whether she'll admit it out loud or not, we bonded in that week I was in here. She has a soft spot for me. With some smooth talking, I'm confident she'd be on my side for an escape.

I glance around her medic room. She has access to many medicines that could be used in our favor. To poison. To subdue. To whatever.

Talme grabs a bowl and begins putting maggots on Sera's infected skin. Sure I've heard of maggot therapy, but I've never actually seen it. I watch for a second as their tiny curly bodies squirm. Hopefully, I'll never have to have maggot therapy. Or if I do, I don't want to know about it.

Back outside I continue to hover in the shadows, watching as everyone slowly imbibes and passes out. Yes, if I were to ever make a move, it would be a time like this.

Night trickles into early morning and I force myself to stay awake. As do Alexior and Ignatius. Apparently they don't trust all the partying either.

Eventually, the sun rises and the place quiets to only the sounds of soft snoring and birds overhead.

Master steps out onto the terrace. "Alexior, bring me Valoria."

I jump from the shadows. "Is Lena here?"

Master nods and disappears back into the villa.

In my chest my heart slowly begins pulsing and then builds to a thumping race until it's all I can feel throughout my body. I race across the training ground, leap over a few naked passed out bodies, and sprint down the tunnel.

Alexior quickly follows.

At the gate, the soldier takes his time pulling out his key and fitting it into the lock.

"Hurry," I urge.

He shoots me a warning look that I completely ignore. I try to count my breaths to calm myself, but it's useless.

The gate opens and I race up the stairs. The soldier at the top takes his time as well and I clamp my teeth together to keep myself from roaring at him.

That gate creaks open and I surge into the villa. Every muscle and capillary in me hums with joy. I'm about to see my sister. I'm about to see Lena!

Master greets me with a forlorn look that clamps me in panic. "Valoria..." his voice trails off and his shoulders lift as he breathes in.

I push past him, deaf, not listening as he begins speaking, trying to explain something. "Where is she?" I shout.

He keeps speaking and the words *medic room* and *Talme* leak into my fear.

Spinning, I fly back down the stairs. I burst into Talme's

room, gulping for air, and there lies Lena with Talme hovering over her.

I don't move. I can't. My feet weigh heavy on the floor. It's Lena. But it's not. Her hair is long, like it has always been, but it's matted with mud and blood.

Beneath her filthy tunic, every bone in her small body juts out in angry starvation. Her chest lifts on a hollow, hoarse breath. She's alive!

From behind me, someone touches my arm. "Valoria." It's Alexior's voice.

I throw his touch off and race over. "Get away from her," I snap at Talme and fold my sister into my arms. I inhale her soiled body odor and bury my face in her crusty neck. "Lena," I sob.

She inhales a high pitched moan that clenches all my organs and has me rocking her. "It's okay, baby girl. It's okay."

Gently I lift up and smooth her tangled hair from her emaciated dirty face. Her black lashes flutter and I smile when her dark eyes meet mine. She lifts a shaky hand and touches the tears trailing hotly down my cheeks. Then her lips quiver, her eyes roll back, and she is gone.

CHAPTER 29

I SWITCH off the engine and turn to my sister. "Stay here. You'll be safe."

Some guy opens my door, and I nearly jump back. He's dressed in a suit with dark glasses and no smile. He nods once, and I take that as my cue to slide out.

Nerves flutter through me and I breathe through them.

I smooth my hands down a pencil skirt I found at Goodwill, double check the tuck on my white blouse, and retighten my long dark ponytail.

Lena hands me the black binder that has only my resume in it, but it looks professional and better than just carrying a sheet of paper.

"You're going to do great," she tells me.

I wink at her and follow the stern suited guy inside. He leads me across a marble foyer and I'm more than aware of my heels echoing in the quiet house. I take the quick moment to look around—up at the vaulted ceiling, to the right at a grand staircase, and out the bank of windows that overlook a pool bordered by palm trees.

Suited guy raps on a closed double door before opening the left panel and motioning me inside.

I take a deep breath and step into the dim interior. Wood —it's the first thing I notice. It's everywhere: the floor, the walls, the ceiling, the desk, the built-in shelves. Shiny dark wood like it's recently been oiled.

Tobacco enters my senses next, and I catch a lazy stream of smoke winding up from the desk where an older gentleman sits. I know from my research he is seventy-two years old. But looking at his salt-and-pepper hair and tan skin, I would guess at least ten years younger.

He gives my entire body a quick once-over, but before I have time to feel uncomfortable he offers a kind smile and indicates I should sit in one of the two chairs in front of his desk.

I tell myself to calm down. The last thing I need to be is a stammering fool.

I hold my hand out, very professional like I practiced. "Hello, Mr. Vasquez. It's a pleasure to meet you." I give his hand a firm shake, take a seat, and immediately open my binder and hand him my resume.

He slides it aside without even looking at it.

He taps two long fingers on the desktop. "I'll review that later. Let's just talk and get to know each other."

My lips curve. "Okay. I've worked all around Miami clean—"

"How old are you?"

"Um, twenty-one." I probably shouldn't have started talking. He's the interviewer not me.

"And you have a younger sister?"

"Yes. Lena."

"And how old is she?"

Why does that matter? "She's thirteen, sir."

"You are her primary caregiver?"

I swallow. "Yes."

"Your mother abandoned you girls, and your father died a couple of years ago. He was a cop, wasn't he?"

Uneasiness squirms its way inside me. These aren't the questions I was expecting. How does he know about my parents? "I'm sorry, Mr. Vasquez. What does this have to do with my qualifications?"

He doesn't answer and instead reaches over, picks his cigar up, and takes a couple of cloudy puffs. Then he gives me another one of those kind smiles, and the uneasiness in me settles a little bit.

"This job comes with a garage apartment," he points out. "Which means you'll be living on my property. If you're living on my property, I'd like to know everything about you. I'm sure you can understand that."

He does have a point. "Yes, sir."

Mr. Vasquez doesn't say anything for several quiet seconds and the only thing that fills the office is the soft ticking of the old timey clock on a shelf behind him.

He raises his finger and it's only then I realize there is a man standing behind me. "Bring in this sister. I'd like to meet her as well."

I go to get up. "I can get her."

Mr. Vasquez nods a go-ahead to the man and picks up my resume. "You stay here and tell me all about this."

Finally. "After our dad died, I got a job at the Red Roof Inn. Last year I moved over to the Hampton Inn. Sir, I really want a better life for me and my sister. With the pay and the accommodations you're offering, it will allow me to enroll her in a better school, and I would like to start taking night classes and putting away money for her college, too."

"Your father didn't leave you any money?"

"Yes." Granted, not much. "I used it to pay off bills."

The office door opens and Lena timidly steps in. The huge security guard behind her only makes her seem even smaller.

I smile and hold my hand out and she eagerly crosses the room to take it. "Mr. Vasquez, this is my sister."

He doesn't greet her and instead looks over our heads and nods. I glance back to see not the one suited guy, but now two. Uneasiness settles once again way down deep and I start to get up.

One of the men grabs me. The other one grabs Lena. She screams. Something pricks me in the neck. And my whole world goes black.

CHAPTER 30

I'VE HEARD that when a slave dies, their body is loaded onto the galleon and dumped into the black water that surrounds us. I can't bear the thought of another stranger handling my sister's body and so I request an audience with Master.

Alexior escorts me through the villa where we find Master at his desk looking through papers. When I enter he quickly closes and latches a soft leather notebook and my eyes linger on it as he slides it into a desk drawer.

I'd give about anything to see what's in that notebook. There's no visible technology on the island, but I'd place a solid bet that's his form of a computer right there.

Master stands and crosses the room to me. With a pitiful expression that doesn't look fake he reaches out and clasps my shoulders, just like he did the last time I was in here and he delivered the news my sister had been found.

"Valoria," he squeezes my shoulders and then releases them, "please know I did everything in my power to bring her safely to you. I did not know she would be delivered in the condition she was. It's important to me that you believe that."

His tone is so convincing I can't help myself *but* believe him. Plus, how would he benefit from killing my sister? He knew she was the only reason I lived. The only reason I fought. The only reason I made him money. The only reason I stood compliant.

I hold my posture rigid and dispassionately ask, "Do you know who had her?"

My tone surprises him, and his eyebrows come down. "Are you okay?" he carefully asks.

Right now I'm nothing. I'm empty. I'm numb. My sister died in my arms while I sobbed. Now I want answers. "Do you know?" I repeat.

"I do not. But I will find out for you because I, too, am very upset. All of my contacts knew I was looking for her."

"Bareket said two men bought Lena. And you told me they took her to Tawain. What did they do to her then?"

"They kept her for a while and then abandoned her. That's where she became untraceable. Often times girls like that get dumped in a whorehouse and they become just another face. That's why it took me so long to locate her."

His words shoot angry pricks through me and suddenly I'm not so numb. Every muscle in my body tenses and it takes every bit of self-control not to spring through the air and claw his face. "Girls. Like. That?"

He holds his hands up. "I'm sorry. Listen, I promise you I will find who had her last, and I will bring him here, and I will let *you* decide what happens. Until then, harness this vengeance, focus this rage, and use both to garner future earnings toward your freedom."

"I don't care about my freedom. Everything I lived for is gone."

"Then set your thoughts on killing whoever did this to your sister. Let that be the reason you live. Everyone in

Saligia is talking about Valoria, the defiant one. You need to ride that victorious wave. You need to use it to your advantage."

"She was innocent! She didn't do anything wrong. She should have never been here."

Master steeples his hands in front of his face and studies me. "What can I do? I already promised to bring you the person who had her last. What else can I do for you? I want you to know how much I value you."

"I don't just want whoever had her last, I want *any* man who touched my sister. And I want Bareket dead. She had Lena first. She's the reason my sister was sold and taken off Saligia."

"Valoria, I can give you anything but Bareket. *Anything.*"

The reason why I came into his office comes back to me and I don't hesitate in requesting, "I want to go with the galleon and see my sister off. I can't bear the thought of anyone else touching her."

Master gives a nod. "Agreed. There, now see, I'm not unreasonable."

He motions to the corner. "I will send Alexior with you. And I'll do one better, I'll allow you access to my private boat." He waves toward the door. "Now go and get your sister ready. You two will leave this afternoon."

He goes back to his desk, and I follow Alexior out of the office and through the villa. As we're about to descend the stairs into the tunnel, a movement catches my attention and I glance over to see Felicia standing in the corner.

Her bad arm lays strapped to her stomach. Bruises trail her other arm and both of her eyes are now swollen. She didn't have the bruises or two swollen eyes when she left the training grounds to come up here. Master or his wife probably did both to her.

Despite my earlier annoyance with Felicia, my steps falter and I try to catch her gaze to return a reassuring look. But she stands like the other house slaves I've seen—a shadow, hazed, waiting for whatever comes next.

"Felicia," I whisper and her face lifts.

The destroyed look she gives me hits me in the gut. She's been beyond abused up here in this villa. Submissively, she looks away, and I see it. She's given up.

"Valoria," Alexior quietly beckons, and I turn my thoughts back to my sister.

Down in Talme's medic room, I take a bowl of water and a rag and soap and meticulously clean Lena's frail body.

Do you believe in God and heaven? She'd asked me the day our father passed.

I don't think so, I'd replied.

Why?

Because if there were a God, I think he'd be nicer to us than he was.

Hm, she'd mumbled. *Well, I think he's plenty nice to us because we have each other.*

My breath hitches, and I close my eyes. My little sister. So wise. "You're right, Lil' Bit. We have each other." I open my eyes and look down into her beautiful face. "And there is a heaven, and you're already there."

A smile creeps into my quivering lips as I imagine her running across a beach filled with sunlight and white sand, giggling, her black hair flying out behind her. I nod. Yes, that's the exact image I want.

I finish cleaning her and braid her hair and put her into a new tunic. Her weight is insignificant, and I easily lift her and carry her down the tunnel and out to the training grounds where Alexior and the cart waits.

All the warriors are lined up to see us off. Even Master and his wife stand up on the terrace, reverently looking down.

I sit in the back cradling Lena in my arms, and as we travel I hum her favorite song.

Some fifteen minutes later we arrive at the dock and I take a few seconds to look around.

The galleon is not here, but there are five smaller wooden sailboats in their own slips. I estimate each one of them to be about thirty feet long. From the immaculate condition they are in, I can only assume certain elite privately own them.

Soldiers line the dock, guarding the boats. I gaze up and down the beach and see only pristine beige sand. I take a second to scan the horizon and the endless ocean with no other land in sight.

But I now know the layout: soldiers, other sailboats, an empty beach, and a galleon when it's in dock.

Alexior climbs from the cart and circles around the back to let me out. "Do you want me to carry her?"

With Lena in my arms, I slide to the sand. "No."

I follow Alexior down the long dock to where a captain and a soldier sit ready on the boat we will take.

Moments later they push off, hoist the sails, and we catch wind out into the dark expanse. With Lena held close, I watch the land get smaller and smaller as we smoothly make our way through an opening in a reef and toward the horizon.

From this view Saligia looks much like I imagined. Sandy beaches leading to a rocky incline of land that spreads to lush lawns and gardens with the grand villas dotting the scenery. Like a private island with an exclusive resort.

To the right I notice something new—a guard tower. It sits at the very tip of the island, tall enough to watch the surrounding waters. Whoever occupies that knows all comings and goings.

And if the reef circles the entirety of Saligia, then they have a natural barrier for protection. No random boat could wander in without bottoming out on the reef.

Thoughts of escape have me looking over my shoulder at Alexior and the soldier and the captain. There is no way I could overpower all three of them. Plus, if I were to jump, where would I swim to? What about Camille and Gem? I can't leave them.

The sails lower, and Alexior nods to me. "Whenever you're ready."

I slide the bracelet off my wrist and back onto Lena's where it belongs. "There," I whisper. "Now I'll be with you always."

I press a tender kiss to Lena's forehead and then gently lower her body until she slides from my arms into the water. She floats away and then back, away and then back, gradually sinking further and further with each lull of the waves. I stare at her body until there's nothing left to see. Then I continue staring even after the sails are hoisted and we move with the wind back toward shore.

With each wave of water that passes between her and me, something inside of me shifts and an unwelcome thought settles in—Saligia is my home now. Everyone I care about is right here.

CHAPTER 31

THAT NIGHT I sit alone on my cot, staring at the dagger I stole. It seems heavier in my hand than last time. What was I thinking taking this thing? I can't overpower this entire place with one single blade.

Camille sits down beside me and nervously glances around. "Put that thing away," she whispers.

I flip it over in my hand and study it. "This is all my fault."

"What are you talking about?"

"I *knew* something was off that day Mr. Vasquez interviewed me for the job."

Camille shakes her head. "I'm lost."

"The day we were taken. During the interview I kept getting a weird vibe from him. And then he asked to see Lena... I should've known. I should've walked right out, climbed in my car, and drove off."

Camille wraps her arm around me. "You know this is not your fault. This is none of our faults. Your sister's death is on the people here in Saligia."

"This is our home now, Camille. It really hit me earlier

on the boat. You and Gem and Razo and Ignatius, you are who I care about now." I sigh. "Even Alexior."

"Not Sera?" Camille jokes, and we both smile.

I push to my feet and hold the dagger up. "I'm giving this to Alexior."

"What?" Camille reaches for me. "No. Please don't do that. He'll tell Master and who the hell knows what will happen to you then."

I hear her words, but I'm not changing my mind. "It's the right thing to do."

"Wait—"

I ignore her and go to find Alexior. He is in his usual spot, standing on the training ground, staring up at the stars. He hears me before he sees me, brings his attention down to my hand holding the dagger, and though it's very slight, I catch him stiffen with alarm.

It's times like these I wonder if he'll lose his temper. I wonder what I have to do to make him snap. He's perfected the art of stoicism. I could take a lesson for sure.

Yes, he's always seemingly very much in control, but I swear there's a hint of something else in his hard eyes—a pensiveness he tries to hide and probably thinks I don't see.

Coming to a stop right in front of him, I stare up into his gray eyes and hold the blade out. "I stole this from one of the villas."

He takes it from my hand, but doesn't respond.

"I'm handing it over as a gesture of my recent realization."

"And what is that?" he asks, sounding almost bored.

"That this is my home now, and the warriors here are my family."

Alexior nods, but doesn't seem inordinately pleased with my newfound insight. "Then this is forgotten."

"Will you tell Master?"

"No."

I take in a relieved breath and blow it out. "Thank you. Goodnight then."

Again, he doesn't respond, just looks at me through eyes that are now level and intense. I take that as my cue to leave, get back across the training ground, and hear, "Valoria?"

I turn and watch as his eyes travel slowly down my body and with it comes a warm irresistible awareness.

Then he lifts the blade by the tip and my whole body stiffens. He flings it at me, and I lock my muscles in place. I could dart out of the way, he knows that. He won't hurt me... will he?

The dagger glints in the moonlight as it sails toward me and grazes straight across the thin skin covering my triceps. My mouth drops open and I look down to see dark red blood oozing.

I bring my irate gaze up to his and anger bursts straight from my mouth, "You son of a bitch!"

He gives me a hard look. "Do not *ever* sneak *anything* in here again. Do you understand me?"

"Yes!"

"Good. I'm glad we comprehend each other."

"I can't believe I actually included you!"

"Included me in what?"

The people I care about. But of course I don't say that.

He lifts his brows, waiting, and I still don't respond. He nods toward the tunnel. "Go see Talme if you need to."

I want to tell him he disgusts me, but I clench my teeth and turn away. Down the tunnel I stomp and push through the medic door and come to a stop. Sera's awake. My pulse jumps in an unexpected pump of joy.

Talme's standing over her, applying something thick

and white to the row of puffy stitches that hold in her guts. She glances over her shoulder at me, and sighs. "What happened to your arm?"

"Alexior and I got in a disagreement," I tell her.

Sera chuckles and then cringes.

I step closer. "Can I help?"

Talme nods to a bowl of water. "Soak a rag and wipe her face."

"When do you think I'll fight again?" Sera hoarsely asks.

"Not for some time. But don't worry about it," Talme reassures her. "Master has given you unlimited healing time."

Sera shakes her head. "You and I both know how that works."

I look between them. "How what works?"

Neither one of them answers, and I begin to wonder why I even asked. I already know the answer. Master isn't generous enough to give anyone unlimited anything. If Sera doesn't get well, she's out of here—whatever that means. Re-auctioned. Banished to The Hole. Or any other number of horrible things I probably still don't know about this place. Despite our mutual dislike, she doesn't deserve that.

Talme tsks. "Don't talk, Sera. Just heal."

Sera closes her eyes and I wipe the wet rag over her sweaty face. I've never been gentle with Sera. It feels... odd and not completely right. "How did you two end up here?" I quietly ask and hold my breath, waiting, *hoping* they respond.

Talme takes in some deep air. "I'd just gotten divorced and wanted to travel the world, start over, rediscover myself. I took a volunteer nursing job with Third World Aid. I fell asleep on the transport and when I woke up, I was here. That was twenty years ago."

I suck in a shocked breath. "Twenty?" This place has been around that long?

Sadly, she nods. "I'll die here."

"But are you 'free'?" Is she like Ignatius? Could she leave if she wanted?

She huffs a sarcastic laugh. "Hasn't anyone told you yet? Unless you die, you're never leaving."

Her words wash through me, numbing me with realization. Yes, Alexior and Sera have both said as much, but somewhere in my brain I still held hope.

I wipe the rag over Sera's forehead. "And you?"

"Like Gem," she croaks, in obvious pain. "My 'contract' was up year one, and I'm still here." She swallows. "Been ten years now."

Oh, Gem. She's never leaving. She'll never see her daughter again. I'm never leaving. None of us are.

"You should be the one on this table," Sera rasps.

I pause in my wiping and stare down at her face. She pries open her one good eye and looks up at me. She's got a point, even if it irritates me. She's been here the longest. She's the one who deserves all the attention of killing Zebulon.

She closes her eye again. "Because of me, you are the victor."

"Because of me," I defend myself, "you're alive."

She grunts. "Look at you talking big and free. Don't let the triumph go to your head. I'll be off this table soon and back in Master' graces."

Done with the gentle thing, I toss the rag beside the bowl.

"I wish you would've died," she mumbles right before drifting back off to sleep.

I scowl down at her. Why in the world did I think anything would be different between us?

"What'd you do to piss off Alexior?" Talme asks.

"Nothing," I say and slide up on an empty table. "Just put a stitch in it or whatever."

CHAPTER 32

THE NEXT MORNING at breakfast the atmosphere is heavy with my sister's death, the rain pelting the sands, Sera still in the medic room, everything...

Across from me sits Camille and Gem, silently eating, liked they're weighed down with the denseness, too.

"How you doing today?" Gem asks me.

Resolutely, I nod. I've always hated that question. I mean, do people really want to know? Do they really want to sit here and listen to me spout off about our crap for a life? What good is it going to do any of us and our morale?

How am I doing? Like shit. My sister's dead. How do they *think* I'm doing? But I know it's a nice thing to ask and that she's being a friend, and so I manage a reassuring smile and then quickly change the subject. "So you and Razo snuck off during our night of debauchery. Anything to tell?"

Gem blushes, and it strikes me as odd. Such an innocent response for this sinful place. She glances over her shoulder to where Razo sits with Ignatius. Razo must sense her look because he glances up and sends her a little smile.

She lets out a tiny giggle and then slaps her hand over

her mouth in embarrassment and turns back to me and Camille. "I can't believe I just giggled."

Jealousy pangs through me, and I frown. But, yeah, I am jealous of the fact she's found a modicum of happiness in this place. Jealous... and pleased, too. Gem is my friend. I want only the best for her.

"Sure we kissed," she tells Camille and me, "but that's all. Mostly we talked. Do you know he was born here?"

"What?" Camille gasps. "That's awful. I can't imagine being raised here."

"Twenty-two years ago to a house slave," Gem tells us. "Master bought him at fifteen and he's been here ever since."

"What about his mother?" I ask.

"As far he knows she's still working in the same villa he grew up in."

I flip my attention over to Razo. This is his world. He's never been beyond these waters. He has no clue what life is really like. Cars and cell phones and TV. And electricity for God's sake. How unbelievably odd. But... if anyone were to know the ins and outs of Saligia it would be Razo.

A scream pierces the air and we all stop what we're doing and look around. Another one shrills through the rain, and I realize it's coming from the terrace.

I jump to my feet, as does most everyone else, and we hurry out onto the training ground.

Naked and bug-eyed, Felicia hangs from a length of rope and from the grayness of her body, I'd guess she's been there several hours if not all night.

Her injured arm is wrapped to her stomach and red welts angrily crisscross her body.

Yet another scream pierces the morning air, and I switch my gaze to Mistress standing on the terrace, staring in shock over the balcony. Clearly, Felicia did this final act on her own.

Master finally comes rushing out onto the terrace. He glances over the side, grabs a knife from his office, cuts Felicia loose, and then wraps his wife in a condoling hug. Felicia's body drops to the wet sand.

Sorrow. Guilt. Anguish. Pity. All of these things course through me. I should've been kinder to Felicia. She took her life to escape this one. At least she's free now. I glance up to Master hugging his wife and anger sparks my blood. They're the reason she hung herself.

A warrior to the left of me snickers. "Wasn't like she was of any use anyway."

My anger morphs to rage. I duck and drive my fist straight into his balls and follow that with a powerful punch to his throat.

He staggers back, gagging, and I hover toward him, ready to tackle and pulverize his snickering face. He brings his arms up in automatic blocking formation. He's ready to fight. Good.

"Enough!" Alexior yells.

My fingers curl into my palms and I shoot the warrior a poisonous look. "That is a human being lying dead. Show some respect!"

He flips me off and stomps away. I turn to Camille and Gem. "Help me."

We head toward Felicia's naked body and as we're leaning down to pick her up, I hear Master say, "Alexior, I want to see Valoria in the holding cell."

I clench my jaw and roll my aggravated eyes to Camille and Gem.

"It's okay," Camille assures me, though her eyes seem more alarmed than anything. "We got this."

I don't even wait for Alexior and instead stalk right past him. Why Master wants to see me in the holding cell, I have no clue. I thought I'd moved beyond this. But, whatever.

I fling open the door, stamp over to the wall, and snap the shackles on. I turn and hold out my wrists and wait for Alexior to lock me up.

He does and goes to stand at his usual spot over in the corner. I glare at him and impassively he moves his eyes over me.

"Well?" I snap.

"Well, what?"

"Oh, I don't know," I spurt. "Why don't we start with the fact you *knifed me*. Or perhaps Felicia hanging herself. Then there's Sera and who the hell knows what will happen to her if she can't fight again. Not to mention she still hates me despite the fact I'm the reason she's alive. Or how about the knowledge Razo was born in this hell."

I rattle the chains. "Or the fact Master wants to see me and I'm FUCKING chained like an animal once again!"

As if on cue Master slams into the cell and storms right over to me. He throws all his weight into a punch that sinks into my lower abdomen and then follows that with one straight in the throat. Just like I did with the warrior a few minutes ago. Minus the ball shot.

I hunch forward with a gag.

He grabs the front of my tunic and pushes me up against the wall. My head thuds against the stone and a sound gurgles from my lips.

He sticks his face right in mine. "Do not *ever* discipline a warrior. That is my job and that is Alexior's job. I heard what he said, and he's right. Felicia was nothing. That warrior is six times her worth. Despite all that, her death has now caused me money. Money *you* will make back for me."

I clench my jaw. "But I'm not the reason she's dead. This place is. Whatever you did to her in the villa pushed her beyond her limits. You and Mistress are the reason she committed suicide."

He pierces me with cruel eyes. "And you? What are your limits?"

"I don't know," I sneer. "But I haven't reached them."

He releases me and slams his palm against the wall with a growl. "After all my generosity with you and this is how you repay me. With more defiance." He steps away and turns to Alexior. "Just leave her here. She needs yet another lesson in humility."

With that he's gone.

"You're a fool," Alexior tells me in disgust.

"Please," I scoff. "He's not going to do anything to me. I'm his champion."

"Your ego is fully intact, I see. I thought you had learned something. If you want to remain his champion, his chosen one, you do what he says. That's the only way you'll get what you want. Because eventually you'll be just like Sera in the medic room with an uncertain life. Then what?"

He doesn't wait for me to respond and instead walks out.

All my frustration erupts from my body in a scream.

I yank at my restraints and my heartbeat elevates to the point it's thudding in my eardrums. The urge to cry overwhelms me, but I don't give in.

I'm in the cell the rest of the day, through the night, and into the next morning. No one comes to check on me. I am left alone to seethe. It's more of a mental exercise to be in here alone, not a physical one. I'd almost prefer physical to this.

Eventually my temper tires me out, and though my

wrists are still shackled to the wall, I manage to slide down to somewhat of a sitting position. It's just me and the stone cell and my thoughts.

I thought you had learned something.

I thought I had too. I thought I'd learned how to "play" this disgusting game. Alexior is right. Of course I know he's right.

If I want to remain Master' chosen one I have to do what he says. Because being his chosen one is the only way I'm killing Bareket and bringing this place down.

Hours later, the door opens and Master and Alexior walk back in.

"I take it you enjoyed your extended stay in this lovely accommodation?" Master sarcastically quips.

Wincing against the awkward angle the shackles have kept my arms at, I slowly get to my feet and try to regain some balance. "I apologize, Master. Between my sister's death and seeing Felicia's suicide, I snapped. Please forgive me. It won't happen again."

He folds his arms in a grand pleased gesture. "Okay, a test. We've recently acquired some *very* special slaves. After your show with Zebulon, I've been commissioned, *you've* been commissioned to publicly kill these slaves."

I close my eyes and swallow every refusal in me. I think of those women slaves who got brutally beat to death by the soldiers and open my eyes so I don't see them in my brain. I clear my throat. "What's so special about these slaves?"

Master grins. "Ever heard of the Candy Duo?"

I think about that for second and slowly I begin to remember. Candy Duo. Twins. Ran a candy store. Also raped and murdered a dozen or more children and buried the bodies in their backyard. The whole thing made national news.

Master laughs. "I can see your excitement."

No, not excited. But if I ever wanted to be in the arena to kill two people, these would be them. They deserve to die. I don't even want to think about what that says of me —*wanting* to go into the arena and kill two people. Who am I that I even think this way now?

"When?" I ask.

"Two days." Master nods for Alexior to unlock me and when he does, both of my shoulders pop.

I cringe and give them a rub.

"You'll wear your new armor, of course. Bets are already being placed. A bonus to you if you make it good and gory. By that I mean blood. Chop off their fingers. Hack their penises. Stab them like you did Zebulon. Decapitate them for all I care."

Master laughs and claps his hands, and wickedness glints in his eyes. "This is going to be *so* great."

It's all I can do not to curl my lip at his obvious delight in the gore. I'll kill them, sure I'll kill them, but I'm not going to purposefully draw it out and painfully mutilate them. That's a line I'm not willing to cross.

CHAPTER 33

"Let blood be shed!" Master shouts and everyone in the small arena stamps their feet.

From my spot behind the iron gate, I watch across the fighting grounds as another gate opens and two men are shoved out. They both stumble forward, dazed, looking around. I remember their faces from the news. This is definitely the Candy Duo.

The crowd immediately begins booing, and I size the duo up. One is tall and skinny with thinning hair and the other is short and heavy with a full gray beard.

Two slaves wheel a cart out loaded with weapons. They dump them all in a loud clatter in the center of the arena before hurrying off the sands. I eye the heap and recognize many of the tortuous tools from those used in The Hole.

My fingers flex around my spears. I hadn't expected my opponents would be given weapons. But of course they would. This "show" wouldn't be fun without it.

I glance again to the two of them and watch as they take a few hesitant steps toward the pile, like they're not sure what they're supposed to do. I wonder if they've been told anything. Probably not. Like me, they were likely sedated, woke up, and here they are. Naturally, I want to question how Master went about getting them out of prison, but nothing surprises me anymore. He and the other rich and elite seem to have connections everywhere.

My gate opens then, and I step through. The crowd sees me and erupts into insanity as they leap to their feet and chant my name. "Va-lor-i-a. Va-lor-i-a."

This is my first public fight in my new armor. I lift both spears high into the air and the decibel level in the place magnifies. I'm sure the warriors back at camp can probably hear.

Closing my eyes, I tilt my head back, and just breathe in the energy. My "test" as Master put it. Fine. I will kill them. Pass this test. And get back in his good graces. Then I will move onto the next phase. Devising a plan to escape and take my friends with me.

My life here in Saligia flashes across my thoughts: the auctioning block; popping Sera's eye; Bareket taunting me with my sister; the violence of The Hole; ending Zebulon's life; Lena dying in my arms; Felicia's hanging body.

My eyes snap open, and I stare straight up to where the elite sit and into Bareket's eyes. I am stronger now than ever. *I am Valoria.* I quietly acknowledge my new name, the defiant one.

My grip tightens on both spears as I yell and charge.

CHAPTER 34

"My God you're like a freak of nature," Camille jokes. "How many fights have you won now?"

"Every one of them," Gem joins in.

Razo grunts. "Yeah, you're making the rest of us look bad."

I smile at their teasing. It's true, fortune has been with me. Or the gods. Or something. Since killing the Candy Duo, I've fought in four other events and won each one. I am the number one requested warrior for everything that goes on here in Saligia.

But I don't abuse it. I don't take it for granted. I use it. I learn from it. I harness it.

Sera gingerly makes her way out of the tunnel and over to the food table. She spoons up meat and vegetables, grabs bread, and sits down beside Ignatius. She's been up for a week now, but she's not training. For that matter, she doesn't really seem to be healing.

Gem leans in. "I hear Master is going to sell Sera."

I've heard the same thing, but I honestly don't want to see her go. Another month or so and she should be back to normal. I would think. She *was* gutted. Something that severe has to take months to heal.

The gate opens and in rolls a cart pulled by two horses. Alexior jumps down from the driver's seat and opens the back. "Out."

Six new slaves, three women and three men, climb down. I didn't realize we were getting new recruits. Alexior unlocks their shackles and indicates they should stand in a line.

I'm immediately reminded of my first day here.

The cart pulls away, the gate to the outbuilding bolts shut, and Alexior nods to all of us warriors sitting in the shade eating lunch.

In unison we stand and make our way out into the sunshine. Several warriors walk up and down the line, jabbing the recruits, sneering at them, telling them they're shit. Sera even joins in.

I use the time to study the six new recruits. Like everyone else here, they stand big and capable, except for one. He is small like me and looks Cuban-American, too. Did Master buy him thinking he would be the male version of me?

Though they're trying hard to be brave, fear rolls off of them in palpable waves. They are confused. Lost. Dirty. Months ago I stood right there. Without reminders like this, it's easy to forget those things that linger in the recesses of the mind.

Sera steps in front of the small man. "What was Master thinking getting *this* one?"

I suppress the unexpected smile that comes to my lips. She'd said the same thing to me.

She throws her head back and laughs, and the small

man kicks her right in the shin and she just laughs and laughs.

"Enough!" Alexior barks.

Sera scowls at the little guy, and he scowls right back. I think I'm going to like this one.

"Greetings!" Master shouts, and we warriors get into formation.

I look up to the terrace to see him and his wife, a couple of the elite, and Bareket. I haven't seen her since the arena when I killed the Candy Duo. Did she leave Saligia and come back? Does Master ever leave? And Vasquez. I wonder if I'll ever see him up on that terrace. Or does he stay in the real world to kidnap and sell people to this place? I wonder how much money he made off me and Lena.

"Welcome to Saligia," Master says. "Each of you are lucky enough to have been brought to this camp. You have been blessed. This is sacred ground. We do not fear death, we embrace it! We are warriors!"

To that, we give our expected guttural war cry that I'm sure completely intimidates the new slaves.

"We are the proud owners of Ignatius, the fire of the arena." He points to the right where Ignatius raises his enormous fist into the air. "And Valoria, the defiant one." He points to me and I do my signature back flip.

He doesn't introduce Sera and I'm sure that pisses her off.

He waves his arm through the air in a grand gesture. "We are a self-sustaining society full of decadence and desires. Sins and fantasies. Debauchery and perversions. All can be explored right here."

He lays a gentle hand on his wife's shoulder. "You will find that this can be a good life. You will be well cared for *if* you do as you're told. Let me ask you, what did you have going for you back home? Food in your stomach? A definite roof over your head at night? No, you probably did not."

Master nods to Alexior. "Alexior is in charge of your training and will turn each of you into the type of warrior that gives us our outstanding reputation. But make no error in judgment. You *will* be executed if you try to escape. Do *not* cross me in any way."

I've heard this speech before. I only hope the recruits are seriously digesting it for the real warning it is.

"Now," Master nods to the rich standing around him, "we have some special guests today. Each of you recruits have been bought by these elite. They are your patrons. When you fight it will be to honor them. They will cover your expenses, but you will stay here to train under the best." He lets out an airy laugh as he looks at them. "Of course I will share in the earnings as part of our agreement."

They all chuckle in response. Just another materialistic way for them to spend their greedy money.

Master spreads his arms. "Well, what do you think of your new purchases?"

Bareket purses her thin lips, glances once at me, and then goes on to peruse the line of slaves. I wonder which one she owns.

"Slaves," she announces. "Disrobe."

Master cuts her an amused glance and then nods to Alexior. He motions us warriors over to the side and then indicates the recruits should undress. I shake my head in disgust at their intimidation tactics.

The recruits strip to their undergarments, and Bareket says, "No, I want naked."

Camille shoots me an equally disgusted look and we stare in mutual antipathy as they strip completely bare. Why aren't they fighting back? I would've. But maybe they've already realized they will suffer if they do not do as they're told.

Bareket giggles and claps her hands like some imbecilic kid playing a game.

Up on the terrace they start discussing their purchases while the slaves stand there naked staring at the ground. I want to walk over and hand each of them their garments, but I don't. What good would it do? It would only get me punished and probably all of them as well.

The fact of the matter is, this is good for them. It'll toughen them up. It'll smack them with the reality of this place.

Gradually the elite leave the balcony, their voices trailing behind them, and Master motions the new slaves can get dressed. "You," he calls to the little man. "What is your name?"

"They told me my name is Niho," the guy states in a bold tone. His deep voice and his little body do not match.

"I want him to train with Valoria," Master tells Alexior.

I was right. He's going to be the male version of me.

CHAPTER 35

THE REST of the afternoon we warriors are each paired with a recruit. I can tell Niho has had some fighting experience. Either because he's small and has had to defend himself or because he's taken some real lessons. Like I had with my dad.

Either way, I'm not kind to him. I am firm and focused. I in no way want him to think this is a friendly place. The sooner he accepts his fate and understands that, the stronger he will be.

Alexior walks among us. "Defend by removing yourself from the opponent's range."

I sweep Niho's legs out from under him with my spear, and he quickly gets back on his feet.

"If you don't remove yourself from their range, then step inside their circle," Alexior continues.

I grab Niho's head and pull it toward me. His eyes widen, and he yanks back.

"Control by remaining within your effectiveness range," Alexior goes on, "and at the same time moving out of your opponent's."

That was easy with a giant like Zebulon, but not someone small like Niho. Our effectiveness range is similar. Still, I back away to taunt him forward. He takes the bait and I lunge, bringing my spear up and under his shield and twisting it free from his hands.

He sighs.

I lean down and pick it up and hand it to him. "Make your opponent believe they have advantage so they will over extend."

Niho nods and arcs his sword to the left to jab me in my ribs. I go toward the jab instead of away, slamming my spear down on his wrist and causing his sword to clunk to the ground.

"Dammit," he swears.

"But being too close can hinder your effectiveness," I tell him as I flick his sword back into the air and catch it. "It all depends on the situation and range of that moment."

I go to hand him his sword, he reaches for it and I rotate it and bop him under the chin.

He glares at me.

Alexior walks up to us. "Range. You were just in hers."

Niho firms his jaw and I can tell he's beyond pissed. Good.

He fiddles with his shield a second. "You know a lot," he begrudgingly admits.

I hand him his sword for real this time. "I do. But I was just like you when I first got here. Practice. Pay attention. Be pissed. Just make sure you channel that pissiness in the right direction. And don't fidget. It makes you look unsure."

"Oh, yes," Sera taunts from the shadows. "Listen to Valoria, the defiant one. She's all knowing."

I ignore her and go back to training with Niho. I'm not

trying to be "all knowing". I really just want to make him into a good fighter. A survivor.

"Oh, that's right," she taunts some more. "I'm no longer champion. You are, and you're too good to speak to me."

I continue to ignore her but my temper crawls slowly through my insides.

"I am still Sera, Serpent of Saligia, and you are just a lucky runt."

Irritation pulses through me, and I narrow my eyes on Niho. His dark ones flick over to Sera and back to me. He's scared I'm going to take it out on him.

A harsh laugh escapes her. "You would have *nothing* without me."

My fist clenches around my spear and I slowly turn to her. What is she doing? She's barely said a word to me over the past couple of weeks. Why the challenge now?

She steps out of the shadows and slowly stalks toward me. In my periphery I see the warriors and the recruits backing away. I don't want to fight her. She's in no condition to go up against me. Surely, she realizes that.

She comes to a stop right in front of me, purposefully towering and intimidating as she sneers down at me. She's uncomfortably close, but she doesn't touch me, as I expected her to.

It's times like these when I am reminded of our size difference. She's not quite twice me, but she's really darn close.

My pulse throbs in my throat as I say, "This isn't a good idea."

Her upper lip arcs into a snarl. "I will regain my status here."

Does she know there's talk of selling her, is that why she's doing this? To impress, to prove she's worth keeping? It doesn't matter. I'm not going to let her win. I will not purposefully take a fall.

She moves quickly then, swinging her fist to uppercut my chin. My teeth crash together, my head snaps back, and I suddenly can't hear anything. But I duck and spin and jab my elbow into her lower abdomen.

My hearing rushes back as she sucks in a raspy breath and stumbles away with blood immediately soaking her tunic. I broke her wound back open. She sucks in another breath and falls to the ground, gripping her stomach and cringing, all the while glaring at me.

Guilt pinches at my gut and I clench my teeth against it. It was low of me to hit her there, but what did she expect challenging me?

"Know your opponent's weakness," Alexior says to the recruits, using this as a teaching moment.

I turn away from him, from Sera, from the whole thing. I hate what I just did.

CHAPTER 36

THAT NIGHT AFTER DINNER, the recruits pace the training ground with small boulders strapped to their hands and wrists, just like we had to do. They haven't eaten all day. I remember all too well the hungry acid that felt like it was eating me from the inside out.

"Remember when we had to do that?" Gem mumbles.

I nod.

She shakes her head. "Who would've ever guessed we'd be on this side of things?"

"Never thought I'd say this, but I see it all now." Camille takes a sip of water, studying the recruits. "The training, pacing with those boulders, the sweat box. Everything. It really has prepared us."

"Hey," Gem turns to me, "don't feel bad about Sera. She brought it on herself."

"I know." But I still hate myself for it.

"Halt!" Alexior yells, and I watch as he walks around and unstraps the ropes from each of their hands and wrists. "Eat."

The recruits stumble over themselves to get to the one

gigantic bowl of rice and lentils that has been put out on the training ground for them. Eagerly, they thrust their dirty hands into the food and shove it into their mouths.

"What's this?" A voice cuts through the night and I turn to see a warrior coming out of the men's quarters. He stomps across the training ground and kicks the bowl through the air.

The recruits watch in agony as it arcs above them and rice flies in every direction.

I step out from the shadows. "Let them be."

The warrior turns on me. "You'll teach them nothing being kind and gentle."

"I agree. But this isn't gentle, this is humanity. They need nourishment."

He snorts his disagreement, gives one of them a shove in the head, and stalks back toward the men's quarters.

Calmly, I look at Alexior. "Can we get more food?"

He doesn't immediately answer and I lift my brows in question.

"Perhaps," he says. "But Master will require you pay for it out of your arena earnings."

I shrug. "Then so be it."

Camille grabs my arm. "What are you doing? They won't die if they starve for the night. God knows we did."

Lena's emaciated body flashes through my mind and I pull my arm away from Camille. "I don't care. They need food." And what else am I going to do with my money?

One of the house slaves comes through the tunnel and straight toward me. It's the first time I've ever seen a house slave down here. I don't recognize her. She looks older than the others up in the villa. Does she have a key?

"Mistress would like to see you and Camille and Gem," she tells us, and we all exchange an apprehensive glance.

"Have you bathed for the night?" the house slave asks us next.

My heart jumps unsteadily, but I answer succinctly, "Yes."

She nods. "Follow me."

CHAPTER 37

I GLANCE over my shoulder to Alexior. Last time I was summoned to the villa by Mistress he saved me from whatever she had planned with Ignatius. Something tells me he won't be able to save me this time.

Halfway down the tunnel, Camille stops us. She grabs each of our hands and squeezes tightly. "Whatever they want, we will do. Do not show emotion. Do not show they have power over us."

I give them both a closed lip reassuring smile. "And imagine slicing their necks open. It's a beautiful thought."

"No matter what," Gem adds. "We will remain friends and allies."

Allies. What an appropriate word.

A soldier at the top of the stairs shackles our wrists. We follow the house slave through the villa and into a back room where Mistress and Bareket and a couple more women lounge among a harem of pillows. The same cat I've seen before lays curled on one of their laps.

Their gossiping and laughter immediately die as the

three of us enter. There are two house slaves, one in each corner, and as usual their gazes are void.

Mistress bites into a plump, ripe strawberry, all the while contemplating us. The last time she summoned me, her husband had no clue. I wonder if he knows now.

She tosses her half eaten fruit aside and takes a sip of wine. "We women have decided the men get all the fun around here. Save for Bareket, the rest of us just live off our men. We're taking our allowances and betting in the fights to make some money of our own."

On my right stands Gem and on my left Camille, and neither one of them moves a muscle.

"What do you think about that?" one of the women asks. "Would it make you proud to make us money?"

As expected, the three of us nod, though pride is definitely not how I would feel.

Bareket slides to her feet and casually strolls over. Her pot and jasmine scent floats up my nostrils and they flare. I hate her smell.

She glides around us, easing her cold fingers along our arms, our necks, our ears. I lock my muscles and concentrate on not showing how much she affects me. Because of her, Lena is dead.

She comes to stand right in front of me. "I was so sorry to hear about your sister."

My jaw clenches and I resist the urge to head butt her.

She tsks. "Such a shame."

I bring my gaze from the spot I've been staring at straight into her demented eyes. I imagine slicing her neck wide open and hope she sees the image reflected in my stare.

Her eyes linger on mine and then she dramatically rolls

hers over to Gem first before going to Camille. "I hear you three are quite the pals now."

My muscles lock even tighter.

Bareket sways back and forth, studying the three of us as she taps her finger to her chin. "What would happen, I wonder, if your little trio was broken up?"

We stay completely silent, and I struggle to suppress the rage scratching its way to the surface.

Mistress laughs. "Oh don't be mean, Bareket."

Bareket's expression narrows to deviance as she brings her eyes back to mine. "Yes, I wonder indeed."

I swallow the words I want to spit at her.

She twirls away and her scent kicks up around us as she throws her arms out. "Okay, which one do you want to keep for tonight's enjoyment?"

All the women brighten.

Camille visibly quivers, and her fear vibrates in the air around us.

"Let's keep the blond one," one of them says.

My pulse leaps that it is not me and then immediately plummets in shame and guilt. I would never wish anything bad for Camille, but I'm so relieved it's not me they're keeping.

"What's her name?" another one asks in this non-purposeful tone that spasms straight through me.

Mistress's face twists into a strange smile. "That one's Camille."

"Yes, let's keep that one," Bareket agrees.

Mistress waggles her fingers. "You two may go."

I turn toward Camille, but she doesn't look at me. "Imagine slicing their throats," I whisper, and she barely nods.

Gem and I are completely silent as we make our way back through the villa and down the stairs to the tunnel. We are silent as we enter the women's quarters and go to sit on Camille's cot. Silence that fills my ears with uneasiness.

Camille.

"Do you think they're going to separate us?" Gem whispers.

Yes. But I don't say that. I lie. "No. It was just a threat. Just another one of their evil games."

We don't say another word as we wait. And wait. And wait for Camille's return. Hours go by and she finally enters the tunnel. Gingerly, she walks the length of it and enters the gate that leads into our quarters. Every organ in my body wrenches as I watch her.

She looks up, sees us waiting, and doesn't say a word. Her face is so full of agony and humiliation that my blood curdles.

She keeps walking right past us and straight to the bathing area. Gem and I don't say a word. We merely follow.

We help Camille undress and step into the water, all the while ignoring the blood smeared along her butt and inner thighs and the welts on her back where she was lashed.

She buries her face in her hands and gives into sobs that come from the depths of her very soul. Sobs that make tears jump into my own eyes. Sobs that make every muscle in my body clench.

Afterwards, we dress her in clean clothes and lead her back to her cot. We stay with her all night, but none of us sleep. None of us talk. Sometimes quiet closeness is the best support friends can give each other.

Camille doesn't tell us what happened and we don't ask.

Yes, separating us will be a mistake the elite will most definitely regret.

CHAPTER 38

"I'm coming to you because I know Camille won't. She was severely mistreated last night and needs a day to rest."

Alexior glances over to where Camille's eating breakfast, and that muscle in his jaw flexes. "I'll put her in charge of cleaning weapons today."

"Thank you." I turn to leave.

"Are you okay?" he quietly asks.

I turn back. "Yes, I'm fine."

His eyes travel over my face—my eyes, my cheeks, my lips—before gently saying, "Good."

His tender look washes through me, relaxing me, and I physically feel my shoulders drop with the ease.

I think about his station here in Saligia. About mine. And I watch as his gaze touches down on my triceps where he flung the dagger at me. Though he doesn't say anything, his expression comes across remorseful.

Yeah, I was pissed. But not now. He did what he was supposed to—discipline me. If it would've been Master, I would've been severely beaten. A nick in my skin is nothing compared to that.

Ducking my head, I catch his eyes and give him a small smile to let him know I'm okay—one that he slowly returns, and I feel myself physically relax with the warmth of it.

Then I walk right past all the recruits sitting on the ground and head toward the tunnel and the medic room. Despite what went down between me and Sera, I want to check on her.

"Valoria?" comes a voice behind me and I turn to see Niho.

"What are you doing?" I ask. He should be with the recruits.

He holds up his hand where a gash runs across his palm. "Alexior has sent me to the medic."

I point down the tunnel. "It's just down here."

"Thank you," he says as he falls in step beside me, "for being kind."

"I'm not kind," I tell him. That's the last word I want him to associate with me or this place.

"If it weren't for you we wouldn't have eaten yesterday. The other warriors are leaving us alone, too. Plus all the instruction with the fighting. I really appreciate it."

I don't say you're welcome, but I do nod my acknowledgment.

"Which makes this even harder to do," he says.

I turn at the exact second he moves, thrusting a knife right into my hip. I gasp and stumble back and he comes right at me.

"I'm sorry," he mumbles and lunges.

Sera comes from the medic room. "Hey!" she yells and charges.

I block his lunge and cringe when the blade slices across my forearm. Sera grabs him and throws him, and the knife flies through the air before she climbs on top of him and pummels his face with her fists.

His screams echo up and down the tunnel and I grip my hip and slide down the wall. Blood oozes between my fingers, fire licks through my bones, and I concentrate on keeping my eyes open so I don't pass out.

People are in the tunnel now, moving around, yelling, trying to figure out what's going on. Sera's in front of me next, staring down at the blood creeping through my fingers. She helps me to my feet and into the medic room.

I look down at her tunic. She's bleeding, too. Her wound has broken open again.

Talme's eyes move over both of us, and she sighs. We both slip out of our clothes and climb up on side-by-side tables. Neither of us speak as Talme starts working.

"It's not near as deep as all that blood makes it seem," she tells me.

"Good." I put my left hand on top of my head and breathe through the stitches she begins giving me in my side. I look over to Sera and awkwardness fills the air between us.

"Why did you help me?" I ask.

"Because that recruit is nothing. You're one of us. You don't deserve to die in a tunnel being stabbed by someone who has been here one day. When you die, *if* you die, it shouldn't be like that."

If you die. I like that she thinks I might not. "But you don't like me. This would have been your chance to be rid of me."

"Like I said, that's not how it should happen."

I grit my teeth as Talme tugs the last stitch and ties it off. "Well, thank you."

Sera doesn't respond. I didn't really think she would.

Talme looks at my forearm. "I'll do that after Sera."

She moves over to work on Sera and while I idly watch, my thoughts drift. She saved me. I probably would not be here right now if it weren't for her. I owe her my life. This is not a comforting thought.

Master flings the door open and steps inside. Alexior comes in behind him. They both take in our stitches, our blood, and Master roars, "*What* the fuck happened? Where did that recruit get a knife?"

Nobody answers him. We don't know.

Master turns on Alexior. "You're supposed to have better control down here."

It's the first time I've ever seen Master talk to Alexior that way. But he doesn't defend himself, only nods and agrees, "You're right. I am sorry, Master. This won't happen again."

What? Alexior has perfect control down here. Why doesn't he say so?

Master sighs. "Banish that recruit to The Hole. He is not to return. Find out where that fucking knife came from and how he got it in here." He turns to Talme. "How long until my champion is ready to resume training."

"A couple of days."

"And Sera?" he asks next.

Talme rolls guilty eyes to Sera before softly admitting to Master, "I'm not sure."

"Fuck!" he yells. "Do you know how much money you're costing me while you *heal*?"

Sera looks down at the blood seeping from her wound and quietly acknowledges, "I do, Master."

"She saved my life," I defend her.

He growls and throws his arms up and turns to leave. I

look from Alexior's frustrated stance to Sera's defeated expression and I know I have to do something.

"Master?" I speak.

He turns back.

"The new recruits. They're owned by other elite. That's what you announced, correct?"

He nods and impatiently waves me on with my point.

"Perhaps whoever owns Niho gave him that knife with instructions to hurt me. I am your champion. You've made a lot of money off of me. I'm sure you're making others jealous over that fact."

Realization slowly creeps into his agitated expression, and he narrows his eyes as he thinks through that. Some extremely quiet seconds go by where no one even seems to breathe. The more I think about what I just said, the more it does makes sense.

Plus, now I've planted doubt in Master' mind about the other elite. Doubt is good. It breaks systems down.

He snaps his fingers and points at me. "You're smarter than I give you credit for." He slaps Alexior on the shoulder. "Load those recruits back up and take them to the market-place. I want them sold and out of here. While you're there, purchase two you think look promising."

I want to ask him who sponsored Niho, but I don't. I'm pretty sure I already know—Bareket.

Which means Master knows, too. Good. Let him hate Bareket over this. Let him keep that nugget of information. Let him use it. I've been around this place long enough to know, he's going to make Bareket pay for this. Somehow he will.

That night I request to see Master and he agrees. Alexior leads me through the villa to the office, and as I enter, Master is sitting staring out at the terrace. Hopefully he's plotting his revenge against Bareket.

Alexior takes his usual spot in the corner, and Master comes around his desk to stand in front of me. He looks down at my tunic to the area where I was knifed and then to my forearm where a row of stitches hold the split skin together. "You are well?"

"Yes, Master, thank you."

"Why did you want to see me?"

"I hear you might be selling Sera."

"Yes," he sighs. "Unfortunately I'm going to have to."

"I've earned a lot with my percentage of the fights." Money I naively thought would purchase my freedom. "I've spent very little."

He nods.

I straighten my spine and look him right in the eyes. "I would like to pay for her expenses so she can stay."

CHAPTER 39

WITH A YELL I CHARGE GEM. Right. Left. Right. Left. Duck. Spin. Kick. Elbow. Over the head with my spear and halting at her head. I turn and move the blade down to her neck. "Your guard is low and I now have your jugular."

She sighs.

I smack her lightly in the side of the neck. "*You*, my friend, are incredibly distracted."

It's been days since everything happened with Camille, and neither she nor Gem have been mentally in the here. Sure we train, we eat, we sleep. All the normal stuff. But their brains are somewhere else, like they're going through the motions without purpose.

Truthfully mine is, too, but I just hide it better.

Gem glances over her shoulder to where Camille trains with the two new recruits Master bought. Twins that I hear are from Poland. A guy and a girl that do seem capable of surviving this lifestyle.

Gem turns back to me, her expression serious. "I can't stop thinking about what happened to Camille and the threat they made about separating us. It could happen any day. You know it could."

I tap my knuckles against her practice shield. "Listen, Master is not going to split us up. Now that Sera's not fighting, we are his three main women warriors. We make him the most money. He's spent a lot of time and investment in us. He's smart. He wouldn't risk it."

She stares at me for a few seconds as this seems to really sink in. "You're right."

I'd said it to reassure myself as well. But now that I have, it really does make sense. Master wouldn't risk the future earnings.

I follow Gem's line of sight as she looks back over to Camille. Together we study her for a few seconds as she fights the twins. Something's different about her today. She's more focused. More intense. Definitely powerful. Like whatever trance she's been in over the last several days has suddenly snapped free.

I watch as she roundhouse kicks one twin in the stomach and blocks the other. With a yell, she jumps up, arcing both of her swords through the air and straight down to simultaneously disarm them.

"Wow," Gem says.

"Yeah," I agree.

"This isn't a real fight," one of the twins grumbles.

Camille grabs the edge of her shield and slings it like a disk straight into that twin's shins and knocks him hard on his ass. With a smirk, she crouches and the pandemonium of adrenaline flashes through her gaze.

In my periphery I see Gem look at me for my reaction, but I don't exchange her glance. I know Camille's expression. She's enjoying the feeling of triumph. Good for her.

She opens her mouth and out comes a slow, deep, powerful chuckle.

"Halt!" Alexior yells. "Eat."

"Oh thank God," Gem says. "I'm starving."

"Valoria," Alexior calls out, "a word."

I grab up all my gear, deposit it in the large wooden boxes, and go to the opposite side of the training ground where Alexior waits. I wipe the sweat off my neck and look up at him. "Yes?"

"It's not in anyone's interest that you discuss your deal with Master regarding Sera."

"I didn't plan on it."

He nods. "Good."

I wait for whatever it is he wants to say next, but he doesn't speak. "Is that it?" I finally prompt.

His gray eyes flick across the training grounds to where everyone is eating and then back to me. "You're going to be in debt to Master a long time. Sera's been here forever and with that comes a huge investment. Money you now have to pay in order for her to stay."

"I know."

He moves a fraction closer and his nearness flushes my skin with heat. "Why?" he asks.

"I thought that was obvious."

The right side of his mouth lifts into a half smile. "Only to you."

"Without her I wouldn't have won against Zebulon. If she weren't there in the tunnel, Niho probably would've killed me. She saved my life. She deserves better than being sold to whomever for whatever malevolent thing they have planned. I have no doubt she will fully recover."

I fold my arms over my chest as a new thought occurs to me. "*And* when that happens, she'll start winning in the arena and now that I pay for her, I'll share in her earnings." Of course I know that will never happen, but still.

His eyes crinkle. "Got it all figured out do you?"

"Not really," I retort with a chuckle. "But it sure sounds convincing."

We both stand, looking at each other, amusement tickling the air around us. I wonder what Alexior would be like outside of this place out in the real world. And then I think about his wife. What happened to her? Will he ever tell me the whole story?

CHAPTER 40

THAT NIGHT I go out onto the training ground. It is empty, as I had hoped. I lay down on the sand and stare up at the multitude of stars. One of them blinks and I smile.

My sister was convinced any kind of twinkle or blink was an angel winking at the person staring up. "Hi Lena," I whisper. "Is that you? Are you my guardian angel?"

A soft moan echoes through the air and I turn my head to the right to see Razo and Gem hidden in the shadows. He has her pressed against the wall while he nuzzles her neck. She slides her leg up to curl around his hip and he grinds into her. Another quiet moan floats toward me and I watch as he slides his hand under her tunic—

"Valoria," Alexior says.

I shoot straight up.

He steps from the tunnel. "Master has sent something for you. Come."

I push to my feet and don't look over at Gem and Razo as I hurry toward the tunnel. "What's going on?" I ask.

Any camaraderie we may have shared earlier is completely gone now. A look that can only be described as disappointment and disgust enters his eyes and makes me pause.

"What's going on?" I hesitantly ask again.

"Just follow me."

"Am I in trouble?" I search my brain. *What did I do now?*

He doesn't answer and instead turns and starts walking down the tunnel. I follow him, my ears tuned to our sandaled feet echoing softly off the stone around us.

We pass the medic room and continue all the way to the end where the gate leads up the stairs into the villa. On the right sits a wooden door I've seen several times and naturally wondered what was on the other side.

Alexior unlocks it and steps inside.

It's a big area with shelving on the left that holds food and wine. On the right, behind a locked iron gate, sits a room with weapons. *Real* weapons. Not the ones we practice with. Swords, spears, shields, knifes, ball-and-chains, clubs, axes, bow and arrows, and tons more.

I eye the gate's three enormous padlocks. Who has the keys?

Straight ahead sits another door. Alexior turns to me. "Master wants to keep his champion happy." He nods to the door. "He said you requested this. When you're ready, go on in."

He turns to leave and I grasp his arm. "I don't understand."

Alexior tugs his arm from my grasp and walks straight past the food and wine and weapons and leaves me in the area alone.

I stand for a few seconds, staring at the door. *I requested this?* I search through my brain, but come up completely empty. I don't recall requesting anything.

Oh, to hell with it. I lift my hand and push the door open.

The smell of citrus hits me first. Subtle and sweet. Like the villa. Colorful hanging cloths decorate the room with enormous bright pillows all over the floor. In the center sits a table with fruit and wine.

On the right is the boy house slave who I saw Master raping in the office. On the left is the girl house slave who I saw giving Master a blow job on the terrace.

Naked, both lay sprawled across the pillows.

"I'm here to please you," the boy says.

I close my eyes and turn away. "Put your clothes on."

"I'm here to please you, too," the girl parrots.

"*Put* your clothes on," I repeat.

Neither one of them move.

"Or we can do each other and you can watch," the boy says.

"Put your GODDAMN clothes on!" I roar.

I hear them both jump up and scuffle around and I draw in a couple of deep breaths. Master is right. I did request this, but not for the reason he thinks.

Back when I killed Zebulon and he was parading me around, promising me anything and everything, I requested a night with a house slave, thinking I could talk to him, learn the inside goings on of the villa.

I honestly didn't think it was a request Master would honor.

I open my eyes and turn around to see them fully clothed and sitting scared and stiff-spined on their individual pillows. It brings out an odd blend of protectiveness and anger in me.

"I'm not going to hurt you," I carefully, calmly assure them. "I just wanted some food and wine. Some company.

A nice cozy place to sleep." And hopefully some information and possibly an ally on the inside.

They exchange a blank glance. They're practiced at hiding emotion.

No wonder Alexior was pissed.

"When Master asks," the girl timidly speaks, "will you tell him we pleased you?"

I give her a gentle smile, "Definitely," and close the door. I sit down in front of the table and grab a slice of mango and motion to the food. "Please eat. Both of you."

They exchange another glance but they don't move. They've never been offered food and wine before. Not like this.

"You're supposed to do whatever I say, right?"

They nod.

"Then pour us all some wine and both of you eat. Please."

Finally, they move, carefully doing as I asked, making sure they don't piss me off. I hate that they're so beaten down. They won't even look at me.

"What's your name?" I ask the girl.

"Hedian," she softly answers.

"That's pretty." I turn to the boy. "And yours?"

"Joseph."

I smile at them both. "Nice to meet you."

The girl's lips curve into a very tiny smile that I'm so glad to finally see.

I let a couple of quiet moments pass so we can all eat, drink, and get used to each other's presence. "How long have you two lived here?" I finally break the silence.

"Four years," Joseph answers, and it curdles my blood.

Four years of living in the villa and being forced to do

unspeakable things. "How old are you two?" I ask next, hoping to hide the turmoil going on inside of me.

"Fifteen," Hedian answers. "We came on the same boat."

They were eleven. *Eleven goddamn years old.* "You two are friends?"

They nod, and I smile. Like me and Camille and Gem.

"Where are you from?"

"We're both from Italy," Joseph answers.

Alexior, Australia. Ignatius, Greece. Gem, Asia. Sera, Africa. Camille, Denmark. The U.S.... yes, Saligia really does have their evil fingers everywhere. "And your parents?" I ask, though I already know the answer.

Joseph shakes his head. "We were both living on the streets. They snatched a bunch of us up."

"Wait, so you knew each other before here?" This is new.

Hedian nods. "There were six of us taken, but..." She glances away before continuing, "We're the only two left."

I glance away, too, not wanting to show them the fury simmering within me. Six children taken and only two still alive. Who knows what happened to the other four. The elite did whatever they wanted. They did what *pleased* them.

We talk for the next hour or so, but every time I steer the conversation in the direction I really want it to go— goings on of the villa, keys to open things, Master' office— they expertly divert things into a safer area.

I can't blame them. They're brainwashed. They're scared. Frankly, they don't trust me.

All I can do is request them again, hope Master allows it, and work on gaining their trust. Because what they see and hear upstairs will be invaluable when it's time to take this place down.

We end up falling asleep and in the morning I tell them both goodbye.

"Will you request us again?" Hedian asks, the eagerness in her voice coming through probably more than she had intended.

"Yes," I assure them both. "I will."

They go back upstairs and I head toward the training ground. Everyone is finishing breakfast, and I grab an apple and a roll of bread.

As I quickly eat, I look toward Alexior who is speaking to Sera. She's holding a practice sword and I wonder if she's going to do some light training today.

Alexior turns to all of us. "Warriors. Recruits. Take note of a true champion returning to training." He looks right at me. "An *honorable* champion returning to training."

I narrow my eyes. He has no idea what he's talking about, and I have no plans on setting him straight. He can think what he wants. All of them can.

The fact is, I can't tell them about my real reasons for being with Hedian and Joseph. What would I say? *I'm gathering inside information so I can overtake this place?*

That thought alone will get me killed. Not to mention Hedian and Joseph.

CHAPTER 41

DRESSED IN OUR ARMOR, me, Camille, and Gem stand at the gate, staring out into the small arena as raindrops softly patter the ground. I watch as several disciplined slaves are dragged from the sands by soldiers. I've never been ordered to participate in maiming the slaves. That's what the soldiers are for. If I'm ever commanded to do it, I will not. I will gladly die first.

The pre-games have come and gone and we are up next. The main event. We've been told we're fighting six men, all violent offenders brought in from some maximum security facility in California.

The irony is not lost on me. If the elite rape and torture and murder, it is part of being in this sick and twisted cosplay. Yet that's exactly what these six men did and now I'm about to end their lives.

The light rain gradually dissipates and the sun comes back out. The gate on the other side of the arena opens and out step six men of varying sizes and ages. The crowd immediately begins booing. The men squint against the brightness and look around in obvious dazed confusion.

"Va-lor-i-a. Va-lor-i-a. Va-lor-i-a," the crowd starts chanting.

Gem glances over at me. "Gem. Gem. Gem." She laughs. "Doesn't have the same ring."

Through Camille's helmet, I study the dark circles under her eyes and her intense expression. "You good?" I ask.

She nods once, giving off an almost weird level of energy. "I'm ready to kill these assholes."

Gem flashes me a surprised, worried look that I agree with but don't return.

The gate opens, and Camille doesn't wait, she yells and charges. Gem and I follow. The crowd leaps to their feet and screams. The six men start to run in different directions. Good, they'll be easier to pick off that way.

We weave through them, purposefully confusing them. One goes down with a stab in the gut. Another with a sliced neck. I fling my spear toward one who is trying to climb the wall out and pierce him straight in the back.

Three down. Three to go.

The crowd roars.

One runs straight toward Gem. I catch her eye and give her the signal and she drops to all fours. I use her back as a spring board and fly through the air to impale the guy right in the heart. I spin to see Camille sliver one from groin to chin.

Five down. One to go.

Gem grabs a long chain and her and Camille sprint toward the last man. He just stands there in a trance, looking at the five other murderers lying dead and bloody on the ground. He knows there is no escape. He knows he is about to die.

Gem dives low, Camille high, and they sling the chain around the guys neck.

They yank hard and the guy gags and claws at the chain as he falls to his knees. They run a wide circle around him, weaving the chain tighter, pulling until his tongue and eyeballs bulge on a last breath.

I have a quick flash of Felicia hanging from the terrace and immediately shake the image from my head.

The crowd stamps their feet and screams and some of the women flash us their tits.

Camille and Gem come to stand beside me. We all link hands and raise our victorious fists into the air, and the crowd transitions into unadulterated craziness.

"I no longer think of life beyond Saligia!" Camille yells. "This *is* my life!"

Violence and power can intoxicate, and my friend is drunk. But I grip her hand harder to let her know I heard her, even though I don't like her words. When it comes time to overtake this place, I need her on my side.

I look up to the Master' private balcony to see him proudly on his feet, cheering. Beside him stands his wife politely applauding. And next to her sits Bareket. She's the only one not on her feet celebrating.

I watch as her eyes travel slowly from Camille to Gem and finally settle on me. She catches me staring and sneers.

That sneer. There's something even more deviant than usual hiding behind it, and I have a feeling I'm going to find out soon what it is.

When we return to the camp, Sera is practicing hard against a wooden post. I watch her form. She's definitely improving, as I knew she would.

"When you're ready for a real opponent," the male twin stupidly taunts, "I'll take you on."

Slowly, Sera turns from the wooden post, and a grin creeps into her face. Other than that, his statement is met by silence.

He straightens a little bit, like he's surprised by Sera's response, or lack thereof, and glances over to Alexior.

Alexior nods. "Begin then."

Sera lifts her sword and shield and crouches into a fighting stance. The twin lifts his, too. He waits for a confused second, like he thinks Sera should move first, and then with a yell, he charges.

She sword plays with him—under, over, down, block— barely expending any energy. He grunts and jabs and curses, flings an ineffective fist, and she catches his wrist and spins him to the ground.

All the warriors laugh. Me, Camille, and Gem exchange an amused look. The twins haven't been here long enough to know what Sera is capable of. Sometimes bravery makes people do stupid things.

Narrowing his eyes, the twin jumps back up and lunges. Sera shoulders her shield straight into his sword and he falls right back down. With a chuckle, Sera turns and walks away.

He grits his teeth and climbs to his feet. "I'm not done with you yet."

Sera turns back around. He throws a handful of sand right into her face and runs at her. Their shields collide. Sera head butts him, uppercuts her fist straight into his jaw, and sends him flying backward.

"Stay. Down," she commands and starts to walk away again.

With a yell, he gets back up and charges. Sera knees him in the groin and punches him hard, twice, in the side of the head. Blood slings from his mouth and he whirls face down into the dirt.

"Stay down," his twin sister whispers.

Unsteadily, he lifts up on all fours, spits a string of blood, and then shakily gets the rest of the way to his feet. He turns, barely able to stand up now, and looks Sera straight in the eyes. "I'm not staying down unless you make me."

Sera stalks over, yanks his shield from his grip, slings it in a wide circle, and rams it directly into his lower gut. The twin gags and buckles forward and Sera flings his shield on top of him.

"Enough!" Alexior snaps.

No one says anything for a few seconds as Sera brushes dirt from her tunic, and the twin rolls over onto his side and grabs his stomach.

Alexior nods to two of the warriors. "Take him to Talme."

One single applause fills the air and we all glance up to the terrace to see Master staring down. "Sera, you are in fine form."

"Thank you, Master," she says.

He looks to Alexior. "I want to see Sera and Valoria in my office. Now."

Alexior puts Ignatius in charge of training and we follow him through the tunnel toward the gate.

"You won't be champion much longer," Sera says to me as we're heading up the stairs that lead into the villa.

I tamp down the urge to provoke her and say simply, "Hm."

CHAPTER 42

MASTER IS SITTING behind his desk when we enter the office. Joseph stands off to the right and behind him. I give him a small smile that he returns.

Alexior takes his usual spot in the corner and me and Sera come to stand right in front of Master. I train my eyes on the papers that he's studying and make out the word *shipment* before he shuffles them around and looks up at us.

From where Joseph stands he could probably read those papers.

"We've got some *very* special guests coming to visit. One of them is the original mastermind behind the creation of Saligia. He's my... boss, for lack of a better phrase. Mr. Vasquez."

My entire body goes numb. *Vasquez...*

"It's very important that he's happy while he's here. I want him to see what a fantastic job I've done of running this camp and Saligia. I'm throwing a welcome party, the biggest yet, and I would like you two," Master looks between me and Sera, "to put on a demonstration right here in the villa."

Beside me Sera straightens even more than she already is and her words come back to me. *You won't be champion much longer.* I'm tempted to remind her this is just a "demonstration".

"Nothing too bloody—okay, maybe a little blood—but more clanking of swords and Valoria, definitely do a couple of those back flips." He looks beyond us to Alexior. "You can work with them on a good show?"

"Yes, Master," he responds.

"Good. Now," he claps his hands, "Sera, Alexior, you may go. Valoria stay." When they are gone, Master indicates the chair in front of his desk. "Sit."

Hesitantly, I do. I've never been in here without Alexior's escort and I've never been allowed to sit.

Master looks over his shoulder to Joseph. "Wine, boy."

Joseph moves, carefully and efficiently pouring us each a goblet. Master lifts his for a toast and I cautiously lean forward to tap.

He laughs. "Relax. Drink. You are in here as my guest."

I smile a little and take a sip and try to settle back into my chair.

He sucks in air through his nose and exhales it slowly through his open mouth, sending his rancid breath to taint the air surrounding us. His gaze traces over to the terrace where the sounds of training filter up.

I chance a quick look at Joseph to see his gaze fastened at a spot above my head.

"You and Camille and Gem put on quite a show today," Master says, bringing his eyes back to mine. "What do you think of Camille? Have you noticed a difference?"

"Yes." *Ever since your wife and her friends tortured her.*

He nods. "Me, too." Another sip of wine. "And Sera?"

"She's healing well. Since I've been paying her

expenses, I expect to profit in her comeback earnings," I joke and hope I don't get in trouble for it.

Master laughs. "Ha!" He toasts me again. "Touché."

I settle back a little more, acting like I'm comfortable with this weird camaraderie, and take another sip.

"Well, don't embarrass her during the demonstration. She *is* the former champion."

"I'll play nice," I joke again, and he laughs.

"Oh, Valoria, you and I are going to accomplish great things together." Another sip. "Just look at us sitting here as almost equals, laughing. Who would've thought I'd feel such a connection to a slave?"

Who would've thought I'd feel such a desire to slice your neck wide open?

Master downs the rest of his wine and holds his empty goblet out to Joseph. "What can I do for you, my champion? I want to keep you happy."

I glance to Joseph again. "When it is convenient, may I have him and Hedian for another night?"

Master chuckles deep and low and dark. "Oh, Valoria, that I can do."

Cold crawls along my spine.

His wife glides into the office and comes to a surprised stop. She looks at me sitting and drinking wine.

"What are you doing?" she snaps at her husband and points at me. "She is a slave and she's sitting there like she's one of us. *Drinking* our wine. Have you lost your wits?" She rips the goblet from my hand and wine sloshes out as she slams it down on the desk. "Get out," she commands me.

I look over to Master to see his teeth clench, and he gives me a brusque nod.

Quietly, I get up and just as quietly leave the office. I expect to hear them yelling when I get in the hall, but I do not. Somehow it didn't occur to me that Master and his wife would ever argue. I like that they are. Especially if it is about me.

But I hate that Joseph is still in there. I hope they don't take this out on him.

"Move," the hallway soldier commands and I keep heading toward the stairs and the tunnel.

As I round the corner a soft cry has me glancing over to the right where a different soldier has Hedian pressed up against the wall.

"Hey!" I call out. "What are you doing?"

The soldier glances over his shoulder and its then I see Hedian's torn tunic and her face streaked with tears. Her eyes widen in fear and she shakes her head.

Screw that. She's been through enough. Some horny soldier isn't going to rape her, too. "Master!" I yell, and the soldier immediately releases her.

Hedian sniffs and lifts her tunic up to cover her bared breasts. She looks straight into my eyes and her lips tremble as she shakes her head again.

I take an intimidating step toward the soldier. "You want to rape someone. Try raping me."

The soldier returns my intimidating step. "Get out of here," he snarls and I notice one of his front teeth is unusually larger than the rest. If I threw a punch, I could easily knock that one single tooth out.

Feet shuffle down the hall behind me, and Master comes around the corner. "What the *hell* is going on?"

I nod to the soldier. "I thought you'd like to know this soldier is trying to rape your house slave. Surely, you don't allow that, Master. She's your property, not his." I honestly don't know if it's allowed or not, but I suspect not.

Master hikes his chin. "Of course it's not allowed." He

points to Hedian. "You, go get cleaned up." Then he points to the soldier. "You want to fuck, you go to one of the whorehouses in the marketplace."

The soldier nods before shooting me a glare and stalking off. It's not a good idea to have a soldier mad at me, but I could care less. He's just another one I'll kill if I have to.

Master turns to me. "And you, do not ever challenge a soldier again. That's grounds for a lashing. My wife reminded me that you are just a slave. I made a mistake inviting you into my office, drinking wine with you, laughing. Remember your station here or I will *gladly* remind you of it."

CHAPTER 43

THE NEXT COUPLE of days go as usual. Training, eating, sleeping. All I can think about is the upcoming party and Vasquez's arrival. Will he remember me? I hope so. Oh, I hope so.

Bareket, Vasquez, Master, and many more elite all in one room. If ever there was a perfect time for revenge...

Joseph and Hedian are not sent to me as I requested and I doubt now that they will be, especially after Mistress reminded her husband of my station. Camille takes to training with Ignatius. Gem and Razo steal intimate moments alone. Alexior only speaks to me when he's commanding something. And me and Sera practice for the demonstration.

Or I should say I practice. She goes about it as if it's a real fight. As if she's planning on more than just a show. It does concern me, but I highly doubt she'll do anything questionable in front of all the elite who are expected at the upcoming gathering.

In front of Vasquez... I cannot *wait* to lay eyes on him.

On the night of the party, we are instructed to bathe,

shave, and dust ourselves with bronze powder. We are given gold leather bikinis to wear and our wrist shackles are polished and gleaming.

Those of us who have hair use scented wax to style it in spikes. We are tattooed with the image of a sword that stretches the length of our left forearm. It's henna and should wear off in a week or so.

We stand in the tunnel as before, lined up according to height. I am in the front and Alexior towers before me, ready to lead us up the stairs and into the villa.

I stare at his broad, bronze-dusted back. He's never without his leather vest and if I look beyond the powder, I can make out his tan line. Such a normal simple thing. It calms me. Until this moment I didn't realize I needed calming. I close my eyes and slowly blow out, relaxing my muscles one at a time, and then open and refocus on the man in front of me.

To signify his station above us, Alexior wears gold pants. His tattooed sword spans his entire bare chest. I wish he would turn around so I could see it closer.

I lean in a fraction and surreptitiously inhale. The men use the same soap as the women, but mixed with his pheromones, it's an entirely different alluring scent.

He shifts a fragment and looks over his shoulder, but not at me, at the door where the weapons are. Where I spent my night with Hedian and Joseph. Like he's reminding me he's repulsed.

The door at the top of the stairs finally opens. Talking, laughing, and the spicy scent of cooked meat flow down the steps to surround us. Despite the fact I've already eaten, my salivary glands still water.

A soldier unlocks the gate at the bottom of the stairs and

a different soldier opens the gate at the top. Alexior leads the way and we quietly follow.

The villa is packed, and I immediately begin searching their faces for Vasquez. There is easily a hundred more here now than the party before. People glance our way as we enter, but the talking, laughing, eating, and drinking continue on. Half of them are already tipsy.

We pass by a row of live statues—men and women painted white and moving in fragments every few seconds.

Like before we come to stand in a line in the room with the shallow pool. The same pool Hedian and some other young girl had rolled around in naked. That was the night I first saw Joseph standing in the corner in a see-through gown.

I glance over my shoulder to that same corner but he is not there this time. Instead there is a naked girl on a table with chunks of fruit laid out all over her. I watch as a couple of the rich and elite pass by, pick a pineapple spear, and continue on.

Wide, dark wood planks have been laid over the pool in the shape of a cross, allowing people to walk back and forth over the water.

A clump of erotic dancers come through the room, suggestively slinking in and around us warriors and doing the same to the elite. One of them runs a finger down Alexior's chest and he looks right into her eyes.

Suggestively she licks her lips and gently traces his belly button before twirling away to follow the pack into the next room.

"Enjoy that, did you?" I snark.

"Yes," he simply replies.

I try to imagine myself suggestively licking my lips and almost snort.

The scent of pot and jasmine burns my nostrils and I know without looking that Bareket is nearby.

As if on cue her disgusting giggle floats past and I glance down the line to see her strolling arm-and-arm with a woman I don't recognize. She must be one of these visiting elite we're celebrating.

They stroll right past me, and Bareket slices me a sideways smirk. Then they continue on across the pool to the other side where they stand and drink, their heads together as they whisper and study us.

She's planning something. I know it. Or if she's trying to intimidate me, to make me think she's conspiring, it's working.

I glance around the packed villa and still don't see Vasquez. Perhaps he is in one of those back rooms making slaves do God knows what. I wonder if he'll even recognize me or if I am just one face of many.

Hedian silently walks down our line, carrying a tray of food. I'm happy to see her dressed in an actual tunic and not something transparent.

"Hi," she shyly says to me.

I smile. "Hi, Hedian. Where's Joseph?"

"He's helping the cook tonight."

"Good." That means he's safe.

She glances around to make sure no one is watching her linger and leans in. "I just wanted to say thank you for the other night with the soldier."

"You are very welcome." I nod her away. "Now keep going. You don't want to get in trouble."

She grants me a sweet smile that warms her eyes before continuing on.

"Soldier?" Alexior asks.

I shrug. "A tiny disagreement."

Master strolls into the room and straight across the pool to the center. "Greetings!" He holds his arms out wide. "Come. Gather. I have something very special planned."

Slowly, those from the other rooms begin to crowd in and Master continues. "Tonight I give you a demonstration of my finest warriors up close and personal here in my villa." He points at me. "We have Valoria, the defiant one."

I step out of line as several people begin politely applauding and do my signature backflip.

Master points both hands down the line. "And we have Sera, the Serpent of Saligia."

Proudly, she comes forward and waggles her tongue and several of the elite step back like they think her tongue is a lethal weapon.

"Actually," a scratchy woman's voice interrupts and everyone turns to see who's speaking. It's one of the new elite. The one who had been strolling with Bareket. The one who *still* stands beside Bareket.

"I would like to see the blonde," the woman points down the line, "fight that one. The Asian looking woman."

I glance over my shoulder. She wants to see Camille and Gem fight. They exchange a curious look and I turn back to Master. Is he going to allow this?

Nervously, he laughs. "Yes, but they are not prepped."

"Are they not slaves?" the woman challenges. "Aren't they supposed to do as I command? I paid good money to be here. I want to see the two of them fight."

I move my eyes from the woman to Bareket who is trying to hide a smile behind her goblet. This is her doing. She coached that woman into making this request.

Master bows. "You are very right." He nods to our line. Me and Sera step back, and Camille and Gem come forward. Master stretches his arms wide again. "Who would like to see these two fight?"

All the elite yell and applaud. The scratchy-voiced woman grins, and her overly white teeth seemingly glow.

The decision is made.

Alexior unlocks Gem and Camille's wrist shackles. "I know you didn't practice for this, but you've sparred against each other plenty. Put on a good show. A little bit of blood. And it will all be over and the party will go on."

The two of them nod and step up to the wooden planks crossing the pool. Master leaves, and they take their place in the middle. A soldier brings them both a polished orna-mental sword and they crouch into a starting stance.

"Begin!" Master calls out.

Their swords collide, and the metal on metal rings through the air. They rotate their swords in a wide arc, holding the other's block, until Gem slices free, spins and comes down on one knee, then nicks Camille in the side.

The appearance of blood draws a collective breath from the crowd.

Camille glances down at the dark red streaking through the bronze powder and then back up at Gem. She narrows her eyes in amusement and Gem gives a very tiny shrug. I've been nicked a million times—as have they—it really is nothing.

Camille moves lightning quick then, twirling, swinging her sword. Gem goes to block and Camille ducks, swerves, and pops her in the side of the head.

The crowd laughs.

This time Gem narrows her eyes and Camille shrugs. A smile tugs at my lips. They're having a bit of sparring fun. Like chess—watching, strategizing, predicting next moves.

Gem takes a few steps back, and Camille follows.

She sweeps her sword along the ground in a fake trip and Gem hops over it. Then she moves forward into a lunge and roundhouses to the right instead of her usual left. Her foot connects in the center of Camille's chest and knocks her right on her ass.

Camille doesn't hesitate a second in snapping to her feet and slamming the butt of her sword against Gem's wrist. Her weapon flies from her grip and plops into the water. Camille steps forward and points her sword at Gem's chest. She's won.

The crowd politely applauds, and my two friends smirk at each other. I can already tell this is going to turn into an ongoing match.

"That's it?" the scratchy-voiced woman yells over the crowd, and the entire room stills. "That's it?" she repeats on a scoff. "That was *nothing*."

With an apprehensive smile, Master looks around the room. "We save the real violence and gore for the arena. This was meant to be a simple entertaining demonstration."

The woman folds her arms. "Well, I don't want to wait for the arena. I want to see something now. Right here. Right in front of me."

Master and his wife exchange a muddled look. Like they're not sure how they lost control of their own party.

Camille and Gem stare into each other's horrified eyes. They know something bad is about to happen.

Bareket flings her hand through the air. "If it's the money you're worried about. I'll reimburse you." She turns to her new pal. "He does love his warriors." She puts her arm around the woman's shoulders. "Now, what is it you would like to see?"

The woman smiles and steeples her fingers in front of her lips as she studies my two friends posed on the planks crossing the pool. Dead seconds go by and with each one something claws inside of me, wearing at me, rubbing me raw.

"I..." she finally speaks, "would like to see the blond one cut the other one's arm off."

Several people gasp. Others chuckle. And every nerve and fiber inside of me suspends in the air surrounding me.

Alexior wraps his fingers around my forearm and squeezes tightly. "Do not speak. Do not move."

Camille's eyes fill with tears and she stares imploringly over to Master. The atmosphere stills with heaviness as the entire villa waits for his response.

Master turns to look through the crowd, and I follow his gaze. There, all the way in the corner and standing by himself, is Vasquez. The room narrows, and my world goes mute. There is the man responsible for everything. The mastermind behind Saligia. The reason why I am here and my sister is dead. He looks exactly the same. Like months haven't passed. Same slicked gray and black hair, same tan and weathered skin, same commanding stature.

I watch as he gives one single nod, and my gaze trails back to Master. He breathes out, getting control of himself, and straightens his shoulders. "Bareket's right. I do love my warriors. I spend a lot of time and money on them. These are two of my best."

Hope springs through me. Maybe Vasquez's nod was for the positive.

"But," he continues, "Saligia is here for your pleasure, not for theirs. If you want to see Camille cut Gem's arm off, then that is what I will give you."

Immediately, I take a step forward and Alexior yanks me right back. "Stop. You will get both of them killed if you do anything."

Every muscle in my body angrily shakes and I clench my fists to try to gain some control. It takes everything in me not to move. Not to storm up there. Not to scream.

In front of me Gem and Camille stare into each other's blurry eyes. Then Gem turns and looks right at Razo.

I glance down the line to see his enormous body shaking just as violently as mine. To see Ignatius gripping his arm just like Alexior grips mine. To see him nod at Gem to let her know it's going to be okay.

Gem lifts her quivering hands to Camille's face and kisses her on the cheek. "I love you. It's going to be okay. You have to do this. They will kill us both if you don't."

Camille lets out a soft sob as tears stream down her cheeks. "I can't," she whispers.

Gem swallows and releases Camille and takes a step back. "Yes. You. Can."

"No," Camille cries.

Master signals the soldiers and they start to move forward. My mouth goes dry.

Gem takes Camille's sword and forces Camille's limp fingers to grip the handle. Camille twists her hand, trying to get it free, and Gem just wrenches it back into place. She lays down in front of Camille and extends her left arm.

"Do it!" Gem yells.

The soldiers move closer. How is this fun for these people? It's just sick. Everything about this place is just so goddamn sick.

"DO IT!" Bareket shouts.

Camille's breath comes fast and she lifts her sword high into the air. With a scream that ricochets through her entire body she swings the blade down in one swift blow.

Gem's shriek echoes through the room and then she blessedly loses consciousness. Red flows over the wood platform and down into the pool, swirling with the bronze powder in bloody juxtaposition. Camille drops the sword and collapses to her knees.

My heart punches my rib cage. Banging. Deep. Reverberating through me. Deafening me.

I look across the room to Bareket and the scratchy-voiced woman. They both have the audacity to cringe. Then they turn away, not even looking at what they caused. What they requested. They go back to drinking, insensibly laughing, and stroll away.

When it comes time, I will start by cutting that woman's arm off and then I'll go from there. Better yet I'll let Camille do it.

I no longer think of life beyond Saligia.

I bet Camille does now.

I glance over to where Vasquez was standing to now see him gone. Correction, I won't start with that woman, I'll start with him. Then I'll move onto Bareket.

CHAPTER 44

EARLY THE NEXT morning I find Camille pacing back and forth on the training ground. I watch her from a distance as she mumbles to herself and throws a punch into the air.

Quietly, I approach.

She spins on me and the crazed look in her eyes, her taut expression, makes me pause.

She screams and runs at the wooden post and pounds it with her fists. Right. Left. Right. Left. She thrashes. Until blood begins to spot the wood. But she doesn't stop and just keeps on and on and on. And then begins kicking it.

I watch her frenzy, my throat swelling, wanting to go to her, but not sure how.

Panting, she moves back to punching and through the early morning darkness I see the blood soaking through her sandals and the skin splitting on her knuckles.

Finally, I move. "Camille."

But she doesn't stop.

Carefully, I touch her shoulder. She whirls on me, her face contorted, and attacks. My face and stomach become that wooden post. My shins take her kicks. I don't fight back. I know she needs this. I have to be her strength.

I go down hard on the ground and she climbs on top of me. She grabs my shoulders and slams me back down into the dirt.

Tears spill out of her eyes and she continues punching, but there's no power behind her fists. Minutes go by and she collapses on top of me, sobbing hard into my chest. I wrap my arms around her and hold her tight.

I don't know how much time passes. Seconds. Minutes. An hour. But finally she rolls off of me and lies in the sand.

"Master had no choice," Alexior's voice comes through the early morning.

I sit straight up. "Who the hell do you think you are defending him?"

"If he hadn't honored the request more damage would have been done."

"Honor?" I scoff. "Nothing about this place has honor."

Alexior ignores me and looks straight at Camille. "You had no choice either."

Camille pushes to her feet. "Is this it? This cycle? Accolades when we do as we're told. Blood or death at someone's whim. Are you going to tell me now that it's going to be okay?" She huffs. "Because things are *far* from okay."

"Sometimes we are forced to do things out of our control," he answers. "Out of our choosing. You have to move beyond it or you'll go insane."

I climb to my feet, too. "I *welcome* the insanity."

He shakes his head. "You'll realize you don't."

I stare at him, unable to figure him out. One day I think he might be on our side and then the next I see nothing but allegiance to Master and Saligia. Alexior perplexes me. I'm never sure which side I'll see.

He looks down at Camille's bloody feet, then up to her fists, and then over to my equally bashed face. "Master wants to see both of you. And he's not going to be happy now."

"Who the fuck cares?" Camille snaps and stalks off.

Alexior and I stand for a few seconds longer, staring at each other like we want to say something, but neither of us knows what it is.

Finally, I follow Camille down the tunnel and on a last thought pause to look back. I see Alexior, like I have many times before, staring up at the just dawning, silent sky. I doubt his thoughts mirror the silence.

Minutes later we stand in Master' office. Everyone has left and out in the villa the slaves clean up from the party that went all night. He takes one look at both of us and sighs. But it's not an angry sigh. It's a defeated one. Almost like he's upset with himself, not us.

"I don't know what to say," he begins. "I'm so sorry. It was supposed to be a fun affair and it spiraled out of control. Some actions carry a very steep price. I don't want what happened to affect our relationship. I feel like we're at a place where we've never been before. You two have turned out to be incredibly valuable to me."

We are only money and power to you, I want to say.

Tenderly, he takes both of our hands, surprising the shit out of me. "Your loyalty means a lot to me and I know I've let you both down. It's important to me that you two know I had to relent to the new elite. The resulting damage would've been too great. You know this, right?"

I nod, as expected, but Camille doesn't. If Master notices her lack of agreement, he doesn't acknowledge it.

"Now let's turn our thoughts to the upcoming fights." He motions to my bloody face, to Camille's mangled hands, and looks down at her bloody sandals. "What happened?"

"Your new elite is what happened," I boldly speak. *Vasquez is what happened.* "We were both enraged over Gem and we took it out on each other."

"It looks more like Camille took it out on you."

Neither one of us responds to that.

He sighs and nods. "I understand. Any other time I would discipline you over this. But to show you my heartfelt apology, I am excusing you from this next round of fights. You two focus on getting well and training."

I don't trust this at all. This is not Master. Something is going on. What kind of game is he playing now?

Master looks at both of our stoic faces and heaves another sigh. "How can I make this right?"

You can let me kill Vasquez and Bareket. But I ask instead, "What of whoever had my sister? You promised me retribution."

His face brightens. "Yes, as a matter of fact. I was going to tell you yesterday but with the party and all, things got lost in my head. I have located the owner of the whorehouse where she got dumped in Tawain. One week from now he will be here. And you can do as you wish."

Retribution pulses through me, energizing me, focusing me, *calming* me. One week. But I also want the two men who bought Lena from Bareket, but I know that won't happen. They're elite. They're untouchable.

"Where's Gem?" Camille asks. "When can we see her?"

Master' brows come together and his eyes slowly fill with anguish as he shakes his head. "I'm sorry. She didn't make it. She bled out."

CHAPTER 45

A DAY GOES BY, and Camille barely speaks. Barely eats. I know she didn't sleep last night either. I heard her pacing.

Now as we spar on the training ground she puts little effort into her swing.

I drop my sword and look down at her wrapped hands. "Do they hurt?"

She shrugs and nods to my beaten face. "No worse than that. I'm sorry by the way. I hope you know that."

"I do." And I really do.

Tears well in her eyes and she blinks them away. She's cried more in the last day than the entire time I've known her. I know she needs a moment so I take her arm and guide her over into the shade where the water barrel sits. I ladle out a cup and give it to her and she drinks.

Together we watch Sera and Razo train with the twins. They will all go in the arena tomorrow instead of what would have been me, Camille, and Gem. The crowd will be disappointed I'm sure.

"Sera's big comeback is tomorrow," I say. "If the twins submit their opponents they will earn the mark of Saligia."

Camille nods, though I know she's not really listening to me.

"I dreamt of her last night," she quietly admits. "She was playing with her little girl. She looked just like Gem with brown hair and those beautiful tilted green eyes."

I smile at that image. "She did have gorgeous eyes."

I glance across the training ground to where Alexior stands. He taps his wrist, indicating we have just another minute or so of rest.

"Razo won't talk to me," Camille painfully mumbles.

"He's angry and he's hurting. It may seem like he blames you, but he doesn't. He just doesn't know how to deal."

Camille nods but I can tell my words don't soothe her. "I wish Master would've let us see her body one last time."

"Me, too." I toss the ladle back into the barrel. "We should get back. Alexior is giving us the stink eye."

This makes Camille chuckle and I'm so pleased to have brought her some joy today. "Every bit of happiness I've had in this place is because of you and Gem." Her chuckle fades to a sad smile, and her bottom lip wobbles. Just the sight of it rips through me. "Please don't leave me," she whispers.

I take a step toward her and take her hand in mine. "I can promise you I will do everything in my power for that not to happen. If it does happen against my will, I will find you. We will find each other."

CHAPTER 46

THE FOLLOWING day every warrior and recruit load up in the cart and head to the arena for the fights. There will be no murderers or rapists brought in for us to mutilate in public. It's our camp against another.

The pre-games come and go. Every warrior and recruit fights but me and Camille. Some win. Some lose. But for the first time ever, no one dies. I'm sure the new elite are not happy with that.

Night settles in, and the crowd knows the final match is about to begin. Sera, Razo, and the twins.

"Va-lor-i-a. Va-lor-i-a. Va-lor-i-a."

Camille and I stand at the gate watching as the four of them enter and the crowd immediately begins booing.

"That's not good," I mumble.

The gate on the other side opens and out struts warriors from another training camp. I size them up. Two I recognize from previous fights and two are new.

Four of them. Four of us.

Master stands up and addresses the crowd and then shouts, "Begin!"

Sera sprints right toward the largest of the four. She leaps and scissors her legs around his neck, rotates her body and his, and cracks his neck to loss of consciousness. She leaps to her feet and waggles her tongue and the crowd goes wild.

One down. Three to go.

"Looks like Sera's back on game," I say.

The male twin back rolls to dodge a spear, comes to his feet, and executes a spinning split in the air. His heel connects with his opponent's chin and sends him sailing back.

The other twin slams her forearm into her opponent's esophagus and he gags.

Razo flips forward, grabs a roped net, and flings it on top of his guy.

My eyes trace back over to the male twin as he drives his foot into the side of his challenger.

On it goes. Punches. Kicks. Leaps. Swordplay. Flying spears. Blood. The female twin has a skip in her step like she's enjoying the blood a little too much.

Then surrender. Surrender. Surrender.

Sera, Razo, and the twins grasp hands and lift their fists into the air and the crowd cheers.

"Guess the twins will get branded tonight," Camille says.

I nod. "Suppose we need to find out their names now that they're warriors. We can't very well go around calling them 'the twins' forever."

"Yana and Willem," Alexior answers. "Their names are Yana and Willem."

The fact that he knows their names twirls a bit of tenderness through me. And guilt.

I should have known their names, too. I should've cared

enough to ask. I've been training side by side with them for weeks. Have I lost the basic civilized ability to ask a person's name—even if it's not their real one? I hope not.

Razo comes through the gate first.

"Well done," Camille says and Razo ignores her.

I grasp her shoulder to let her know it's going to be okay, but she shrugs it away and goes to stand with the other warriors waiting on the cart to go back.

Sera struts through second, cutting me a sly, conquering look with her one eye. I arch my brow and return the cunning glare more because I know she expects it than I feel it.

There's much celebration on the way home, but all I can do is stare at the faint lights of distant villas and smaller homes and farms. The galleon is not on the docks tonight. I turn away and glance to the left where Camille sits. Her expression remains guarded as she looks at the back of Razo's shaved head.

Something beyond her catches my eye and I squint into the darkness. Over to the west where the tall wall is located and the trees beyond, I see a light blink. I squeeze my eyes shut, reopen them, and strain for clarity.

Sure enough. Not just one light, but lots. They're torches. And they're moving. All over. Back and forth and up and down. Why would there be moving torches? I've seen that wall and the woods beyond several times now, but I thought it was a barrier to keep us from escaping off Saligia. Now I'm not so sure.

CHAPTER 47

I want to nudge Camille and show her the lights, but I don't dare. I don't want to draw attention to myself.

How did I miss them? All these times I've been in this cart and I've never noticed. I want to ask Razo about those moving lights. He was born here. He would probably know. I want to ask Alexior. Sera. Ignatius. Surely, one of them knows something. But none of them are good options. I don't want anything getting back to Master.

What I need is Hedian and Joseph. They exist in the shadows. Master likely speaks freely in front of them. They know more then they probably realize. Joseph stands behind Master at the desk. Joseph has probably read more than one paper on that desk.

Our cart pulls through the gate into the training ground. Everyone files out and into their different directions.

The twins, correction, Yana and Willem, go with Alexior to get branded. I linger on the training ground enjoying the ocean breeze that seems more prevalent tonight than usual. Perhaps there's a storm on the way.

I close my eyes and let the saltiness wash over me. I

imagine coming face to face with the man who had Lena. What will I say to him? I don't think I'll say anything. I'll just pick up a spear and end his life.

Before Saligia I would've never had that thought. Now it's my nature.

I think of Vasquez next. I don't want to end his life with a spear. I want to be right in his face. I want him to know his time of reckoning has come. And then Bareket...

I don't know how much time passes as I stand here, but this weird sense of peace settles over me that I know has everything to do with the upcoming vengeance for my sister.

"Valoria?"

I turn in the darkness to where Alexior stands at the tunnel. "Master has sent Hedian and Joseph for you again."

"Why? I didn't even fight tonight. Why am I being rewarded?"

"He says he wants to keep his champion happy."

Maybe this is lingering guilt over Gem. Or maybe he feels he took too long in bringing me my sister's killer. Perhaps a thank you for paying for Sera's upkeep, which has now paid off. Or maybe an apology for his wife throwing me out of the office.

Who the hell knows why, but I don't question it any further as I follow Alexior down the tunnel, through the locked door, past all the weapons, and come to a stop at the room where Hedian and Joseph wait.

Alexior doesn't open the door and instead turns to me. "I don't know what it is you do in there with them, but after hearing yours and Hedian's exchange at the party, I suspect it's not what Master thinks you do."

I'm pleased he doesn't think me some sexual deviant, but I still shrug. "I don't know what you're talking about."

Alexior sighs. "You will get both of them disciplined, *harshly*, if Master finds out you are doing anything other than what he thinks."

"Well, he won't know unless you tell him. Right?"

A muscle in the right side of his jaw ticks and my eyes go straight to it. I stare at it as it ticks a second time. A third. My vision narrows to just that one hard muscle, and warmth flushes through me. The muscle stops ticking and instead locks into tense attention.

I swallow, and my gaze trails down to his throat to see it constrict, too. The puffy vein in his neck draws my attention next and I watch as it thumps. Thumps. Thumps.

He moves a fraction closer and I draw in his unique Alexior scent. He shifts, and I realize he's opening the door.

I don't bring my eyes back to his. I don't want him to see whatever it is that is going on inside of me right now. I don't want to face the possibility there is nothing going on inside of him.

He grabs my upper arm and squeezes almost too tightly and then roughly trails his hand down the length of my arm and around to my lower back. So low he's touching the top of my ass. He turns me and presses me forward into the room.

Finally, I look, glancing over my shoulder, but I only catch the side of his face as he closes the door. I reach back and touch the warmth still lingering on my lower back.

"Valoria?" Joseph tentatively speaks and I blink out of whatever trance Alexior just had me in.

I look to Joseph first, who hesitantly smiles, and then Hedian. My eyes trace over her bowed head, her submissive posture, and my heart breaks.

Something's wrong. She won't even look at me.

I cross the room to where she sits and crouch at her feet.

I take her hands between both of mine and press as much comfort into them as I can.

I wait. But she doesn't speak.

"Hedian?" I prompt. "You can talk freely. I won't say anything."

Still she says nothing and I glance to Joseph for help.

"The night of the party... after what happened to Gem and the warriors left, one of the new elite took her into the gang room, and this is how she's been ever since."

I look between them. "The gang room... What—" The realization smacks me and I am shocked completely mute.

I pull her slumped body into my arms and I hold her tightly. I squeeze my eyes against the images of what she must have endured. I am reminded of my sister and the horrors she went through and my skin burns with the injustice of it all.

A few seconds later, I pull back from Hedian and look to Joseph. "Have you ever been in the gang room?"

He shakes his head, and relief flows through me. Thank God.

Gently I reach up and cup her cheeks in my palms. I lift her face to look at me, but there is nothing there. Her green eyes are tearless and void. She's given up.

"She tried to kill herself," Joseph says, nodding to her wrists.

I look down at the wide leather bracelets that I assumed were decoration. I untie one and look beneath to the bandage wrapping her delicate wrist.

"Who found her?" I ask.

"I did," Joseph tells me. "I didn't tell anyone, though. I cleaned her up and bandaged her. She hadn't lost much blood."

"Good. Don't tell Master." The bastard would probably

discipline her for trying to take her life over a gang room his friends made her go into.

Hedian pulls away from me and curls onto her side, facing the wall, not looking at me or Joseph.

I turn to Joseph. "I can trust you, can't I?"

CHAPTER 48

JOSEPH'S BROWS come down into a level of seriousness, a level of commitment that tells me everything I need to know. He loves Hedian. He knows what goes on around here is wrong. He just doesn't know a way out. "Yes, you can trust me."

"Do you remember life before Saligia?" I ask.

He nods.

"I want to get back to that life. I want *all* of us to get back to it."

"I remember being hungry and scared. It's the same here except I have food and I have a bed." He shrugs. "There's no difference really."

I can certainly see his point. It's a point others will likely have, too. Lena and I went hungry many days. And I had more nights of being scared than not. So, yeah, I get it. Saligia's the first time I've had this level of worth. Though it's entirely everything I never wanted.

I move over to sit beside him. "Yes, there is a difference. There's freedom. You would never have to do anything you didn't want to do ever again. If I'm with you, if we're all together, you won't be scared and abused. We'll be each other's family."

I say the words. I hear them. The delivery is confident. But now I wonder. How *will* we all make it? None of us have anything to go back to. We'll leave Saligia and return to our homes and then what?

I'll tell everyone who will listen about this place, as I'm sure others will. Saligia will be brought down, there's no doubt in my mind of that fact. But I have no clue who on the outside is involved in all of this. Other than Vasquez, I don't know real names. Who is Master really?

It would be impossible for the authorities to catch and prosecute everyone involved. Unless... there's some sort of master list.

I take Joseph's hand and show him nothing but the defiance I was named after. "That leather binder on Master' desk. Can you get it?"

He thinks about that for a second. "I think I can probably get a page or two."

"Good."

"He also has this small rectangular thing that I know is a computer but I've never seen anything like it."

"What do you mean?"

"He moves his finger over the screen. There isn't a keyboard."

I smile. "It's called an iPad. That's right. You wouldn't have any clue what that is."

"I've also heard him say he only uses it for bank trans-actions."

That would makes sense. All the people involved are kept in a ledger for security and the money moving in and out of this place is done electronically. I'm sure through some off-shore account that no one can trace. But... if he has an iPad, then there's connectivity somewhere on this island. Not that it would matter. With as tightly as Saligia is run, I'm sure his iPad is the one and only device in this place.

I squeeze Joseph's hand. "When it comes time, I want you and Hedian to go with me."

"But how? No one has ever escaped and those who try get banished to The Hunts."

"The Hunts?"

"It's a nighttime 'game' they play behind the wall. They release slaves and then they're hunted." Joseph looks over to Hedian's back. "I hear it's worse than The Hole."

The lights I saw. The Hunts. I take in a breath and blow it out slowly. This place just gets worse and worse.

I give his hand another squeeze. "I know you're scared. But I also know you're a survivor. Eventually we will have many people on our side and then it will be time for action. Warriors. House slaves. We will outnumber the elite and the soldiers. We will take this place over. Then we will move on to the next villa and the next. Until we Mistresste Saligia."

Hedian turns then and looks at me and Joseph. Gone is the empty look that was in her eyes and in its place gleams retaliation and determination. "You tell me what you need me to do and I'll do it."

I return her look with one equally unwavering. "Good."

She sits up. "You need to know something."

I nod. "Okay."

Pressing her lips together, she looks away. "We are taught to be silent. To never say a word. But I don't care anymore."

Hedian brings her eyes back to mine. "Your sister... Bareket sold your sister to Master. She was here the whole time. He kept her in a private chamber where he starved, raped, and repeatedly beat her. He is the reason why she is dead."

Silence drops over the room. I replay the words Hedian just said. The words sink in. Then something builds inside of me, hot and fiery, and erupts from my mouth in a scream that vibrates through every muscle in my entire body and echoes off the walls of the room.

I lurch off the cushion and sling the bowl of strawberries against the wall. I grab the goblets of wine and hurl them at the door. I rip the bolts of colorful fabric from the ceiling and claw them to shreds. I punch and kick and punch and kick the stone wall, striking hard, until my toes burn, my knuckles redden, and heat races through my shoulders.

I clench my jaw to keep from screaming again. Every limb in my body infuses with rigidity, and I raise my clawed shaking hands and scrape hard across my scalp.

I turn a circle, looking for anything else to beat. I open my mouth to take in a breath and instead several wheeze out.

"Valoria?" Joseph hesitantly says.

Whipping around, I stare at both of them as they warily, cautiously stare back. I don't move and instead just hold their unblinking gazes. Joseph slides over to sit beside Hedian, ready to protect. My God, do they really think I would hurt them?

Neither say anything, and I concentrate on uncurling my fists to alleviate their fear. Seconds pass, and I hold up my hands to show them I won't hurt them. That I'm done.

I take a step away and turn to look around the upended room. The sight makes me uneasy. No wonder I scared them. I can't lose control like this. Ever again. My emotions cannot bleed into my actions. They cannot.

Joseph stands and with sure feet begins quickly moving

around the room. "We need to put this back together. Nobody can find it like this."

I hear his words, but they're garbled. I watch as Hedian stands and hurriedly begins helping. Neither of them look at me. Several minutes pass but I don't help. I merely stand and watch and breathe.

When all the work is done and the torn fabric is stuffed inside several pillows to hide it, they both go to leave.

"Thank you," I croak.

Joseph nods. "You have both of us," he pledges, "any time you're ready."

The door opens, surprising all three of us, and a soldier fills the opening. These walls are made of stone and the room is tucked down beneath the villa. Surely no one heard me.

The soldier steps aside and Master enters. I automatically put my hands behind my back to hide my raw knuckles. He looks around the room that is now back in order before settling his gaze on me. I hope he doesn't notice the fabric is missing.

"Are you done with my slaves?" he asks.

"Yes, Master."

He nods his head to Hedian and Joseph and they both leave. "I trust they pleased you?"

I nod my head.

He looks around the room again before tracking his eyes back to mine. Behind my back I dig my short nails into the skin covering my palms so I don't fly across the room and dig his eyes out.

I will kill you. And I will make it painful.

CHAPTER 49

THREE DAYS HAVE GONE by and every day I request an audience with Master. Every day he refuses. It's like he *knows* I have an ulterior motive. Like he knows I'm ready to kill him.

Finally, I ask Alexior, "Why won't Master see me?"

"Because you are a slave," he placidly reminds me. "You forget that. *He* doesn't do as you ask. *You* do as he requests."

This is just Master' passive aggressive way of reminding me of my station. Okay, that's fine. I promised myself to rein in my emotions. I will wait. I will be smart. And when it's time, lethal.

Today we are to go to the arena for a special event but we're not told what that is. We are handpicked. Only me, Sera, and Ignatius go, accompanied by Alexior.

The four of us stand at the gate looking out over the sand and up into the seats.

I crane my neck to the right where Master sits. He is there, of course, with his wife. I see Bareket surrounded by the new elite, including the scratchy-voiced woman who ordered Gem's arm be severed.

Behind them stand their slaves. For the first time ever Joseph and Hedian are in attendance. Why are they here?

But in the center of them all sits Mr. Vasquez. My eyes narrow in on him. It's the first time he's ever attended the arena fights.

The gate across from us opens and out stumble two soldiers who have been stripped of their armor. I study them and remember the one from a villa I visited during my tour right after Zebulon's death. I don't recognize the other one.

Vasquez stands and addresses the crowd, "Today's special event is about reminding everyone of their place in Saligia. It is about reminding everyone of the rules. We have our own laws on this island and you will follow them. This is a decadent society. You don't just come here and do what you want. That is not how Saligia operates. These two men severely beat several incoming slaves to the point that they are now dead. No one beats a slave unless given a direct order from an elite. Now they will die."

You don't just come here and do what you want. Yet it seems to me everyone around here can. Again, the irony. You can do what you want as long as you're one of the rich and elite. Not even a soldier is safe. As evidence by what is about to go down.

Our gate opens and Alexior says, "All yours Sera."

She grabs two swords, "Gladly," and charges out into the arena.

Minutes go by and Sera returns covered in blood. The two men are dragged off the sands.

Through the opposing gate next steps two slaves. Two boys. They don't look any older than Joseph. I glance up to Master' balcony to see both Joseph and Hedian staring down with huge eyes.

Vasquez addresses the crowd again, "Here we have two

house slaves who have been in Saligia for years. Yesterday they tried to take the life of their master. Today they will die for all to see."

Our gate opens, and none of us move. None of us speak. We all know it is Ignatius' turn and that he should step forward.

Heads in the crowd begin to turn.

"No," Ignatius says. "I will not. They are just boys."

"Master will discipline you for this," Alexior says.

Ignatius firms his scarred jaw. "I don't care."

The crowd silently stares toward our gate. But Ignatius doesn't move. Several seconds go by, and Vasquez finally signals two soldiers. They run onto the sand and brutally slaughter the house boys.

I glance up to Hedian and Joseph to see them both staring off to the side, too horrified to look. The two boys are dragged off, the gate opens again, and out steps one of the elite.

"Holy damn," I breathe.

Vasquez addresses the crowd one last time. "To prove no one is above our rules, I give you one of us. He has been in Saligia for an extended six month vacation. He has lied, he has stolen, he tried to leak information to the outside world, and two days ago he killed his own wife in their villa. Today he dies."

I would bet anything the "leaking information" is the real reason he is about to be killed. Our gate opens a final time, and Alexior gives me a nudge. "All yours."

I step onto the sand and the crowd erupts in their normal chant. *Va-lor-i-a.* But I can tell it's because they know it's expected, not because they really want to. They're about to watch one of their own get murdered as a lesson.

I don't race toward the elite. I just walk until I'm face to face with him.

He's crying. Good. And shaking. Even better.

"You're not armed," I point out.

"Will you make it quick?" he asks.

I shrug. I really am indifferent. "Perhaps."

"You should know your sister was in that villa the whole time."

Though I already know this, fury resurfaces and nudges through me.

"You should also know," he continues, "that one who lost her arm—"

My heart pauses a beat. "Gem."

"She's alive."

I get right in his face. "What did you just say?"

The crowd begins booing.

Several soldiers start marching toward us and the man kneeling in front of me casts them a fervent look. "Please kill me. They will torture me if you don't do it."

I step back and rotate my spear in a wide circle, silently telling the soldiers to back off. I turn to the man. "What else?"

The crowd starts throwing stuff and booing even louder and the soldiers approach again.

The man shakes his head. "Kill me."

The soldiers start to move again. No, this kill is mine. In one smooth, swift movement, I bring my spear back and ram it forward straight up under his chin until it comes out the top of his head. His blood splatters my face.

I turn toward Master and Vasquez as expected. They are standing, but they're not cheering, and instead have their eyes leveled on mine. I wonder if Vasquez recognizes me now.

CHAPTER 50

THAT NIGHT when I get back, I pull Razo and Camille aside and deliver the good news, "Gem's alive."

Neither one of them immediately responds, then Camille moves first, nearly staggering to the side. "*What? How? Are you sure?*"

Quickly, I tell them how I know. "And I doubt the elite was lying. Why would he? He had nothing to lose."

Razo presses his palms into his eye sockets and groans.

I grip his forearm. "We will find her, Razo. We will."

He shakes his head and mumbles miserably, "No, we won't," before walking off.

I stare at his back, tempted to tell him the lies about my sister, too. Tempted to feel him out about my plan of attack and escape, but I sense that now isn't the time.

I do decide to finally tell Camille.

"He had your sister the whole time?" she asks with as much shock as I felt at the time. "When did you find this out?"

"A few days ago. Hedian and Joseph told me."

"Why didn't you tell me?"

"Because of Gem. You had a lot you were dealing with. I didn't want to burden you with this, too." I grab her hand. "Tell me you're still with me. I have Hedian and Joseph on the inside. I know I'll have Razo now that he realizes Gem's out there."

"Of course I'm still with you. We need Ignatius and Sera. If we get them, the rest of the warriors will follow."

I nod and think of how Ignatius defied Master' orders earlier. "I have a feeling that might happen sooner than we think."

Camille leans in. "Why? What happened?"

"Valoria," Alexior calls from the tunnel. "You have visitors."

I give Camille a quick hug. "That would be Joseph and Hedian." I squeeze her harder. "Gem's alive."

She squeezes me back. "We *will* find her."

I follow Alexior down the tunnel feeling a sense of victory that is very near. He doesn't walk with me the entire way, as he usually does, and I can tell there is something on his mind.

"You okay?" I ask.

He shakes his head, turns, and walks off. I watch his broad back for a few seconds until it disappears completely into the shadows. As always I am curious what his brain is processing.

"We were sent to distract you," Joseph tells me a few minutes later.

"Distract me from what?"

"From the fact Master is ignoring your requests to see him."

I sit down on one of the cushions. "And why is he?"

Joseph sits down beside me. "We don't know."

Hedian hovers near the door and I give her a quizzical

look, waiting.

Joseph glances over to her, too, and sighs. "She doesn't want to help us now. She's scared."

I nod. I understand. "From what you saw in the arena today?"

"Yes," she timidly answers.

"Don't you understand that's exactly why they did it?" I ask. "Vasquez had to remind everyone to be scared. Fear is a powerful tool. But we have to be brave. We have to take a chance for the things that we know are right. Why do you think Ignatius refused to enter that arena?" I point out. "He knew it was wrong. His actions showed such power in front of everyone. He basically said 'fuck you' to Vasquez and Master and Saligia by refusing to step out. They're scared. That's the only reason for that little show today."

"But can you promise we won't die?" she asks.

I take a breath in and blow it out smoothly. "I wish I could. But I can't. I might die. You might. Camille might. But that's something I'm willing to take a chance on in order to do what's right. You need to make that decision for yourself."

All expression washes from her face as she shakes her head. "I can't. I'm sorry." She opens the door and slips out.

I turn to Joseph. "I know she doesn't feel she can rely on anybody. Tell her not to be sorry. Tell her to be smart and to do what makes her feel good and right."

"I'll talk to her," he assures me. "In the meantime, what can I do?"

"What about the leather notebook? Any luck?"

Joseph shakes his head. "Not yet. Master keeps it guarded."

Evidence that whatever is in there will be good. "What about the other house slaves? What does your gut tell you?"

"Some will think like Hedian and others like me. I truly believe they will turn on the elite if enough of us ban together, if given a chance. They want to be free, too." He stands. "I'm sorry. I have to get back. Master only gave us thirty minutes."

"Okay," I nod. "Be safe."

After he leaves I sit, and I just think.

About Gem, now alive. *I'm sorry she didn't make it. She bled out.*

About my first day in the villa. *You fight for me and I'll find your sister.*

About Bareket's visit. *Indeed they enjoyed her so much.*

About Lena dying in my arms. *I will find the man who did this and bring him to you.*

Familiar anger and betrayal scratches inside of me, and I breathe through it, harnessing it.

The door unexpectedly opens and Alexior steps in. I glance behind him and see that we are alone.

Alone.

He doesn't say anything and instead stands in the doorway, looking down at me sitting on a cushion. I have a quick flash of him down on this cushion with me, stretched out on top of me, and my entire body warms. I want him whispering against my ear in that wonderful accent of his. What would he do if I reached my hand out and beckoned him? What would he do if I stood, walked over to him, and pressed my lips to his neck?

He swallows, and I wonder if he is having the same thoughts. "Master wants to see you."

Oh... But that doesn't make any sense. He just sent Hedian and Joseph to distract me. Why does he want to see me only moments later?

Alexior holds up shackles. "He wants these on you."

CHAPTER 51

"What? Why?" Though I know why. Like the arena, he's reminding everyone of their station.

I stand and Alexior shackles me. As I follow him out of the room, I glance to the left where the weapons are. I need to ask Joseph who has that key.

A soldier leads me up. I walk through the villa, studying every slave. Some of them look at me. Others don't. I wonder which ones would pick up a knife and stab someone.

I am led into Master' empty office and a soldier stands in the corner where Alexior usually does. I look over to the terrace and then down to his desk. There is a brown pencil. I could easily stab his eye out with that.

I glance over my shoulder to the soldier and the sword he wears on his hip. Even in my wrist shackles I am confident I could take that sword and slice his head off.

In walks Master. "Valoria!" he cheerfully greets, like he hasn't been ignoring me. Like he hasn't just demanded I be placed in shackles. "What can I do for you?"

My eyes track back over to the pencil. Stab him in the

eye. Spin and get the sword. Slice the soldier's neck. Knife Master in the gut.

He slaps me on the back. "Let me guess you're here to request Joseph and Hedian on a weekly basis."

No. Sword first. Slice neck. Stab Master. No pencil needed.

Master sits down at his desk. "Why don't you first tell me what deep conversation you were having out there in the arena earlier?" He chuckles. "Was he confessing all of his sins?"

Now that he's sitting I move closer to the desk and the pencil. "He was pleading for mercy."

This makes Master laugh.

The door to the office opens and in walks a young Asian girl. She's the smallest I've seen yet. Younger than even Hedian and Joseph when they came here. She seems incredibly frail.

Carrying a tray of fruit, she trips over her own feet and the pears roll onto the floor.

Master sighs. "Joseph!" he yells and in runs my friend.

He takes one look at me, down to the girl, and hurries over. She's crying now, shaking, and he whispers soothing words as he helps her get things cleaned up.

I step away from the desk and the pencil, the soldier and the sword, and bow my head. There's no way I can attack with a child in here. "Yes, I was indeed here to inquire about weekly visits, but I realize now that is an unreasonable thing to request."

"Good, because the answer is no." He laughs and waves his arms in the air. "Now off with you. I have a ton to do."

In my wrist shackles I make my way back through the villa toward the stairs and tunnel. As I round the last corner

I see Hedian kneeling and scrubbing the marble floor. I come to a stop right beside her.

"Hedian," I whisper. "When did that little girl arrive?"

Hedian glances around to make sure no one is listening. "That's Gem's daughter."

CHAPTER 52

THE NEXT AFTERNOON Razo aggressively practices against the wooden post. His deep grunts fill the space around him and sweat drops in big globs to dot the sand at his feet.

Around and around the post he goes, knifing it, ducking, swerving, punching. I've never seen him so fiercely focused. I know Gem has to be on his mind.

Sera strolls by. "Trying to take the champion spot?" she jeers in a joking tone.

He ignores her and keeps going.

I debate whether to tell him about Gem's daughter and decide to wait until he's calmer and more likely to accept that news as well as my plans of escape.

I pick up a practice sword and search out Camille, but she's training with Ignatius again. I look to Sera who is speaking with Alexior and then my gaze falls on the twins, Yana and Willem. I have yet to spar with them. I'd like to see their level of skill.

I walk over. "How about sparring with a *real* fighter?" I tease and they both smile.

The three of us begin going through the basic formations. They try a few tricks that I quickly divert. I try a few of my own that, as expected, catch them off guard. They're good, though. I'd put them on the level of Gem's expertise.

The female twin, Yana, is light on her feet, as I noted in the arena when she seemed to skip across the sand. I want to know their story. More importantly, I want to know if they'll be on my side when it's time.

A half hour or so in, I suggest, "Water break."

The three of us walk over to the shade and ladle out some water. We stand, sipping, looking at everyone sparring. Even though I already know the answer to this, I prompt, "Where are you two from?"

"Poland," Willem answers.

"So how'd you end up here?" I ask.

Willem sighs. "Because we're idiots."

I look to his sister for clarification, and she says, "We've been in trouble our whole lives. Runaways. Group homes. Living on the streets. Selling drugs. Stealing. You name it and we've done it. We both spent our nineteenth year in prison for petty theft. Anyway, there was this ad for a reality show and we answered it. Figured we were twins and that we would be a shoe in. We got 'cast', showed up for our first day, knocked out, woke up, and here we are." She scoffs. "Some reality show."

Willem shrugs. "Whatever. First chance we get, we're outa here. We're totally planning to escape."

I nearly smile. Mission accomplished.

"Warriors!" Master shouts from the balcony. "Formation!"

We line up as expected, and I look up to the balcony to see Master, his wife, Bareket, and several more elite. Vasquez, like before, stands right in the center. Behind them in the shadow of the terrace hovers Joseph, Hedian, and a few other house slaves, including Gem's daughter.

Razo is on my left. Camille stands on the right. Now is the time. "That little girl," I whisper, "is Gem's daughter."

Camille gasps and looks at me. Razo's body goes even stiffer. I glance at him from the side of my eyes to see him staring up and right at the little girl. His hands curl into two white knuckled fists and his triceps twitch to muscled knots.

"Disrobe," Vasquez commands, and we all take our tunics off and drop them on the ground in front of us. He nods to Master, like he's giving him permission to take over, to proceed.

What's going on?

Master stretches his right arm out to motion to the other elite filling the terrace. "As evidence from the arena yesterday, we are reminding everyone of how Saligia is supposed to operate. I have been far too generous and lenient with my warriors. Each of you need to be reminded of exactly who you are. You are slaves. Do you hear me? Slaves! You do as I say. Never the other way around. Yesterday I was embarrassed and humiliated when Ignatius refused a direct order to enter the arena. Now, as everyone knows, Ignatius is free. The last time he refused a direct order I banished him to The Hole. This time because of his freedom, I cannot. However," Master' voice lowers, "every one of you will suffer while he watches."

I exchange a anxious glance with Camille.

Ignatius steps out of line, his expression desperate. "Master please."

Master nods to the gate. It opens, and in march a dozen soldiers carrying shackles and whips. *Whips?*

Down the line I hear Yana, frantic, crying, "No. No. What's going on?"

Automatically Camille and I edge closer to one another. We reach over and death grip the other's hand, just like we did that first day in the marketplace. The soldiers begin shackling ankles and wrists, and I still myself for whatever atrocity is about to happen.

"Master," Alexior calls out and I swerve my gaze to him. What is he doing? "I implore you," he keeps going. "Is there no other way to exercise your authority?"

"No," Master snaps. "There is not."

My gaze flicks to Vasquez who stands, chin high, staring down his nose at us. He's the reason for this—whatever this is. Clearly Master got in some kind of trouble for not running Saligia correctly, and Vasquez is making him exert even more authority.

A soldier rips mine and Camille's hands apart and shackles our wrists. I glance over to Ignatius and see his muscles visibly quivering.

"Master," Ignatius tries again. "I will do anything you request. *Anything!*"

"No. You will watch and then I am banishing you from this camp and Saligia. Go out into the real world and see how you do there. Just look at you. You're a monster. No one will want you." Master turns away from Ignatius and runs his dark gaze down our line. His eyes glint with a maliciousness that sends a chill flittering across my skin. Despite the balmy weather, I shiver.

"*Kneel* before me." He motions to Vasquez and the other elite. "*Kneel* before all of us."

"Oh my God," Camille mutters. "Oh, shit."

I fall to my knees in the sand, my wrists in front of me. I don't look up at the terrace. I keep my eyes down and make myself submissive, hoping it will placate, if just a little.

I'm sure they are up there, eyes bright, giddy, triumph

racing through them. I lift my gaze and look to the left where Alexior stands to see him helplessly staring back.

I feel nothing. No heartbeat. No breath. Nothing but a slight prickle across my scalp. Like my soul is leaving my body, to be joined later when it is time to feel again. His eyes glass over and he takes a step forward only to have a soldier block his path.

"Begin!" Master shouts.

Simultaneously the whips crack through the warm air. I hear a gasp. I hear a yell. A grunt. A scream. I don't take my eyes off of Alexior as the leather strips rip through air and tear into my back.

I'm aware Camille falls forward. I'm aware Razo does. But still I kneel and keep my eyes glued to Alexior. I need to focus on something and he seems the only thing I'm able to hold. His face clenches into a multitude of hard planes and he fights everything in himself not to intercede, not to cry, not to yell.

There's nothing anyone can do. We are shackled. We are outnumbered. There is nothing Alexior can do, but keep his focus on me like I am on him as the whip lashes across my skin. Again. And again. And again.

Eventually it is over and I am now cheek down in the sand, my wrists underneath me. My eyes still directed on Alexior, but I no longer see a clear image. He is hazy and blurry. My scalp prickles again, and I wonder if that means my soul is merging back with my body.

Pain comes next, coursing along my back, vicious and licking a fiery path along my nerve endings. With a cringe, I stifle a groan. Bitterness tangs my mouth and nauseates me. I hear my shallow breaths—slow, raspy, in, out.

Faint laughter and conversation filter through my senses

next, coming from the terrace. Fading, and I know they are heading back into the villa.

Finally, I close my eyes and drift with the pain. I am aware someone unlocks my shackles. I am aware but I don't open my eyes to see.

I hear a tight voice, "Leave her alone," and know it is Alexior.

Careful hands are on me next, gently touching my cheek. Despite it all, gratefulness hovers over me and gradually settles in. This is exactly what we needed. The truth about my sister. About Gem. Her daughter. Ignatius being banished. The whipping.

Desperation can be powerful in its motivation and lure to a dark place. There isn't one warrior here who won't be motivated to kill every one of them now and escape with me.

CHAPTER 53

TALME SPENDS hours tending to our wounds. As does Alexior and one of the house slaves Master sent down. The place is eerily quiet as afternoon transitions into evening and the moon finally appears in the sky.

Ignatius was escorted away without being granted the right to speak to any of us. I have no clue where he'll go, what he'll do. *No one is ever free.* Everyone down here knows something else has happened to him. Banished to The Hunts perhaps or something equally foul. I don't even want to think about it. It's too horrible to process right now.

I look over to Sera to see her staring at the gate, like she's willing Ignatius to come back. I'm sure her thoughts mirror my own. She knows he hasn't been freed either.

After Talme is done with the last of us, she comes to stand in front. "No one put your tunics on. Sleep on your stomachs tonight. These wounds need air to heal."

I push up off the wooden bench and walk across the training ground, more to see how I feel than anything. I swing my arms a little bit and arch my back.

Whatever she put on us smells, as usual, like crap. The

least she could do is throw an herb in there to make it tolerable. There is no mirror, so I haven't seen my back. But I've seen everyone else's and imagine I look the same. Red and swollen, skin split in a crisscross pattern.

I pace in a circle and turn back to see the other warriors heading into the men's and women's quarters. I start to follow and glance to the left where Alexior stands in the dark beneath the awning where the water barrel sits.

He's staring right at me, and his intense gaze thumps straight through me.

I cross the sand to step under the awning and come to a stop in front of him. I look up at the shadows cast by his cheekbones and into his conflicted eyes, and something deep inside of me stirs.

He lifts a hand and runs his fingers through my short dark hair. He caresses my eyebrows, down the length of my nose, across my cheekbones, then trails his index finger over my bottom lip. I close my eyes and soak in the warmth and comfort of his touch.

Cupping the back of my head, he brings me closer. His lips move over my cheek and down to my neck to nuzzle in, and I breathe out on a quiet sigh.

Lifting my hands, I curl my fingers into his hips, and he shifts his face, and our lips meet in a simultaneous open mouthed kiss. There is no preliminary peck. Our tongues dive deep. Circling. Pulsing. Devouring. Our bodies move closer until we are pressed from chest to hip, and every minute nerve in my body awakens.

His erection surges against me, and I go on pure instinct as I reach between us and grasp it. He pushes it into my hand, our tongues delve deeper, and I stifle the moan I so desperately want to let out.

He backs up, pulling me further into the darkness, and

sits down on a bench. Our lips never part. I reach into his pants and free him, pull my underwear aside, and climb on top.

My pulse stammers as I slide straight down on top of him and let out a breath that he sucks in and swallows. I want his hands all over me, in me, under me, on top of me, but he's aware of my wounds and grips my thighs instead.

Our lips finally leave each other, and I drop my head back and start to move. Liquid heat permeates my skin and I'm on fire with need, with desire, with want.

Gently, he bites down on one of my nipples and I move faster. He lifts his hips, and I feel him nudging everything inside of me. Neither one of us makes a sound. We know we can't. But I pace quicker. And quicker. And quicker.

He scrapes his teeth against my nipple again and I lose it. Something inside of me opens and each particle in my body becomes alive and abuzz.

I dig my fingernails into his shoulders and ride the spasms that pulse through my core and dizzies me. Eyes closed, I feel him grab my hips, lift his own, and sail into his own release.

Opening my eyes, I watch as he swallows and then opens his. He's still inside of me, and my inner muscles flex in an involuntary spasm that makes us both jump with the sensitivity.

I wish we could do something normal like hold each other, or take a bath, or curl up and sleep. But we can't.

In the shadows of our hiding spot, we stare, taking in the confusion swirling in each other's eyes. What does this mean for him and his job here at the camp? What does this me when I kill these bastards and escape? Will Alexior come with us?

He moves first, placing a kiss in the center of my chest. The gentleness of his touch melts my heart.

I lift off of him and immediately shiver at the loss of his thickness inside of me. I look down at his lap and watch as he tucks himself back inside.

After I straighten my underwear, he reaches out and takes my hand and presses a soft kiss to my knuckles, and my heart melts even more.

"Go," he whispers, his lips moving against my skin.

It's the first thing he's said to me.

I nod and step out from the darkness onto the training ground to see Master on the terrace staring down. I forget to breathe. I resist the urge to look back at Alexior. Did Master see anything?

I step further out and nod my head and concentrate on not having a strained voice. "Master," I loudly say, more to make sure Alexior knows not to come out.

"In the morning I would like to see you," he tells me.

I nod again.

"Where is your tunic?" he asks.

I turn around to let him see my back, cutting my eyes over to the right where Alexior still sits. I can just barely make him out. But from the terrace the awning would obstruct anyone underneath. I hope.

I turn back around. "Talme thought it best we let air hit us for the night."

"Very well. I will see you in the morning after your meal." He disappears back into the villa.

I don't chance any look back and instead head straight for the tunnel and the women's quarters. It's only after I wash myself and lay face down on my cot that I breathe.

How can this be? How can I be attracted to Alexior? He's not one of them. But he's not one of us either.

CHAPTER 54

WHEN I WAKE up in the morning my back aches, but it no longer burns with the hot rawness of the lashing. After Talme checks our skin and reapplies ointment, we are given thin tank tops to wear under our tunics as protective bandages.

I skip breakfast and decide to see Master instead. I'm more than curious what he wants. Once again I am shackled, and Alexior doesn't escort me, but a soldier does.

"You are well today?" Master asks from behind his desk.

As well as a person can be after being whipped. "Yes."

He folds his hands and looks up at me. "I'm sorry you had to endure that."

I don't respond. I know he's not sorry.

"It had to be done," he tells me.

Weight settles on my shoulders at how much I despise this man. "Yes, Master."

He breathes out on a smile.

I glance down to his clasped hands and the papers they rest on top of. But the writing is small and I can't make anything out.

"Did you know my wife and I have an anniversary coming up?"

I shake my head. Why would I know that? Why would I care?

"We're going to have a small and intimate gathering here in our villa. Only our closest friends are being invited. Several have requested that you and Sera put on that demonstration that you didn't get a chance to before."

I want to remind him *why* we didn't get a chance and what happened as a result, but of course I refrain. I also want to ask if Mr. Vasquez will be in attendance. Somehow I doubt it. Master and Vasquez do not strike me as being close friends.

Master doesn't immediately follow that up with anything and instead eyes me for several contemplative seconds. I don't like it when he keeps his eyes trained on me with that vacant yet scheming look. Whatever follows is never good.

"Valoria, what would you say if I asked you to kill Sera during this demonstration? Even if she surrenders, I still want her dead. What would you say to that?"

I would say I'm going to tell Sera. Between this and Ignatius, there is no way she won't be on our side. "How can you be sure she won't kill me?"

He smiles. "Oh, believe me, I would assure it."

I don't like the sound of that. "What's at stake?"

Master laughs. "You think like a warrior now. And you know me too well. What's at stake? More money than I've ever made in one single fight."

Of course. "And for me?"

"I will build you your own private quarters downstairs. I will allow you to come and go as you please. As long as you are here every day to train and present whenever you are requested to fight." He unclasps his hands and reclasps them. "How does that sound?"

I give him a smile that I know he expects. "You've got yourself a deal."

He slams his palms down on the desk and lurches to his feet. "Ha! You and me are going to make one *hell* of a team." He waves me toward the door. "You may go."

As I'm making my way back through the villa, Joseph catches my attention. With a quick glance around to make sure no one is looking, I step into the corner where he is hidden.

"The night of the anniversary party," I whisper. "I need you to open the gates to the tunnel. Can you do that?"

"The soldier has the key and he's always there," he whispers back.

Guilt twinges inside of me that I have to say, "Then kill the soldier and take the key."

Joseph glances away before quickly bringing his eyes back to mine. "I'll figure it out," he assures me.

"I never said this was going to be easy," I try to soften the killing blow.

"I know." He takes my hand, and his is cold when he presses a folded piece of paper into my palm. "That's all I could get from Master' office."

Hope surges inside of me, and I clench my fingers around the paper. "Thank you."

"There are a few names on there that I recognize, that's why I grabbed it."

A soldier rounds the hall and I immediately step from the corner and keep walking toward the tunnel. When I reach it and glance back, Joseph is gone and the soldier approaches me. He unlocks my shackles and then the gate, and I make my way down the stairs.

Halfway through the tunnel, I hear, "Valoria," and turn to see Alexior coming from the medic room. I immediately recall last night.

"What did Master want?" he asks.

"To tell me about an anniversary party and another demonstration." Sweat dampens my palm and I shift the paper slightly.

A few awkward seconds pass as we stare at each other in the tunnel's dimness. We had amazing sex last night, and I wonder if either of us is going to say anything about it.

"My wife was my world," he softly says. "She meant everything to me."

Was. Meant. Both past tense. "Is she... dead?"

He shakes his head. "No."

Can he be any more vague? "Are you upset about last night? Are you feeling guilty?"

"Yes. No." He sighs. "Yes." He sighs again. "I don't know."

He takes a step toward me and all I can think about is the paper in my palm. I want to have this conversation with him, but I want to look at this paper more.

"When they brought us here, it quickly became evident I was who they really wanted."

"I don't understand."

"In Australia I was a cage fighter. I was good. At eighteen I was already ranked at the top and making decent money. So when I came here the fighting was natural for me, and I started teaching others what I knew so they could survive. Not only was I winning in the arena, but all the warriors here began winning. Eventually Master approached me with a deal: my life for my wife. She goes free and I stay to train others." He stops a second, like he's thinking about his next words. "That was seven years ago."

I reach for his hand and massage my fingers into his calloused skin. "Alexior, that is the most honorable thing I have ever heard. You are amazing."

"As long as I stay, she remains safe and free away from Saligia."

"But... are you sure she *is* really free?"

He nods. "Every year I get a letter from her. She's fine."

So when he said no one is ever really free, he meant him. Sure his wife is, but he will never be. With this being why he is here, he won't leave. He has to stay. He won't be on our side when we kill these bastards.

I squeeze his hand to let him know I heard him, I'm listening, but I really don't know what to say. To be honest my mind is occupied with the next steps.

He releases my hand. "You missed the morning meal. Eat. Training will be light today with everyone's injuries."

I'm torn with staying. With going. There are things that need to be said, but I don't know what they are and how to say them so I settle with, "Thank you for last night. It was truly wonderful."

He smiles, just a little. "For me, too."

CHAPTER 55

As I'm sparring with Yana, I tell her the plan. "They'll be celebrating their anniversary. Joseph will get the gate open. We'll move inside then."

"What of the weapons that are locked up?"

To my knowledge, Alexior is the one who has that key. But I don't want anyone else to know that. I don't want Alexior harmed. "We'll use our practice weapons and disarm the soldiers and get their swords."

"I can't wait to kill these fuckers." She looks across the training ground to where Alexior stands. "Him included."

Heat flashes through my face. "No. He is not to be touched. He is not one of them." I jab her in the shoulder to make sure she heard me. "You got that?"

She holds up her hands. "Yeah. Fine. Whatever."

I nod to Willem. "Now go spar with your brother and fill him in. And keep your voice down."

I spy Sera over at the water barrel standing alone and head over. I grab a ladle and stand silently, letting her get used to my presence beside her. I think about making small talk and decide to just dive in.

"Master had my sister all along," I tell her without looking at her. "He tortured, raped, and beat her until moments before the end of her life. Gem did not die. She is alive. That new little girl in the villa is her daughter. You know as well as I do that Ignatius has not really been set free. And lastly... Master met with me this morning and told me to kill you in an upcoming exhibition. He says that he will *assure* that it will happen."

In my periphery I watch as she takes a sip of water and continues staring out at the training going on.

"I want to kill them," I tell her, "and escape, and I want to know if you're with me."

"And Alexior?" she simply asks.

"He doesn't know any of this."

She steps out into the sunshine and I note for the first time the dirt streaking her dark cheeks. Was she crying before I came over here to talk? Was she thinking of Ignatius?

"You tell him," she says. "If he's in, then I'm with you. Every single warrior will be, too."

CHAPTER 56

LATE THAT NIGHT I meet with Razo and Camille. In the darkness with our voices hushed to a barely audible level, I update them on everything: the twins, Joseph, the anniversary party, Sera... we discuss it all in detail and when I finish I pull out the paper Joseph gave me and unfold it.

I give it to Razo. "You've been here longer than anyone. I've looked this over and I don't recognize any of the names. Will you tell me if you do?"

He hands it right back. "I can't read."

Razo was born here. Of course they wouldn't teach him to read. And now I feel stupid for asking. I take the paper back and begin quietly reading the names of people I do not know. Beside each name is basic data: Sex, age, where they came from, who was in charge of bringing them in, money involved, and where they went once they arrived here in Saligia. On that list I see the familiar HOLE and HUNTS and various villa names as well as this place.

When I'm done reading the list I look at Razo. "Anything sound familiar?"

"Yeah. Show that to Alexior and he will definitely be on our side."

The next morning I go straight up to Alexior at breakfast. "Can we talk?"

He glances up to the terrace and then around at all the warriors sitting and eating.

"Privately," I tell him. "I need to show you something."

"Tonight. We'll talk in the room where you met Hedian and Joseph. We won't have long so whatever it is you need to say has to be quick."

I nod, and as I turn I glance up to see Master stepping out onto the terrace. He stretches and gazes around. In a few days I'll never have to look up and see his disgusting self ever again.

My meeting with Alexior is all I can think about as I train, as I eat, as I bathe. I recite over and over everything I want to say to him.

I'll handle it like I did Sera. I'll just go straight in to the details and I'll end with showing him the paper. I can only hope whatever is on it has the effect Razo thinks it will.

It seems to take forever for night to settle in and *finally* it is time to meet Alexior in the private room.

He's already here when I arrive.

"Alexior—"

"I was serious. This has to be quick."

"Okay." I force myself to take a fortifying breath and then I open my mouth and spare no small detail. The truth about my sister is the first thing I tell him. Then about Gem and her daughter. I speak of Master' request of me to kill

Sera. I detail out the current plan of escape, and I end with handing him the paper torn from Master' notebook.

I hold my breath while he carefully unfolds it and begins reading. About half way down I notice a change in him. A tenseness. An anger. A fierceness I've never seen in him before. He crumbles the paper into his tight fist and whirls away from me.

I hold my breath and wait.

"Aaarrrggghhh!" he erupts into a muted roar.

I take a cautious step back.

"God. DAMN!" he hisses and throws the paper at the wall. "Goddamn fucking shit!" He digs his fingers into his bald head and every one of his muscles bunch into angry knots.

He whirls back around and lasers me with two manic gray eyes. "My FUCKING wife *runs* The Hunts!"

CHAPTER 57

OVER THE NEXT few days in stolen moments and hushed whispers the warriors make plans. I'm able to pass those plans to Joseph in one last rendezvous that Master "treats" me to before the demonstration at his anniversary. The demonstration in which I am supposed to murder Sera.

"I would ask that you refrain from telling anybody, not even Hedian," I say to Joseph. "We can't risk someone on the inside going to Master for favor with the information. Once we take control of the villa, the house slaves will see what is going on and they can decide if they want to join us."

Joseph gives me a hug. "Thank you." He squeezes me tight and whispers again, "Thank you," before pulling back. "I know with the new plan you don't need me to kill the soldier, but know I'm ready for anything."

I nod. "Good."

The day of the anniversary, I remind Sera, "Be careful today. Master said he would assure your death. Just... be careful. Be watchful."

"I'll be fine." She widens her stance and folds her arms

and looks down at me. "Listen, I know you're the reason why I'm here. I know you paid for my expenses while I was healing."

I slant her a guiltless look. "I don't know what you're talking about."

She turns to fully face me and extends her arm. It takes me a second to realize what she wants, and I return the favor by shaking her hand.

"No matter what happens tonight," she tells me, "I'm proud to have trained beside you."

I tighten my grip. "Likewise."

Sera releases first and walks off. It wasn't a thank you, but it's the closest thing to a truce we'll likely ever have. No matter what happens tonight and in the days to come, I know we now have each other's backs.

As I go to get my practice spear for some sparring with Camille, I glance across the training ground to Alexior. He walks among the warriors, giving direction, his focus even more concentrated than usual.

He and I haven't really spoken since he found out about his wife. He's been even *more* to himself than usual. I wonder what will happen when, *if*, they see each other again. Maybe there's a good explanation. Then again this is Saligia, so probably not.

He gave his life for his wife. He's been lied to and manipulated. What I don't understand is, how did she become the leader of The Hunts? My suspicions tell me it was all a setup from the start. She tricked him. I'm sure Alexior is probably realizing that, too.

I hate this for him. Yet I'm also glad. He would never have been on our side if this hadn't happened.

The day comes to a close and our last meal is served. Sera and I know we are to eat, bathe, and dress in formal armor for our villa performance. Alexior is to accompany us which means Razo and Camille will be in charge of everything down here.

This is the first time since coming to Saligia that I feel true hope. True power. Unification. Justice to be done. From the way the others carry themselves and proudly interact, I can tell they feel it, too. I only hope Master hasn't picked up on the vibe in the air.

As planned, after our meal several warriors linger on the training grounds. If Master steps onto his terrace and looks down, things will appear as normal.

Sera and I bathe and dress in our armor and meet Alexior in the weapons room. He unlocks the iron gate and the three of us choose weapons to hide under our armor. He leaves the gate open for the others when it is time.

He shackles Sera first and then me. As he does I stare at the strong line of his neck, wanting to wrap my arms around him and pull him to me for what very well may be the last time. But I don't.

He snaps the last lock into place on my wrists and pauses a second. Slowly, his gaze moves from my wrists to my chest, and then up into my eyes. I'm so glad his aren't empty. Instead they whirl with ferocious determination and something else that looks suspiciously like regret and sorrow.

Leaning forward he touches his forehead to mine, and my lungs burn with the sudden desire to cry.

We ascend the steps. At the top, the soldier opens the door and unlocks the gate. Sera and I step into the villa and pause to block sight as Alexior yanks the soldier down the steps and cracks his neck.

Willem is in the tunnel and ready. He strips the soldier

and hides his body, before redressing and taking the soldier's spot at the steps.

It's quiet. It's quick. No one hears or sees a thing.

If someone comes by and recognizes Willem, he will stab them and throw their body down the steps to where the other warriors wait for the signal.

Alexior, me, and Sera move through the villa and come to a stop in the room with the pool. Master is in the room, along with his wife and Bareket, plus twenty of the elite, including the scratchy-voiced one. All supposedly their closest friends.

But not Vasquez. I'm not surprised. Like I said, they didn't strike me as friendly. More authoritative father to errant child.

All of them lounge on chaises while being hand fed by house slaves. The air smells like Bareket—pot and jasmine—and I wonder if they've been smoking.

This would have been more effective if it was one of his big parties, but we'll kill all of them and the soldiers, too, and anyone else who stops us. Then we'll move on to the next villa and the next until every slave on Saligia is free.

Master throws his arms out. "Ah! Here they are. My two greatest warriors." He turns back to his guests. "Eat, drink. I have a little *show* when the time is right."

He claps his hands and out dance several naked men and women. I recognize them all from the party he threw us down on the training grounds. Slaves trained to entertain. They slink into the pool, roll around in the rose petals and water, and begin an orgy.

In the corner stands Joseph and I move my eyes to him. Thank God he wasn't made to get in that pool. He nods ever so slightly, and I see it in his eyes. The same energy from the warriors waiting down below. He's ready.

The night goes on and we stand shackled and at attention waiting, waiting, waiting. They're laughing, eating, drinking, watching the orgy.

With each second, minute, hour that goes by, my muscles grow tauter with tension, with anticipation. I know everyone down in the tunnel has got to be just as anxious.

Finally, Master stands and holds his hands up. "Good friends, I now give you tonight's main event."

The men and women leave the pool, soldiers lay wooden slats down across the water, and as Alexior unshackles me and Sera, everything in me sparks to life. He pauses a second to look me one last time in the eyes, and his severe gaze tells it all.

Kill every one of them.

A soldier gives us each an ornamental sword and shield and we take our spots above the pool.

"Begin!" shouts Master, and excitement zings through me.

CHAPTER 58

Sᴇʀᴀ ᴀɴᴅ I ᴛᴜʀɴ, pick out a soldier, and lob our swords through the air. End over end they fly and pierce the two soldiers straight in the neck. Screaming, the elite jump to their feet and scatter at the same time soldiers rush in from every direction.

Sera and I reach inside our armor, pull out our hidden weapons, and leap from the pool. In my periphery I see it all. Warriors rushing into the villa. Slaves running. Elite running. Screams. Yelling. Blood.

Yana tosses me a spear, I twirl it in my hand, and sling it across the villa. It stabs an elite right through the back.

Camille grabs Bareket's hair and yanks. "What shall I do to you," she taunts. "Shall I ram this up your ass like you rammed your rod up mine?"

"Please," Bareket begs and the sound of her shaky voice electrifies me.

I want to kill Bareket. She had Lena. She sold Lena to Master. But as I stand rooted, watching Camille's brutal expression, I know my friend deserves this. Bareket tortured her.

"Please," Bareket tries again. "I'll give you anything."

"Too late," Camille hisses and slowly slides her blade into Bareket's spine.

Bareket lets out a scream that fuels my blood and I watch as she falls to her side. Camille slides her blade free, rolls Bareket onto her back, and stabs her straight in the heart.

Lifting her eyes, Camille immediately finds mine and in them flashes the retribution she so justly deserves. She grips the handle of the blade, yanks it out, and whirls. Her eyes land on the scratchy-voiced one desperately trying to flee. I know without looking she'll chop her arm off and let her bleed out.

To the left I catch Mistress slinking into a room and I sprint after her. A soldier steps into my path. My fist connects with his jaw, and I slice his knees right out from under him. I leap over and charge into the room. Mistress has her back to the wall, her eyes wildly looking around. I look down and see a knife clenched in her fist.

"What are you going to do with that?" I taunt.

She lifts it up and I note her shaky hands. "Stay back."

I stalk right toward her and lunge, throwing my forearm against her throat and squeezing her wrist until she yelps and releases the knife to clank against the marble floor. I get right up in her face and let my eyes purposefully trace and absorb her frightened features.

Good, let her be scared.

"Can I?" comes a hesitant voice from behind me. I glance over my shoulder to see Hedian standing a cautious distance away.

No. I shake my head. Hedian has been through enough. Yes, she's been abused by Mistress for years, but this will make Hedian a murderer. *No.* She doesn't know what she's asking.

"Hedian," Mistress pleads. "Please. You've always been my favorite. Please help me."

In my peripheral vision I see Hedian lunge. I rip Mistress's arm behind her back and turn at the exact second Hedian plunges a small dagger into Mistress's stomach.

Shaking, Hedian takes it out and plunges it again.

Out and again.

And then she takes a step back and doesn't say a word as she stares down at her bloody hands.

"It's okay," I tell her. "It's okay."

A gasp, a gurgled wheeze, and Mistress goes limp in my arms. As I let her body fall, I reach for Hedian and pull her into my arms.

"You okay?" I ask.

She doesn't respond.

"It's okay." I kiss her forehead. "Go hide somewhere. Only come out when you hear me." I pull her away and look into her eyes. "Okay?"

She nods and sniffs. I give her one last hug and I'm gone.

Out in the villa the slaughter continues. I trace my eyes over the dead bodies. Elite. Soldiers. My heart stutters when I see slaves and a couple of warriors lying in their own blood. I knew we wouldn't all get out alive.

Over in the corner I see Joseph. He's alive!

But I don't see Master.

I slide a sword from a dead soldier and make my way to the office. I open the door and step inside to see Master on the terrace, Gem's daughter clasped in front of him with a knife to her neck.

I look at her face and the tears streaming down her

cheeks and everything in me clenches. So help me God if he hurts her, I will mutilate him like nothing he's ever experienced in his life.

"I am your Master!" he shouts. "You will listen to me!"

"Really?" I scoff. "That is what you have for me?"

Behind me I am aware of the room slowly filling. Alexior. Sera. Razo. Joseph. Yana. Willem. Camille. Slaves. Warriors.

Master' eyes widen in realization that everyone is dead. We are alive. And he will die.

"Where's Vasquez?" I ask.

Master huffs a chuckle. "Fuck you, Valoria."

He's right. Fuck me. He's not going to tell me a thing.

From the right a tiny knife sails through the air and pierces him in the shoulder. He hunches to the side with a scream and releases Gem's daughter, and I watch as she races from the terrace straight into Joseph's arms.

I glance back, ready to advance, and Master is gone.

One second passes. Then two. And I snap back. *No!* I whip my gaze around the office before racing out onto the terrace. I peer over the balcony down the twenty or so feet to see nothing. An empty training ground.

Where did he go?

Grabbing the railing, I don't think twice and I leap. Air rushes past me as I fall the twenty or so feet and land with a jarring thud.

Quickly, my gaze touches on everything. The awning where we drink water. The tables where we eat. The shed. The training ground. The men's quarters. The women's. Where is he? WHERE IS HE?

I race everywhere, looking, searching, weapon drawn and ready. But he's nowhere. Nowhere! I check the gate. It's still locked.

Alexior grasps my arm. "Valoria."

I yank away. "Where is he?"

"He's gone."

"No. No!" How? How is he gone?

"We'll find him," Alexior promises. "We will."

In my peripheral vision I catch sight of everyone moving through the tunnel and out onto the training grounds where I stand. I look at each of them, my friends, my family. We are covered in blood. We are alive.

And they are ready. Ready for what is next.

A single war cry goes up that is quickly joined by the others. It fills the outdoor area until it transforms into a primal roar.

I lift my fist into the air. "*We* are in control now!"

CHAPTER 59

WE GATHER as many weapons as we can and we leave the villa. Outside I stand and look out across the island blanketed in darkness. There are no stars and no moon in the cloud filled sky, like an omen of what is to come. Master's villa and attached camp sit right in the center with at least an acre of land surrounding it. I don't know where Master ran to but wherever it is, he's alerting others that we're free.

We need to move fast.

Turning west, I look in the direction of The Hunts, but can barely make the wall out in this darkness. I do see the lights, though. The hunts are on. Though I don't know for sure, I'd say that's where Gem and Ignatius are.

Alexior steps up beside me. "Where to first?" he quietly asks.

It feels strange him asking me when he's always been the one in charge. But he knows this is me. I started this rebellion. So I turn to face everyone, and no one speaks as they stare back at me, covered in blood, waiting for my direction. My leadership. I count roughly thirty of us, half warriors, half house slaves.

Sera steps forward. "I'm going to find Ignatius. Who's with me?"

Everyone hesitantly looks around.

"Wait." I hold my hand up. "We can't divide. We have to stay as one. We're more powerful that way."

"Agreed," Camille speaks.

Sera hikes her chin. "You don't even know what you want." She nods to the notebook. "Let me see that. I want to see where Ignatius is."

I straighten my shoulders. She's correct. The last thing I should show right now is indecisiveness. "With Master on the run it's only a matter of minutes before everyone knows we're free. We definitely need some who can watch the docks. I don't want anyone leaving this island." I point to the left where the nearest villa sits. "Let's start there and make our way around the island. By the time we hit all the villas and the other *ludi* our numbers will more than triple."

"Yeah, but look at us," Yana challenges. "Half of us are trained warriors and the other half are house slaves who have never used a weapon in their lives."

"She's right," Joseph agrees. "How are we even going to get in to the villas? If it's like this one there're soldiers, there's a gate..."

"First of all, every warrior standing here is as powerful as two people. Second, I saw every one of you house slaves use knives just now." I motion to all of our weapons. "How are we going to do it? We'll kill whoever tries to stop us." I look at all their faces. Some determined, others scared, and yet others unconvinced. "Let's stay as one," I repeat what I said a few seconds ago. "We're more powerful that way."

"I, too, agree," Alexior says.

Inside, I breathe with relief. His support will convince everyone. I step up to Sera and hand her the leather notebook to show her how serious I am. "Go ahead. Look. I'm not stopping you."

She does, flipping through the pages, perusing them, and then tossing it back. "Ignatius is with The Hunts."

As I thought.

Razo kneels down and grabs the book and hands it to Camille. "See where Gem is."

Everyone quietly waits while Camille looks, and a few seconds later she lifts her horrified gaze to mine. "She's in The Hole."

The Hole...

"Fuck this, I'm going there!" Razo grabs a couple of swords and charges off.

"What's The Hole?" comes a timid voice, and I glance through the group and down to where Gem's daughter stands. I don't even know her name. What the hell are we going to do with a little girl?

I turn. "Razo, wait!"

With his fists clenched around the handles of two swords, he slowly turns back. "*What?*"

I take in the stern set of his jaw. I look beyond him to the marketplace where Gem is. My gaze touches on all the villas dotting the landscape, then over to The Hunts where Ignatius is before I turn back to the group. "Let's go get Gem and all those captive in the marketplace. Then we're going to raid every villa and set the slaves free. *Then* with our increased numbers we'll overtake The Hunts and find Ignatius." I look right at Sera because I really do need her on my side. "Agreed?"

Her jaw flexes. I know she wants to go straight to The Hunts. But I also know she's smart. She knows we are more powerful as one. "Yes," she says. "Let's go."

CHAPTER 60

THE WARRIOR I ball shot the morning of Felicia's suicide agrees to watch the dock. He takes a couple of house slaves with him. The rest of us head across the island to the marketplace.

It's alive with nighttime activity—crowded with elite out partying. Drinking. Dancing. Laughing. Music. Clearly word of our upheaval hasn't reached here yet.

Hovering in the shadows I give my group a quick perusal, looking for Gem's daughter and Hedian. They're standing beside each other next to Sera.

I crouch down in front of Gem's daughter. "What's your name, sweetheart?"

"My real name is Early," she tells me.

"Early? That's a peculiar name."

"Mommy said it's because I came early."

I smile at that when everything inside of me is panging at the "Mommy" part. Such an innocent little word. But Gem's not going to be the mommy she remembers.

"Do you have a weapon?" I ask Hedian, and she shows me the dagger that she stabbed Mistress with. "Take Early and hide," I tell her. "Do not come out until one of us comes to get you. Okay?"

She nods.

Alexior comes up behind me. "I know where they can hide."

"Good." I watch as the three of them disappear around a corner and a minute or so later Alexior is back.

"I hid them in the fruit shed," he tells me. "They'll be safe."

With a nod, I turn to our group. "Nice and quiet. Stealth. Deadly. Kill anyone you need to."

In the darkness I see nods. I see weapons ready. I see set faces. That's all I need.

I lead the way along the outer wall of the marketplace, careful to keep in the shadows until I come to a stop at the main entrance where two soldiers stand. Alexior and Razo step around me. They each take a soldier, silently snapping their necks and dragging their bodies out of the entrance.

There's a passageway that runs the entire circumference of the marketplace. Save for the occasional passed out drunk, everyone is in the center of the marketplace partying —in the same place I stood atop a block and was auctioned off. My gaze quickly runs across them and I estimate roughly fifty people. They outnumber us, but we have the element of surprise.

In the center there are three tied up slaves—one man and two women—naked, being taunted by the partiers.

Ducking into the passage, I take a group to the right and Alexior does to the left until we've surrounded the place. In the center people continue drinking, dancing, oblivious as to what is about to go down. Silently, we move as one, stepping from the shadows, coming up from behind, and using our weapons to slice necks, to stab, to kill.

It happens slowly, us silently killing, people gradually realizing what's going on, screams, scrambling for their own weapons, climbing over each other to run free, futilely fighting back, blood...

When it's done, we don't linger. We don't pause. We don't think. We go straight to our next objective—The Hole.

Like before the smell hits me first. Putrid. Then the sounds. Whimpers. Screams. Laughter. Everything in me tightens as I lead the way down the steps.

Two soldiers at the bottom see us coming, draw their weapons, and call out, "Halt!"

Me and Razo slice both of their necks.

The rest of us jump over their bodies and spread out. Like we did up top, we surround the gathered elite. None of us pause to consider, to think. We block out the sounds, the smells, and we kill them all and then we set every slave free.

I find Razo in the last corner, pulverizing a man's face. "Where is she?" he angrily demands.

"I don't know," the man blubbers.

Razo crashes his fist into the man's nose and blood flies.

"Please," the man whimpers. "She was here. But someone took her. That's all I know. I promise."

Razo lifts his sword up and with a yell, brings it straight down into the man's chest. "FUCK YOU!" he screams.

Agony clenches my gut. *Gem's not here.*

Razo shoves past me and sprints up the stairs and out of this abominable place. All around me I'm aware of movement, of quiet sobs, of those who came with me helping all the slaves from their restraints. Gradually the smell trickles back into my senses, and my stomach rolls.

Camille tugs my arm. "Let's go. We'll find Gem. We will."

Back up top I step from the The Hole's archway and

immediately take a breath. It's not fresh but it's a lot better than down there. Alexior is already standing across the marketplace and among the dead bodies. His face. His dirty, handsome face brings me such comfort. Such relief. He's still alive.

The three slaves who were tied up in the center of the marketplace now stand clothed with tunics they stripped off dead bodies and gripping weapons they found. They're ready for whatever comes next.

From behind me trickles all those we set free. I step into the center of the marketplace and immediately sense something is different in me. All these new faces. What I just revisited in The Hole. I can only imagine the horrors waiting for us throughout the rest of this night.

Heat blazes through me and loudly I say, "We are taking over this island tonight. And then we will sail to freedom." I hold my spear up. "Gather all the weapons and let's go!"

Over the next several hours we take down the villas, their outbuildings, and their dungeons. We raid the entire island, slaughtering anyone in our path and setting every slave free. A few people try to swim to safety but end up drowning in their escape. Our numbers grow to the hundreds, astounding me with just how many people were being held captive.

Gem is still missing, and Vasquez and Master are nowhere to be found. If they somehow escaped off Saligia, I will still find them. I don't doubt that for a second.

As the sun is just coming up I find myself standing back in the center of the island at our camp, looking west toward the wall and The Hunts. Next to me are Sera, Camille, Razo, and Alexior. All around us hover the freed slaves, the other warriors, Willem, Yana, Joseph...

Suddenly, the heaviness of the entire night comes down on me. The blood. The screams. The slaughter. All the slaves. It seems all I can feel and my shoulders slump with the weight.

Alexior is standing to my right, and quietly he moves toward me until our bodies touch—shoulders, hips, and feet, letting me know he's here. Closing my eyes, I breathe in his presence, his comfort. I soak in the heavy warmness that his nearness brings me. Both sweet and aching at the same time. I can do this. That's what he's silently telling me. This is almost done.

Everything left is on the other side of that wall, including Alexior's wife.

"These people," he softly says, "they are both master-minds and sadists. It takes the combination to run a place like Saligia."

Well put.

I open my eyes. "Tell me what you know about The Hunts."

"There's only one way in—a gate. The wall is approxi-mately nine meters tall. Slaves are released, and they're immediately on the run. They hide wherever they can. They live off the land. They turn on each other. They do whatever they have to in order to survive. The villa inside is enormous and more like a resort. It's where the elite stay while they're hunting. There are horses, and they hunt with bow and arrow and spears. The terrain is thick with woods."

The reality is Gem, without an arm, is probably dead. Ignatius could very well be alive still. He could probably endure that environment. Hell, he's the longest survivor of The Hole.

"The hunts occur at night?" I confirm.

"Correct. But with what's happened on this side of the

wall tonight, they no doubt know we're coming and are ready."

I roll my neck, rotate my shoulders, and tighten my sore fists around my two spears. There is no element of surprise. He's right they know we're coming.

"But," he continues, "I know them. I know how they think. They'll have whatever elite are left barricaded in the villa with soldiers standing guard. There will also be soldiers at the gate because they think their wall is impenetrable. They don't think anybody can get over it."

I cut him a sly look. "Then we're going over the wall."

CHAPTER 61

No one speaks as we cross the eerily quiet island to the wall. I am reminded of all those times I rode back and forth in the cart. The island never sat still. There was always movement. Elite here and there. Slaves trailing behind or out working the grounds.

We come to a stop at the stone wall. I glance up the thirty or so feet, then to the right and to the left where it stretches a good mile in both directions, eventually wrapping around to barricade the entire hunting grounds.

Behind me, slaves begin dragging wooden ladders that they pulled from the villas and propping them up against the wall. Only four ladders are tall enough to reach, and when they are in place, me, Alexior, Sera, and Razo begin the ascent. Halfway up, I'm aware Camille has begun her ascent on my ladder as has Willem and Yana on the others. As we near the top we ready our weapons, not sure what's on the other side.

Together we slide up and over, weapons poised, but I see only woods and dunes and thick underbrush. No slaves.

No soldiers. No movement at all. In fact, I can't even see the villa through all the foliage.

From the top we drop and as Alexior taught us in training, we roll. Behind us Camille and the others do the same. One by one the other warriors come up and over, and then everyone else who is able follows, jumping and us assisting them with the landing.

Before the last few slaves can jump, I say, "Grab the ladders and prop them on this side." We may need them to get back over.

When that is done we quietly begin creeping into the woods. I want to yell to all the slaves to come out of hiding. That they are safe. To join us. But I keep silent, my eyes flicking from tree to bush to shadow.

Movement to my left causes me to pause. When I stop walking, so does everyone else. I wait, but don't see the movement again. Going on instinct, I softly say, "Whoever you are, you can come out. You're free now." I take a breath and hold it and wait. Beside me, I sense Sera doing the same.

Then gradually, it happens. First one person, then another, and then another. Slowly, they emerge from the shadows, from the underbrush, one even jumps down from a tree, and with each one, something twinges inside of me.

Rags cover their emaciated bodies. Dirt and blood mats and trails their hair and skin. Their eyes stare glassy and wide with fear, with relief, with caution. Men. Women. Boys. Girls.

"Oh my God," Camille whispers.

I make myself stay calm, and stepping forward, I hand them whatever weapons I can spare as do the others. "Go, go tell everyone else they're free. We're taking down the villa and then we're sailing away from this place."

One of the women falls to her knees, shaking, crying, babbling, "The shed and the sacrifices and those hiding in the dunes..."

My insides wrench with her desperate voice and frantic words. "We'll get them all," I assure her.

They take the weapons we give them and disappear back into the shadows as we continue our trek through the hunting grounds. With each step I take, I think about these people. Hunted. Scared. Barely surviving. Every kill I made last night, I did for this. For them. For us.

A gasp to my right has me pausing, looking, listening. A woman who was a house slave in one of the villas catches my eye and points. There, through the dense foliage, I see it. A stone building.

We approach, and on the outskirts, we sink into a crouch and take in the solid weathered structure that has no windows. Perhaps it is simply a storage area.

I circle it and locate a metal padlocked door. With a rap of my knuckles, I whisper, "Hello? Is anyone in there?"

Silence.

"Hello?"

Silence.

Razo grabs an oversized stone and begins hammering the lock with it.

Bang. Bang. Bang.

The lock breaks open, and Razo grabs the handle. He swings the door wide, and we catch a collective breath.

It's pitch black inside and the stench of rot rushes out and surrounds us. So thick and encompassing, it is hard to breathe. Behind me someone gags.

I don't wait, I rush right in. There are bodies every-where. Prone. Hunched over. Hanging. Though I can't see clearly, I can smell they are filthy with dirt and feces, urine and blood.

I reach down and grab the first thing my hand falls on. I go to drag the person from the building and the skin comes off in my fingers. I wince. Bile swells in my mouth, and I repress the urge to gag as I grip with two hands and finish pulling the body out into the night. It's a man. He is dead, his decayed skin hanging from his body in long peels that have clearly been fileted with a knife.

"Jesus," mutters Sera.

Everyone joins in, and one by one we pull the mangled bodies from the building. Some dead. Some barely alive. Others with their tongues removed and yet others like the first, with shredded skin.

"Some they would catch and throw in here," one of the slaves says. "Once a week they burn the bodies and listen to them scream."

Razo kneels down next to a soiled body and I realize with a jolt that it is Gem. I watch him gently pick her up and hold her to his chest. She's unconscious, but she's breathing. I look at her missing arm where someone tried to cauterize it. It is swollen and badly infected with red spreading up across her shoulder.

I drop down beside them both, gently clasping her bony fingers. She needs help now. She can't wait.

Alexior moves in beside us. "Razo, take Talme and go back to our camp. Let her do what she can with Gem until it's time to leave."

I nod. I completely agree. I look around our group that has grown even more with those slaves from The Hunts who have now joined us. I pick out ten healthy ones and instruct them to get the injured and go with Razo and Talme.

With one last look to my dear friend, Gem, I pick up my spear and continue on. Behind the stone building a trail appears, then gradually becomes less and less until it merges back with the landscape. Overhead the trees come together blocking out the rising sun. Other than the sound of us hacking our way through the brush, things remain eerily calm. I wonder what they're doing in the villa right now. I hope they're scared. I hope they know we're coming.

A clearing opens and in the center lays a mangled dead body, obviously killed in the hunts. Another trail opens to the right and we merge onto the narrow path. Foliage lines each side and a little ways up sits a wooden post with horses tied off.

I walk over and undo the horses, give them a pat on their rumps, and they trot off. We continue past and cut through more brush to another clearing where several slaves have been gutted and hung. Flies zing in and out, feasting on the organs and exposed meat.

I want to cover my mouth and nose, but I don't. I make myself smell the rot. I let it burn through my senses. I let the sight of it gnaw at my insides. Yet another reminder of everything vile about this place.

Camille wrinkles her nose and blows out a steady breath, and I know she's doing the same. She starts walking first this time, cutting down the next trail.

Another small clearing opens with one single cross in the center. On it hangs Ignatius. Pure joy dances through my blood as I stare up into his angry narrowed eyes.

"Get me the fuck off this thing!" he demands, and for the first time in I-don't-know-how-long, we all laugh.

They caught him and they strung him up on this cross with rope. Other than his clearly pissed off mood, he is unharmed. They would've come back tonight for sure. Tomorrow Ignatius would've been dead.

Alexior and Sera rush over and cut him down. He lands with a heavy thud on the sand and immediately comes to his feet. He's ready.

Sera punches him. "You asshole," she says with obvious tears in her eyes. "I thought you were dead."

It's the second time I've seen Sera almost cry. Maybe she really is a big softie way down inside that irritable body of hers. Then again maybe not.

Alexior hands Ignatius a sword, and together we head toward the villa.

Way in the distance I hear a *thump-thump-thump*. I glance over to Alexior, and he shakes his head, clearly not recognizing the sound.

Tilting my head, I tune into the far away *thump-thump-thump* realizing... "That's a helicopter! Master and Vasquez are about to escape!"

CHAPTER 62

I SPRINT through the woods with everyone following listening to that *thump-thump-thump* as it draws closer.

Pushing through the last bunch of brush, we emerge outside of the villa. It stands isolated and pristine, sprawling nearly an acre of land with several levels with archways and balconies, looming like some grand king in this desolate place. It makes me want to make it dirty. A six foot wall surrounds it, with soldiers stationed every ten feet or so, armed and ready, just as Alexior predicted.

As the hundreds of us spread out, the soldiers lift their swords.

"You will not survive!" one of them yells.

I simply smile and I lift my spear and yell, "Now!"

We rush the villa from every direction, yelling, screaming with the adrenaline of everything that has happened and everything that will be. Screaming with the fact this is the end.

In my peripheral vision I see four young slave girls attack a soldier, shrieking, their fists flying up and down with daggers. Stabbing him over. And over. And over again.

Others are already up and over the wall and rushing the villa. I slice a soldier's neck and use his body to spring board over the wall, too. With a weapon in each hand I sprint across the lawn to the villa already flooded with warriors and slaves as they race from room to room and floor to floor. The air is filled with violence. Panic. Hysteria. It fuels me.

Thump-thump-thump. I hear it getting closer.

As I race though an archway, I catch sight of a slave boy cowering in the corner. Immediately I go to him, "Where are the elite hiding?" I ask. Because I know they are.

Shakily he points his finger straight up.

"Do you have some place you can hide?" I ask him.

Frantically, he nods.

"Go then. And only come out when you hear all this is over." I extend my hand and pull him to his feet and watch as he scurries off.

A shadow flicks and I spin at the exact second a soldier raises his sword. I don't hesitate a second as I ram my spear through his gut.

Camille emerges from a side hallway. She's bloody. She's filthy. But she's breathing. She's alive.

I nod to a spiral stairwell. "Up here."

We take them two at a time and come to a landing. A hallway stretches all the way to the end where a large wooden door sits closed. My breaths grow faster as I head straight toward it. Sera comes from a hallway on the left, Alexior from one on the right, and Ignatius moves in behind us. Like we all knew instinctively where to meet.

Together we ram our shoulders into the door. We ram again. And then again. On our fourth try the door breaks open, and we all step inside.

Thump-thump-thump. Closer.

A line of soldiers greet us. All around me fighting erupts

as we chop our way through, injuring, killing. I take a stab in the thigh, but I block the pain. Minutes go by and the place falls quiet.

Behind me the muted sounds of fighting filter up the stairs and down the hall. Inside I look around the enormous master suite. The terrace that overlooks Saligia and the surrounding waters. The king-size bed. The sprawling bath with a tub large enough to hold ten people. The chaise lounges.

The scent of flowers float through my senses, and I glance beside the bed where several large arrangements sit, pretty and perfect, a stark contrast to the horrors outside.

It's then that I see them, cowering in the corner. Vasquez, Master, and a woman I don't recognize. Just the sight of them races cold down my spine. I turn to fully face them.

The woman has long blond hair, fair skin, and red lips. Her frightened eyes move over each one of us before falling on Alexior. They widen in shock, in recognition, in horror, in realization of what is about to transpire.

"Hello, Nadine," Alexior greets her with a voice hard and terse.

This is his wife. This is the woman who runs The Hunts. This is the woman who betrayed him.

Thump-thump-thump. It's nearly on top of us now.

From behind her back Nadine pulls a gun. It takes me a second to register what it is. She raises it and points it right at me. Time seems to slow in motion as I lunge. Sera shoves me aside. The gun explodes. And Sera takes a shot straight to the heart.

"NO!" I scream.

Sera falls straight back.

"Sera!" I drop to my knees.

I'm aware of Camille throwing a dagger at Nadine and the gun clanking to the floor. Of Vasquez trying to get to the terrace where the helicopter is now landing. Of Alexior blocking his path. Of Willem picking the gun up and charging out onto the terrace. Of Yana moving in on Master. Of Ignatius dropping down beside me. Of Sera's blood spreading on the marble floor. Of another gunshot. Yelling. Fighting. I'm aware of it all and I can't stop any of it. I can't stop it! That bullet was meant for me!

I press my hands against the wound on Sera's chest, trying to stop the blood flow, and Ignatius grabs my wrists. "She's dead."

I yank away and press my palms to her chest anyway. "No!" *Nooo...* I look at the blood and then into her slack face. I pound the floor. I pound it again. I shove to my feet and scream.

I grab Sera's sword and charge across the room to the cowering elite. Behind me I hear Ignatius stifle a quiet sob. That bullet was meant for me. *For me.*

I point her sword at Master. "*You* made us into what we are. Look around. We were outnumbered and we *still* took this place down. You turned us into animals. And now it has all backfired." I step closer. "You will die first."

He casts a look out to the terrace where the helicopter is now sitting idle. Willem killed whoever was piloting it.

"Your ride is dead," I tell Master.

Visibly shaking, he starts to back away and Vasquez pushes him forward. Behind me I sense more than see other people filtering into the room. I glance over my shoulder. A group of them are the house slaves from our camp, including Joseph. They deserve this. Lena does. We all do. I want to kill Master. I want to gut him. I want to make him pay for every single thing he did to my sister.

But—I turn to the gathered slaves—they deserve it, too. He repeatedly raped and beat every one of them. They need this justice. I grab Master and shove him toward the awaiting group. "Have at him," I tell them.

They surround him, circling him, taunting him, and I watch and listen as they slowly make him suffer and pay for every single thing he did to them. Until he is just a pile of skin and bones and organs and blood.

For you, Lena.

I turn back to Vasquez and Nadine and watch as her eyes drag away from Master' maimed body to land on Alexior. She drops to her knees in front of him, hands clasped, pleading, begging, her arm bleeding from where Camille hit her with a dagger.

He stands in front of her, staring down, as she imploringly stares back. "Please," she whispers, pathetic and hurt.

He points his sword right at her throat. "Please what? Fall in love with you? Believe in you? Give up my life so that you would be set free? Which one, Nadine? Huh?"

Her bottom lip quivers. "I'm sorry."

"What exactly are you sorry for? Running The Hunts? Being responsible for all those dead innocent people?"

"I'm sorry," she whimpers again.

"No you're not." With that, he inserts the tip of his sword into her throat, and when he's halfway in, he rotates it. She gurgles and thrashes and falls to her side.

My pulse throbs the vein in my neck as I watch her life go. All this killing, and my body still reacts in revulsion. Good. If I ever *stop* reacting, then I know I'm gone. I've lost all humanity. It's a thought I've had before, and it strikes me right now as I watch.

When her eyes go wide and blankly stare up, Alexior

removes his sword and takes a step back. He looks over to me and simply nods.

I point my spear at Vasquez, the mastermind behind this hell. "How does it feel to see all your hard work die? How does it feel to know *you're* about to die?" I point out to the terrace where the helicopter sits. "How does it feel to know you almost got away?"

He focuses his dark eyes on mine and I am propelled back in time to his office. The interview he scheduled with me. The new life I thought I would have. *Lena* and I would have.

I take a step toward him and stop right in front of him, tightening my fists around my weapons. "You. You are the reason for all of this. You picked the wrong woman to kidnap."

Vasquez takes in my hair, my face, my body. He doesn't even remember me. What does that say? He's taken so many over the years I am just a blur of a face.

I step closer. "My sister is dead because of you. I am a beast because of you."

Something in his eyes changes, a realization, a recognition, and he slowly smiles. *Fucking smiles.*

"Yes," he murmurs. "I do remember you and that darling little sister."

Tears unexpectedly blur my eyes, and I move at the exact second he does. Lightning quick, he yanks a knife from behind his back and stabs me deep in the side. Hot pain flashes across my stomach, through my ribs, and singes my lower back. I scream. My hands flex open and both of my weapons clang to the marble floor.

I wrap my fingers around the knife in my side, wrench it free, and ram it straight into his lower gut. I clench my jaw and hold my eyes to his and jerk the knife to the left, rotate it, and then jerk it back to the right. He reaches for me, gasping, gurgling, and I grit my teeth and shove the knife further in.

Slowly, Vasquez's body slumps at my feet. With one last thrust of the knife, I fall on top of him.

CHAPTER 63

"TAKE HER," Alexior says. "Get her to the galleon. I need to go get the rest."

I reach for him. Don't go.

Alexior presses his lips to my forehead. "I'll see you soon."

Ignatius picks me up. "Hang in there."

Trees. Leaves. Familiar voices. Camille. Joseph. Willem. Yana.

The sound of a seagull. The smell of salt.

"Put her here," says Talme, and her lips purse as she cuts away my tunic.

Footsteps. Crying.

I hiss. Talme... What is she doing? Something wet plops onto my cheek. Rain?

I go to sleep. I wake.

We're moving. We're sailing. Alexior! I try to sit up. I try to focus.

I squint, confused. Where are we?

Ignatius puts his hand on my shoulder. "Stay still."

CHAPTER 64

FIVE YEARS HAVE PASSED since we sailed free of Saligia and landed on the shores of Kenya. In the days, weeks, months, and years that followed, anyone on the outside who was involved in Saligia were brought to justice. Thanks to Master' notebook and the iPad that was found hidden in his office.

Royalty. Government officials. Businessmen and women. Entrepreneurs. It went deep and stunned the world.

The isle of Saligia was cleared and to this day still stands vacant in the Indian Ocean and for sale, cursed by the evils that existed.

Funds were established for all those who suffered. Money to get us back on our feet. Housing. Education. Employment. Emotional and physical help.

Many stayed together those first months and then slowly trickled off to start a new life. To distance themselves from the rumors, the reporters, the microscope the world still has on us to this day.

My new family—Camille (whose real name is Inga),

Ignatius (Aaron), Razo, Gem (Fuji), Early, Joseph (Sergio), Talme (Edna), and Hedian (Gabriella)—bought a farm in Costa Rica. It is a simple life. A non-violent one. Full of hard work, quiet, peace, dinners together, and laughter. Willem and Yana stayed with us for a while and then branched out on their own.

We never talk about Saligia.

Sometimes at night I stand and stare up at the stars, and I remember Lena and Sera...

"Katalina?"

I turn to see Liam (Alexior) descending the sea wall to where I sit in the sand. I love his blond hair grown out and his trim goatee.

"Dinner," he says.

I nod. "Be right there."

Katalina. That is my name.

ABOUT THE AUTHOR

S. E. Green is the award-winning, best-selling author of young adult and adult fiction. She grew up in TN where she dreaded all things reading and writing. She didn't read her first book for enjoyment until she was 25. After that she was hooked! She now lives on the coast in FL where a rogue armadillo frequents her backyard.

BOOKS BY S. E. GREEN

Killers Among

Lane swore never to be like her late mother. But now she too is a serial killer.

Monster

When the police need to crawl inside the mind of a monster, they call Caroline.

The Third Son

All he wants is a loving family to belong to, to manipulate, to control...

Mother May I

Meet Nora: Flawless. Enigmatic. Conniving. Ruthless.

Vanquished

First Edition: July 2015

Second Edition: January 2019

Cover and Formatting: Streetlight Graphics (first edition)

Cover and Formatting: Steven Novak (second edition)